The Warden Wore Pink

Tekla Dennison Miller

Foreword by Perry Johnson

Biddle Publishing Company
Brunswick, Maine

Publisher's Cataloging in Publication Data
1. Miller, Tekla Dennison
2. The Warden Wore Pink
3. Prisoners and Prisons
4. Corrections, Administation
5. Women: Equality in Employment
6. Women in Corrections

Cover Design by Karen Robbins

Library of Congress Catalog Card No. 96-83321

ISBN 1-879418-24-X

This book is printed on recycled paper.

Published in the United States of America by
        Biddle Publishing Company
        PO Box 1305
        Brunswick, Maine 04011
        207-833-5016

DEDICATION

*to the women working in corrections
and juvenile justice*

TABLE OF CONTENTS

FOREWORD

When I first met Tekla Miller, nearly 20 years ago, she had just been appointed Supervisor of a camp in the Michigan prison system—Camp Pontiac, the ramshackle collection of military-style barracks she describes so well in this book. As we approached her office, her immediate boss, John Mills, said, "Director, put Tekla on your short list [of prospects for top management]; she is very bright, tough although a bit feisty, and has a natural talent for prison work."

That his impression was right on—especially about the bright and feisty part—you will soon learn. You will also learn that she has a great sense of humor—a quality that served her well in tense situations and when she wanted to make a controversial point. Beneath the toughness and humor, however, was to be found a deep sense of concern and compassion for people—especially for those less fortunate. The unmistakable humanity and substance of this book reflect these qualities in its author.

The Warden Wore Pink presents an often humorous, occasionally tragic, but always illuminating account of prison life and the struggle of an exceptionally gifted woman to forge new frontiers in a previously all-male domain. The vignettes of people Tekla Miller came to know during her career provide true insight into the nature of both the keepers and the kept—portraits which are sometimes noble, too often sordid, but always real. I am sure you will find this book to be both entertaining and instructive, and that is true whether you come to it as a lay citizen or as a corrections professional in whom some of these adventures will strike a familiar cord. And funny? The account of Sergeant Ozzie Hernandez's unique introduction to the supervision of women prisoners is one of the most hilarious anecdotes I've heard in forty years of prison work.

Beneath the humor there is a more serious and somber cord: this book puts a human face on the injustice of discrimination and brings home to all of us the demeaning consequences of sexual harassment. I may be able to add a little historical perspective here, since many of the events you will be reading about happened on my watch as Director of Corrections in Michigan from 1972 to 1984. When Tekla started in this business in the early 70's, policy in Michigan, as in most other states, specifically prohibited women from working inside the security perimeters of prisons, from supervising male parolees or probationers, or even from applying for a corrections officer's job in a male facility. And, of course, without entry level positions for women, none could qualify to be supervisors in these institutions. In other words, while racial discrimination, where it existed, was covert, unofficial and denied, discrimination based on gender was the officially proclaimed policy of the State, of Civil Service, and of the Department of Corrections.

I was soon to find that as Director of the Department, changing this official policy was the easy part—but changing the ingrained culture was tougher than I had ever imagined it could be. Resistance and sly insubordination soon became manifest, even by trusted staff— including a warden or two. Women pioneering in the corrections world were subjected to almost total social and professional isolation by their male counterparts. Incidents of sexual harassment and intentional set-ups for failure were part of the routine. Then there were the lawsuits from inmates, unions, and staff, all objecting to the employment of women in traditionally male positions. Some brutal assaults on female employees, and even one rape murder, unquestionably owed in no small part to the indifference and sometimes even malice of male colleagues.

I have long known what a trial it was for those of us on the management team who were trying to deal with these problems in that turbulent time. But until I read this book I did not fully realize how much more agonizing and difficult that struggle was for individuals like Tekla who not only lived with these conditions on a daily basis, but through tenacity, courage, and a sometimes rueful humor, managed in the long run to prevail over them.

Gender bias and discrimination, and the conditions they spawn, have not, of course, vanished from the field of corrections. Women everywhere must still battle those who think they do not belong in this profession, but Tekla and those like her have, I think, made the beachhead secure, and her successors will not now be turned back.

Perry Johnson

Perry Johnson served in many positions in the Michigan Department of Corrections before being appointed its director. During the twelve years he served as director, Michigan was considered among the most progressive states for corrections policy and programs. Mr. Johnson was among the first corrections leaders to aggressively hire and promote minorities and women. Since retiring, Mr. Johnson has been an internationally known corrections consultant and served a two-year term as the President of the American Correctional Association(ACA). He has received the E.R. Cass Award, the highest tribute given by the ACA to a corrections practitioner. Mr. Johnson is the author of Understanding Prisons *and several other books.*

PROLOGUE

"Life is a daring adventure or nothing." Helen Keller

May 28, 1990

I maneuvered our sailboat, *Wildflower*, into slip number 9. The marina in Charlevoix, Michigan, had been our summer home for the past eight years. My husband, Chet, jumped from the boat to secure the lines, shouting, "Flawless landing after a perfect day of sailing! Another ho hum day in paradise. Life is good!"

Our dock mate peered out of his companionway and yelled to me, "I just caught the tail end of the news. Something about Huron Valley Prison. Isn't that yours, Tekla?"

It was Memorial Day afternoon, and though I wasn't on call that weekend—the deputy warden was—a knot began forming in my stomach and my knees felt weak. I was the warden at the men's maximum security, one of the two Huron Valley Prisons. And I knew without asking which prison was in the news.

I watched Chet secure the lines, waiting for his reaction. He looked at me with his mouth turned down and shook his head. "Not again."

With a shrug, I shut off the engine, went below and grabbed my telephone card. As I jumped onto the dock, I told Chet, "Got to call in. Be back in a few minutes."

On the way to the pay phone on shore, all sorts of scenarios went through my head—an officer assaulted by a prisoner, a prisoner barricaded in his room that he had set afire, an attempted escape, a suicide, drugs or maybe just a fight in the visiting room. Tempers always flared during holidays. My hand shook as I dialed. Waiting for the phone to ring, I looked out at the dark green rolling hills surrounding Lake Charlevoix. An afternoon breeze accompanied the kaleidoscopic northern Michigan sunset. The only other sound besides the ringing of the phone was the wind whistling through the masts of the sailboats at rest in the harbor.

A male voice on the other end of the telephone announced in clear, deep tones, "Huron Valley Men's Facility. Officer Turner speaking."

"This is Warden Miller. Is Deputy Bentley there?"

"Yes, Ma'am. Please hold and I'll transfer."

Sam Bentley had been appointed deputy by my predecessor, and during the two years we'd worked together, I'd found him to be bright, dependable, bullheaded, and a workaholic. When Bentley answered the phone, he explained with tension in his voice, "I was called at home at about eight this morning and told that a prisoner was holding Officer Lisa Reynolds hostage. It was Larner. He'd made a shank from a piece of the radiator in his cell and used it to grab her. He raped her."

Larner was housed in Unit 1, the most secure segregation unit, in cell C-103 where he had been moved after breaking out of C-113. Both cells were supposed to be among the safest in that unit. He was on Out-Patient Mental Health Status and segregated because of several previous assaults on staff.

Bentley sounded exhausted. He sighed and continued, "You know Reynolds. She's the white, rookie officer who's been at Huron Valley Men's Prison about a year."

"How the hell did Larner get her?"

"Well, she went off her wing to go to the supply closet. Officers Tucker and Wilson stayed at their station until they heard the porter yell for help. By the time Tucker and Wilson got to Larner's door, it was barricaded from inside, and Larner had Reynolds inside with a shank at her throat."

I'd heard enough to know it meant dropping everything and getting to the prison fast. I needed more details, and I needed to see if I could help Lisa Reynolds.

The anger that I felt as I listened to Deputy Bentley began to be replaced by feelings of helplessness, nausea and guilt—guilt because I'd been on a holiday when the crisis happened, even though my presence at the prison might not have prevented either the hostage-taking or the rape.

It was only the second hostage-taking incident at Huron Valley Men's Prison while I had been warden. The other ended successfully.

The hostage taker was the same prisoner, Larner, a violent offender who looked for any opportunity to attack.

After I hung up the phone, I walked back to the boat feeling a pain over my right eye. I ignored the sunset. I wondered if other wardens waded through these same haunting emotions, or if only women care too much. Are we weak and too quick to take the blame?

I was sure that the gruesome assault on a rookie female officer by an aggressive male prisoner would be fodder for State Senator Jack Welborn's committee. Welborn, chair of the Corrections Committee, had been waiting for something to validate his oft-repeated contention that women should not run men's prisons, especially a max, or, in fact, work in any position in a men's prison.

By the time our car entered I-75 at Gaylord, an hour from Charlevoix, the pain over my right eye had become a migraine. We were heading south, going toward home for Chet and the prison for me. I didn't want to face the extensive investigation that awaited me, but it was my job.

As a child I dreamed of being a ballerina. Corrections and criminal justice were terms that never entered my vocabulary until I needed a job. At that point I didn't think corrections would be too far removed from the work I'd done with slum kids and Army misfits. Nor did I think of it as being an "unsuitable job for women." Once employed in corrections, however, I discovered that women in the system, both offenders and employees, were not treated the same as men.

Before 1972, virtually no women had worked as corrections officers in men's prisons in the United States. As a result of a court order, women corrections officers in Michigan began working in men's housing units in the early 1980's. Without that assignment, women corrections officers could not get the experience needed for promotions.

Progress has been made in increasing the number of women working in men's prisons. Today, approximately 13% of officers in men's prisons in the United States are women. Slower to increase are the numbers of women wardens in men's institutions and women administrators at all levels. There were 644 federal and state prisons for men in 1990, at the time I left corrections. I was then one of only 53 women wardens of male prisons in the United States.

I credit any success I've had to my determination to overcome three obstacles that life had thrown at me.

The first and most profound was the suicide of my mother, Marion Kolk Dennison, in July, 1956. She was forty-one. My father had died four years earlier when I was nine years old. So at the age of thirteen, I became an orphan.

Lessons I learned from my mother during her short life motivated me to search for excellence and influenced the direction I traveled in both my career and personal life. My mother created an environment filled with classical music, opera, and wonderful books. Although she never went beyond the eighth grade in school, her lack of education did not intimidate her. She went to the library every week, borrowed seven books and read one a night. I could not make sense of my mother's suicide, but the words she had dished up along with the morning doses of oatmeal echoed in my ears: "Education will be your ticket out of poverty. You can be anything you want with the right education."

Through books, ballet, opera, and yes, even baseball, my mother encouraged us to explore the world and its options. I don't recall my mother ever saying that gender would obstruct any goal I wished to achieve. She assured my self esteem by allowing me to be a person within my own right, and to choose my own future.

The second thing that influenced my destiny was becoming my sister's ward upon the death of my mother. At that time, my sister, Alyce, was twenty-three years old, married and the mother of two young boys. Her relationship with her husband was not only based on 1950's mores, but on her fear of being beaten—a regular occurrence—and on having nowhere else to go.

Many times I watched my sister trying to cover her bruised face with makeup, or comb her hair over one of her eyes to hide the discoloration and swelling, signs of the previous night's combat. In my eyes, her husband's dominance was insured by his huge physique and intense temper. I feared and hated him. He made me a victim by never hiding his abuse of Alyce and their sons, and by allowing his motorcycle buddies the privilege of entering my bedroom whenever they wanted.

In the summer of 1959, however, my sister left her abusive husband and packed her two children, me, and a few important items and fled to Los Angeles, California. She was twenty-five years old and I was fifteen. Her courage was amazing.

The third event that changed the direction of my life happened when I tried to purchase a 1974 Orange Volkswagen "Bug."

"If you want to purchase the Volkswagen, you will have to have a co-signer," the car salesman said as he smirked.

I was newly divorced, and to the salesman that made me a credit risk. It did not matter that I worked full time at a well paying and stable job as a probation officer. "The car only costs $3000 for Pete's sake," I retorted, feeling both anger and humiliation.

His lip curled as he traced my body with his eyes. "I repeat, you will have to have a co-signer."

I wanted the car, the first in my own name, and so I stooped to having my ex-husband co-sign for it. On the day I drove the Orange Volkswagen from the dealership, I clearly understood that discrimination included gender bias. And because of that degrading event, I became determined to help change women's negative place in society.

The orange Volkswagen took me down many roads and will always remind me of my personal awakening. It was my vehicle to freedom on an insatiable quest for achievement.

When I graduated from the University of California, I never dreamed that I would enter the world of criminal justice. That world forced me to face another reality—that not all corrupt, perverted, ignorant, incompetent, and addicted persons are convicted criminals. Some of them are the employees in corrections and the penal system. There are, however, employees, supervisors, and even prisoners who are exemplary individuals. Through them, I was able to see light in even the darkest prison cell.

These experiences, however, were very much in the future in 1971, when I was the first woman probation officer hired in Oakland County Circuit Court, and one of the first women in the United States to manage men on her caseload.

14

PART 1

Probation Office
Oakland County Circuit Court

I

July, 1971

"Are you taking the pill?" asked the interviewer, a white male in his mid forties who leered at me over his glasses. He was the chief probation officer, Mack Langford.

"Have you had a vasectomy?" I countered. "I don't see the relevance of your question to the posted qualifications for the position of probation officer." A job I know nothing about, I added to myself. But I did not want to be a substitute teacher again this year. I wanted a real fulltime job, even if I didn't know what it was all about.

Langford fidgeted with his tie and explained, "Well, uh, we want to be sure of your availability and ensure your safety if you are now or should become pregnant." He leaned back in his desk chair. "We also would like to interview your husband."

I sat for a moment trying to look puzzled and innocent, a difficult task for me. Then I leaned forward and looked straight at Langford. "I didn't know that my husband applied for this position. I thought he was very happy with the job he has."

"Oh, no, no. Your husband didn't apply. But we... we have to be sure he understands the possible dangers in this job and the type of people you'll be working with, and that he'll allow you to do this work."

"Look," I explained, "I have just returned from Germany where I worked with a special group of enlisted men. Only a fourth of them could be allowed off the base at any given time due to their propensity for trouble and fights. I used to watch them being delivered to the infirmary on Friday nights by the truckload. I was outnumbered three thousand to one, and there was little that I did not hear or see. You should also know that because of my husband's sudden transfer to Detroit, I was forced to turn down a position managing the day care center in Pruit Igo in St. Louis, a notorious crime-ridden and poverty-stricken high-rise residential project."

I paused just long enough to catch my breath and continued, "By the way, are the wives interviewed?"

Langford stared at me with mouth slightly opened. After a few moments of silence, he closed his mouth and whispered, "Well, well." Then he stood up. "We'll let you know what our decision is. We should know in a few days."

He didn't shake my hand or answer my question or identify whom he meant by "we."

Later that day, when I described the interview to my husband, I told him not to count on me getting the job, so I was surprised that evening when I got a telephone call from Langford offering me the position. I accepted his offer, and within a few days I took the oath of office, becoming the first woman probation officer for Oakland County Circuit Court.

My husband was never interviewed.

Langford never told me why he hired me, but I learned later that he was forced to hire a woman in order to meet the emerging affirmative action mandates. At the time, I felt that my bold remarks during the interview and my work history convinced him that I could handle convicted felons on probation. But after several months working for him, I realized he saw me as an experiment that he hoped would fail so he would not have to hire more women.

Oakland County is the most affluent county in Michigan and is predominantly Republican. It's on the northern border of Wayne County, home to Detroit. The line of demarkation between the "Haves" of Oakland County and the "Have Nots" of Wayne County is Eight Mile Road.

Detroit's Mayor Coleman Young and Brooks Patterson, the Oakland County prosecutor during my tenure as a probation officer, often threw insults at each other across Eight Mile Road. Mayor Young blamed Patterson for white urban flight, and Patterson blamed Young for the increasing crime in Oakland County. In either case, my job as a probation officer was interesting because, though I worked in Oakland County, most of my caseload was in Detroit and Wayne County.

"This is your office, your road book. Your report day is Wednesday," explained the less than enthusiastic male probation supervisor to whom I was assigned. The probation offices were located on the top floor of a beige brick four-story building, which also contained the circuit and probate courts and their support offices, the prosecutor's office (employing twelve white male assistant prosecutors), and the law

17

library.

Training consisted of little more than the initial introduction. My supervisor offered no details and ended the fifteen minute orientation on my first day with, "If you have any questions, let me know. Oh yeah, you must make home calls to everyone on your caseload."

He forced a smile and left my office before I could ask, "What's a home call?"

No offer to give me a tour of the courthouse or jail was forthcoming, but he did introduce me to the receptionist and women in the typing pool. My isolation, as the only female probation officer, led to a close relationship with these women. I relied on them for most of the important information I needed, such as where the prosecutor's office and jail were and a definition of home calls. They were always helpful and happy to finally have a woman as a probation officer, and I was glad not to be the only woman in the office.

I could not tell whether my supervisor's apathy was toward his profession or toward me because I was a woman—one he, too, hoped would fail. I was especially aware that I was the first woman ever hired as a probation officer, and so was afraid to ask questions for fear of looking stupid. I may not have been stupid, but I sure was ignorant about what the job entailed.

I came to my office on the first Wednesday armed with information to dictate on my "Report Day," which I assumed was the day on which one prepared reports for the court, etc. To my astonishment, I found a waiting room filled with lethargic male probationers waiting to see me. I realized at that moment that I'd never asked who reported what, and my supervisor had never told me. It was their day to report to me, not my day to do reports. The smiles on each probationer's face when I introduced myself indicated they were equally as surprised, but pleased to discover that I would be their P.O. (Probation Officer).

It was obvious to me after a day of interviewing those men that they had expected I would be intimidated. Their expectations were thwarted. In spite of my long blond hair and mini skirts, I was not about to be manipulated. A group of male colleagues hovered around my office door along with the probationers, waiting to see how I would handle the surly men on my caseload. Obviously, they were hopeful that something interesting would happen on this first report day, something that would prove me different from the others in this white male bastion.

A few colleagues ventured questions, like:

"Do they swear at you? They do at us. For that matter, are we allowed to swear now that you're here?"

"Have any of 'em asked you out?"

"They all look happy when they leave your office. They never look that way when they leave ours. Must be your perfume."

I survived that and many future report days relatively unscathed and eventually was accepted as just "one of the P.O.'s."

II

Most of the one hundred probationers on my caseload were men. The male probation officers were disheartened by this fact. They had hoped I was hired to handle all the women probation cases. My supervisor was among the disappointed ones and explained, "The women are always whining and crying. They're nothing but a bunch of dopers and prostitutes. Most of them hit on us and have got a few of us in trouble. They wouldn't do that with you."

I knew it was more prestigious to work with men because they were perceived as real criminals and more dangerous. But I actually wanted to work with women since I could see the inequities of their treatment by the whole criminal justice system. For instance, at the Oakland County Jail there were no programs for women for a GED (general education diploma), trusty status, or work assignment, even in the kitchen; the men had all these available to them. If sentenced to probation, little effort was made to help women become employed or educated, and the problems of mothers who were single heads of households were not addressed at all. I was determined to help all the probationers on my caseload, but I admit I placed emphasis on helping the women succeed.

One of the first new cases assigned to me shortly after I was hired was Maria, a petite, forty year old Italian woman. She was the mother of four and never had so much as a traffic ticket before she was arrested and prosecuted for murdering her husband, Bubba. Maria,

Bubba and their three-year-old son, Luke, had lived in a two-story bungalow in a quiet, residential, blue-collar neighborhood. Maria's other children were grown and had left home.

I showed my naivete during the initial interview with Maria when I asked, "Why didn't you leave this man if he was a threat and beat you?"

Maria stared at me for a long time, sizing me up before she answered. "When Bubba went to the bar that night, I knew he'd come home drunk again and beat me. He called me a whore, lazy, dumb, whatever it took to build his ego. I've never been any of those things. I've always been a solid Catholic and raised all four of my children to respect the Church. I was tired of the beatings and of Bubba throwing me into the street no matter what the weather, or who was watching, or that I had no clothes or anything. I'd stay with a friend or family 'til Bubba came after me. After the first few times this happened, I stopped reporting the beatings to the police because nothing ever changed. Some beatings even put me in the hospital. But I did run away from Bubba three times, and actually filed for divorce twice. I moved out of the state, changed my name and got work, waitressing mostly."

Maria paused; her face looked tired and drawn. She began to cry as she continued, "But Bubba always found me, caused trouble at my jobs so that they'd fire me, and then he'd drag me back to our house, only to start the whole thing over."

She stopped again and took a deep breath. "So, like I said, when he went to the bar that night I'd had enough. I went into the basement, loaded his shotgun, sat in a chair facing the front door in the living room, and waited for him to come home. He did at about 2:30 in the morning and I shot him. The only thing I didn't count on was my son waking up and seeing it. I'm...." She lowered her head and cried. "I'm guilty, but I don't regret ridding the world of that man. I do regret that Luke saw it and will have to live with that the rest of his life, maybe even hate me."

Everyone that I interviewed for the pre-sentence report (the report prepared for the judge which would determine the offender's sentence) confirmed that Bubba was "the basic scum of the earth." Even the police detective assigned to the case said, "It could'na happened to a better person." According to his report, there had been several complaints about Bubba from other people as well, but nothing was ever considered serious enough to put him in jail.

Although Maria's candid account pointed to first-degree murder which carries a natural life sentence without parole, she was charged with and plead guilty to manslaughter for which she was sentenced to thirty days in Oakland County jail and five years probation. She and her son were placed in therapy, and she returned to full time work, free, finally, of Bubba's brutal interference.

Kathy, like Maria, was among the few women on my caseload that first year. The day I met her, she was seated alone in the attorney's booth waiting for me. She was dressed in an ill-fitting, waistless, drab blue jail dress which swamped her small frame.

Kathy's auburn shoulder length hair shone in the harsh jail light that also emphasized her flawless complexion. She sat facing the door on the stainless steel stool with her back against the wall. She was twenty-five years old and the mother of three children. She was staring into the distance when I entered the attorney's booth and sat down opposite her.

Kathy had been convicted of armed robbery during which one of the co-defendants and the victim were wounded. She drove the getaway car. Neither male co-defendant was her husband, Billy. He had planned the crime, but remained safely at home while the crime was executed. The robbery was committed by Kathy to finance Billy's drug habit and support their three children.

As the interview progressed, I found it difficult to separate my role as a woman from that of a probation officer, and I asked, "Why would you risk getting into trouble, maybe even killed, for a man that sits home and shoots up?"

"I don't know any other life." Kathy put her head into her small hands and cried. "Billy's the only man I've known. He hasn't worked since our first kid, Kevin, was born. He's ten now. Billy's an addict and I've never worked. I don't have any education and don't know any other way."

She stared at the wall beyond me, attempting to compose herself, and continued, "If I don't do as he says, he will beat me. He'll leave me and the kids. I tried to get help from my mother, but she said

I've made my bed and must lay in it. There's nothing I can do. Nothing!"

I asked her, "Don't you think you could make it on your own? Get an education? Work?"

Kathy appeared to look through me. She resumed speaking in a monotone, "What would I do without my husband, Billy? I've been with him since I was fourteen. What would he do without me? He can't make it. Maybe I'm to blame for this. Maybe I wanted too much. No other man would ever want me, especially with three kids. What do I have to offer? I've failed at everything I've done, except having babies."

I felt overwhelmed and silenced by her feelings of hopelessness. Kathy lifted her tired eyes, looked at me and asked, "Why should I ask for more from my life? It's no worse than my mother's."

"What about your kids, Kathy? Don't they deserve more?"

"They're okay. Kevin takes care of the others. He makes them breakfast, gets them to school, and watches them when I'm gone. He even helps them with their homework. I can't. He don't seem to mind. He's always smiling and acts like a grown man, more responsible than Billy."

Kathy received a five year probation period after serving a short jail sentence. I had to help her without belittling Billy. I knew she was very intelligent and thirsted for a more meaningful and rewarding life, qualities that made my task much easier. We embarked on Kathy's "rebirth", taking small steady steps. Most of my counseling urged Kathy to get a GED, which was the first step toward developing her self esteem and independence. Obtaining a GED was just one of many ways she gained the confidence she needed to eventually dump Billy and get out of a relationship which was dragging her forever downward.

Two years into Kathy's five year probation term, she appeared in my office unexpectedly. A broad smile covered her face. "I passed! I got my GED!"

After several moments of exuberant hugs, she blurted out, "I told Billy to leave and not return unless he got help. I told him I didn't want to see him 'til he could prove he can stay off drugs."

Eventually, Kathy obtained an associate degree at a local community college while receiving funds from a special welfare program.

She won a scholarship to a Michigan university and was able to receive Aid-to-Dependent-Children monthly until she graduated. The last time I spoke with her she was working as an accountant, studying for the CPA exam and was dating Billy. Her decision to eliminate Billy from her life had motivated him to change his. Although Billy had remained drug free for several years and was also attending college, Kathy remained cautious about rekindling a permanent relationship.

It is hard for me to think about Maria and Kathy without also remembering Mack Langford's remarks after Kathy was sentenced and placed on my caseload. Langford came into my office, put his arm around my shoulder, and leaned his head close to mine. "You're a little soft on these women, aren't yah? You need to toughen up some. You can't keep taking their side just because they're women."

He squeezed my shoulder, winked at me, and then left. I froze, suffused with anger, because Langford had treated me like a child rather than a professional. I didn't realize that it was only the beginning of his physical overtures toward me, disguised as paternal concern.

I finally decided I was tired of dodging Langford's touches and crude remarks and went to his office unannounced to confront him. I walked in, closed the door, looked straight into his eyes and stated, "I know you were forced to hire me. You hoped that I'd fail so that there'd be no more women P.O.'s, and that I'd help you prove your point that women don't belong in this business. Well, I am here to tell you that you've hired the wrong woman!"

Langford sat behind his massive desk stacked with piles of paper. He stared at me over those damn glasses just as he did the day he interviewed me, but said nothing. I spun around, head held high, and left his office, determined to succeed. Mark Langford didn't touch me again after that session, but he never changed his patronizing attitude toward me or the women that were hired after me.

III

Maria and Kathy were among the most memorable women on my caseload at the beginning of my career, and Jimmie was one of the men I recall vividly. He was twenty-two years old then, and a drug addict. I met him about a year after I became a probation officer. What I remember most clearly was the last day I saw him. He came to my office at 8 a. m., as he had been directed, and sat in the chair opposite my desk.

I handed him the papers that listed the rules for the in-patient program he had agreed to enter. His hands shook as he held the papers and stared at them. His head was lowered so that his chin almost touched his chest. "You know I can't read these, Mrs. Miller."

I pulled my chair next to his and sat down. "Give them to me. We'll go over them together. You'll have to sign them before you can be admitted."

After I read the final statement, "I agree to adhere to all the above rules and have not been coerced into this decision," Jimmie signed his name in a child's scribble. He looked up at me with tears welling in his eyes and asked, "Will they shave my head and make fun of me because I'm fat and stupid?"

I returned to my desk and sat down. I stared at him for a moment. "Well, Jimmie, they may shave your head. Some of the things they do and some of their rules may seem harsh, but all of it is meant to help you get rid of the heavy baggage that has been weighing you down. Oh, by the way, you can't get admitted until one o'clock today."

He jerked his head up and his mouth dropped open. "What'll I do 'til then?"

"Well, I have to make some home calls. I guess you'll have to come with me." I wasn't going to give Jimmie any excuse to back out now, remembering how long it took me to convince him to enter the drug program. I packed my paperwork into my attache case, grabbed my lunch, and loaded them and Jimmie into my car.

As I traveled, Jimmie slept on a sleeping bag in the back seat of my Volkswagen. Glancing at him in the rear view mirror, I thought he looked angelic, when in fact he was an addict who had committed numerous robberies to support his habit. His plump physique was topped by a round, flushed freckled face crowned with red curly hair. He had had no contact with his family in years. I thought of the many conversations we'd had about his parents during the year he was on my caseload.

"I hate my parents," Jimmie had claimed the first day I met him. "Both of them are drinkers, and my father beats the shit outta everybody. Big fuckin' man. Neither one ever cared if I was alive or dead. I got hooked on 'hairon' [heroin] and got kicked outta the house when I was sixteen. Been hustlin' ever since."

He shook his head as he dropped it to his chest. "I really hate them."

"You can't choose your parents," I said. "And no one ever guaranteed that you'd like them. But that's no reason to punish yourself or feel guilty. You can't change who they are, but you can change who you are. It's really okay."

In the back of the car, Jimmie awakened and let out a loud yawn, which brought me back to the mission at hand. We shared my lunch in a park, and I dropped him off at exactly 1 p.m., thankful that my intuition about him was correct—I was unharmed and still in possession of my car. I never saw him again, but years later when I was appointed the warden of the Huron Valley Women's Prison, Jimmie telephoned.

"Hi, Mrs. Miller! This is Jimmie. Do you remember me?"

"How could I forget you, Jimmie?" I was shocked, but glad to hear from him.

"I really think you deserve the warden's job. You saved my life. You know, I'm married and have three kids. I've kept a job for five years and haven't used drugs in ten. I really want you to know that I made it. I live in Dundee, 'bout ten miles from the prison. Maybe one day I'll stop by."

I was proud to think that I had played a part in Jimmie's recovery and journey into a stable life. He sounded confident, happy and proud. I choked up a bit when I responded, "Jimmie, you really made my day. It's so rare to hear from anyone who was on my caseload who succeeded. Usually, I only hear from the ones who end up in prison. I'm happy for you, and me."

Mondays in most businesses are dreadful. Probation was no exception. Monday was when you found out who from your caseload had been arrested over the weekend, meaning a mound of paper work, court appearances, and unending telephone and home calls and road work to sort out what happened, only to have a judge return the violator to your caseload, starting the whole process all over again.

Monday brought new cases from Friday's court hearings, which meant reorganizing my calendar to squeeze in the needed interviews and research in time to complete the pre-sentence reports as scheduled by the judges' clerks. One Monday morning brought me Bob and Jerry, two drug-addicted co-defendants. They were charged with attempted armed robbery after going to three separate liquor stores, claiming to be armed with a gun and demanding money. In fact, Bob was armed with a black plastic toy handgun.

On that day in the brutally cold month of February, this duo entered a party store in the first of three robbery attempts. They were careful not to choose a store in the neighborhood where they lived, even though it meant schlepping against bitter winds through snow and slush because neither owned a car. But neither made any effort to hide his face. After browsing in the liquor store to make sure that the young female cashier was alone, Bob approached her and pointed the toy gun at her through his coat pocket. "Don't make any wrong moves. I have a gun. Give me all your money."

Jerry stood behind him, but said nothing.

The cashier stared at the two of them for a few moments and then turned away from the register. "I have to go to the back room for something." She left the cash register counter and walked slowly to the rear of the building.

Bob and Jerry watched as she disappeared into a room at the back. Jerry yelled at Bob, "Do somethin', for Chrissakes!"

Bob shouted back, "What? Point my plastic pistol at her and yell 'bang, bang, you're dead'?"

Bob and Jerry left that store and walked to another about a mile away and prepared for their next attempt. It went pretty much the same as the first one.

They walked to their third and final liquor store. This time Jerry took the gun and did all the talking. When Jerry finished his demand for money while pointing the plastic gun through his coat pocket, the middle aged female cashier laughed and insisted on seeing the gun. When none was produced, she grabbed a .32 caliber handgun from under the counter and pointed it at the perpetrators who spun around and ran for the door. The cashier pursued them down the middle of Ten Mile Road, shooting the gun.

Bob and Jerry's brief life of crime came to an abrupt halt when they were arrested a few blocks from the third attempted robbery scene, which was within walking distance of the Hazel Park Police Station. Out of breath, Bob admitted to the police, "This is not our day. We need to find some other kind of work."

They were sentenced to probation in front of a courtroom filled with attorneys, probation officers, family members and judge, all trying to keep a straight face as the details of the case were presented.

IV

Judges, prosecuting attorneys, and my colleagues called me naive and questioned the unabashed, fearless and somewhat nurturing methods I displayed as a probation officer. That was especially true on the day I arrived in Judge Gilbert Thornton's Court with a dangerous male probationer, Thomas King, and his luggage. King had been brought to court weeks earlier as a result of a warrant I'd requested for his violation of his probation agreement. He had committed a new felony, armed robbery and rape of a thirteen year old girl. His mother, against my advice, posted bail again by using her house as collateral. King had already stolen everything else from her.

If a director were casting the sleazy con part for a movie, King would have been selected without hesitation. On the day of his sentencing, he dressed in faded, torn blue jeans and a plaid short sleeved shirt exposing several tattoos, mostly of naked women, dragons, girls' names and "Mom". He had red rimmed eyes and sandy colored hair that hung in greasy strings to his shoulders. His slouched posture, toothless smirk and the three fingers missing on his right hand completed the picture.

King's probation term had been revoked and he was about to be sentenced to prison. Since I knew he didn't have a car, I picked him up, crammed him and his luggage into my orange Volkswagen, and delivered him to the judge. Later, as I had promised, I took his luggage to a friend for storage because he wasn't allowed to bring personal property with him to jail.

Judge Thornton was presiding on the day of King's sentencing, something I did not look forward to, as the judge's dislike of the probation department was well publicized, mostly by him. He was stern faced, clean shaven and always wore a perfectly knotted black tie which emerged from the top of his official black robe. He sat behind a towering mahogany bench surrounded by his faithful court servants, including a court reporter, the prosecuting attorney, the bailiff, a deputy sheriff and a Court Clerk. Judge Thornton's awesome demeanor was not diminished by the sudden movement of his right hand to slide his glasses to the tip of his nose, a sure signal that a tongue lashing was about to be delivered.

I approached the bench when called by the clerk. Judge Thornton looked down on me and boomed, "Mrs. Miller! Just what do you think you are doing transporting a dangerous criminal, a rapist at that, around in your car? Aren't you rather trusting? Are you that naive to think nothing could happen to you? Do you think you can play God, young lady?"

"No, only you can play God," I mumbled under my breath.

I looked up at Judge Thornton. "Nothing did happen, your honor. I think his anger is directed toward his court appointed attorney. He feels his lawyer let him down because he didn't get him out of this jam. It's never crossed King's mind that he's guilty."

I was confident about King being spineless when confronted with someone who appeared stronger and in control, which is how I envisioned myself. He'd run into my office a few weeks earlier screaming, "I've been robbed! Right in the alley behind my apartment. The guy took all my money. What'll I do?"

"How does it feel? It couldn't have happened to a nicer guy," I responded.

"I'm not saying that I didn't get what was comin' to me, but what'll I do for food and things?"

"What others do. How about a real job, or get temporary assistance, in your case, a loan from us." He never paid it back.

As I thought about King's predictable behavior, Judge Thornton returned his glasses to their less threatening position at the bridge of his nose. He turned to King's court appointed attorney, Brooks Patterson. "And what do you have to say on behalf of your client, Mr. Patterson?"

"There is really little to say. Mr. King has pled guilty. We beg the court's leniency."

I often found myself in a confrontation when I appeared before Judge Thornton, even though he described me as "gutsy" in a speech to the probation department. That didn't stop him from delivering another verbal thrashing to me during a probation violation hearing for a female offender. On that day, I almost talked my way into the county jail.

"Judge Thornton, this woman is an addict who supports her habit by prostituting. She never reports and never keeps the same address. It's impossible to find her and a waste of time and money to keep issuing absconder warrants for her. Thirty days in the county jail and cut her loose is my recommendation."

Thornton glared down at me from the bench, (a situation I was getting used to). "Who will care for her children if she serves a jail sentence, Mrs. Miller? She is foremost a mother."

"Who cares for them when she is on the streets or with her pimp or high? I really think you would be wrong to put her back on probation."

"I could find you in contempt of court for your insolence, you know, Mrs. Miller," the judge shouted.

"I will gladly go to jail and take the press with me."

I was not held in contempt, but the female offender was assigned probation for the third time. She disappeared within a few days of her sentence, leaving her two children with a neighbor, a fact the judge never wanted to discuss.

Sometimes, however, I had to admit Judge Thornton was correct when he described me as naive, because he saw me as a person who thought everyone could be saved. It was true that I felt most people wanted to be saved and that they were basically good. I also felt that if they knew I was only trying to help them, no harm would come to me. These feelings were to be challenged during the months and years ahead.

V

Home calls were mandatory and lumped with other tasks relegated to a probation officer on her road days, days spent investigating for pre-sentence reports and visiting probationers' residences and employers. These visits produced a gnawing, sick feeling in me, as I steeled myself to face the disorder of many impoverished homes. The smell, somewhere between mildew and feces, lingered in my nostrils for days. Cockroaches were abundant and I was afraid to sit on any furniture. I shook out all my clothes before going into my own house at the end of each road day. Children, mostly poor and black in tattered clothes, played in alleys overrun by rats, and ate pop corn on porches, ignoring the roaches which paraded over the food.

Yes, I do believe Judge Thornton was right when he called me naive, at least in the beginning of my career. Mack Langford also felt I needed to be protected. He wanted me to be accompanied by a male probation officer when I made home calls in a notorious crime filled neighborhood of Pontiac. I rejected the offer, knowing male P. O.'s were not escorted, and claimed that the area was "a piece of cake." In fact, I was quite impressed with the way everyone seemed to know my name and were friendly and polite, a clue I chose to ignore. "Good morning, Mrs. Miller. How are you today? Can we help you find someone?" Once I even found a group of men actually polishing my car while it was parked outside the apartment building in which a probationer lived.

After weeks of feeling euphoric about my effect on this neighborhood, I discovered that one of the men on my caseload was the kingpin for drug trafficking in the Pontiac Projects. He had put out the word that not a hair on my head was to be touched or an insulting word mumbled in my direction.

This kingpin telephoned me from the county jail about a year after he'd become part of my caseload. He began apologizing, "Mrs. Miller, I'm really sorry that I got busted again. It wasn't your fault. You did what yah could. Maybe I'll see yah when I get out." I really missed him when he was sentenced to prison. My home calls were never quite the same.

Most of my caseload was from the metropolitan Detroit area. Those of us working in that area had to take special precautions and to be aware that we could be victims at any time. I dressed in casual clothes, usually slacks and sweater or blouse, and did not carry a purse. I carried my ID and a small amount of money in my pockets and wore little jewelry, nothing to tempt a would-be assailant.

I never rolled the windows down in my car until I was on a freeway, no matter how hot it was. That was the unwritten rule. Thieves were known to reach through the open window and grab whatever they could see of value, whether on the seat next to you or on your body; sometimes they even stole the car.

Many of the cars I drove didn't have air conditioning, which meant I spent hot days traveling around town with my clothes stuck to my body, face glistening with sweat and an irritable personality. That was one reason I made home calls in the cool of the mornings in summer if I could. Another unwritten rule was to make all home calls before ten o'clock, since most of the people we would visit lived in neighborhoods where the population slept late. Home calls were safer when people were sleeping.

I was forced to break the unwritten rule for a reason I've since forgotten and to make a home call in the late afternoon. It was winter and there had been a heavy snowfall the night before. As usual, the side streets had not been plowed and tire tracks had carved huge ruts in the streets. It was dusk, and I was feeling a little nervous.

I successfully parallel parked, although it was difficult because my Volkswagen was in the repair shop and I was driving my husband's van which slid easily on snow covered roads.

Once I completed my home call, I ran to the van, anxious to get underway and cuddle up with my husband in front of the TV in the safety of my warm home. I started the van and, rubbing my hands together as I waited for the engine to warm, watched my breath form clouds on the windshield. I put the van in gear, but it would not move. The tires just spun. The van was stuck and darkness was fast approaching.

I was a well-trained Michigander and carried emergency supplies in the car for such occasions. I shoveled and placed ashes behind the tires in the areas where I cleared the snow. I then got back in the van, started it and attempted to free it, but, again, the tires just spun. My futile maneuvers—digging, ashing, starting the vehicle—were repeated a dozen times, without luck. Nothing worked.

I felt exhausted and disheartened. I was kicking the right rear tire and fighting back tears when I heard a door close at the house across the street. I turned in the direction of the sound and saw three men walking down the porch stairs toward me. Every horrible vision ran through my mind—rape! murder! robbery! I began shoveling again faster and faster, more in an effort to let them know I had a potential weapon than to free my car. My heart pounded harder as they got closer. I was scared.

The tall one, who wore a brown felt hat and a brown, full length, leather coat with a fur collar spoke. "Can we give you a hand? You've been here a long time."

I answered with a quiver in my voice, "Thank you. I could sure use the help." I hoped I appeared in control.

Within a few minutes of this trio's shoveling and pushing, the car was freed and I was able to drive away. I felt foolish for my knee-jerk fears, but I discovered the men weren't just being chivalrous. The car that I was parked behind, putting it in a vulnerable position, was a brand new pink Cadillac with all the bells and whistles. It was owned by the man in the brown leather coat.

I breathed a huge sigh of relief as I drove away. It was at that moment I noticed how much my hands were shaking. I thought I was lucky once again as I drove down the freeway entrance ramp. I recalled another time when I didn't make a scheduled home call because, when I drove onto the scene, a group of men who didn't look very innocent were standing around outside the house. I decided I wasn't going to take the chance of finding myself a police statistic and made a fast retreat. I rescheduled that home call.

Fear of what field (parole and probation) agents might confront on the streets has increased over the years as these streets become meaner. Field agents in Michigan are now allowed to carry hand guns, supposedly to calm such fears. Those who opposed the authorization of hand guns felt guns would give an agent a false sense of security. Unless an agent practiced on a regular basis with the weapon (most did not), the gun could be used against him or her because the agent would not be fast enough to handle it. Issues not debated, but ones about which I was concerned, were the over-reaction to a situation in which an innocent person could be critically or fatally shot, or crimes of passion of which all of us are capable. Agents carrying hand guns make themselves more susceptible to both.

After six years working as a probation officer for the Oakland County Circuit Court, I realized there was little room for promotion. Supervisory positions at that time were held by young men, which meant there would be few vacancies in the near future. And if there was a vacancy, I felt sure it would not be filled by a woman. I was ready for a new experience, so I joined the Michigan Department of Corrections (MDOC) and embarked upon my career in the prison system.

I wanted to stay in the corrections field and knew that Region I (Detroit and Wayne Counties) needed field agents in parole, probation and corrections centers. Most MDOC employees did not want to work there because of large caseloads and dangerous neighborhoods. Since I was used to those neighborhoods from my Oakland County caseload, I volunteered to work as an agent in the Northeast Corrections Center. No one else would take the position, but I knew it would make me more visible for promotion.

I studied state correctional policies and procedures for days in preparation for my interview with Alan Gagne, Regional Administrator of Region I. Gagne never changed during the thirteen years that I knew him. He wore glasses, was a stocky 5'9", had gray hair, and was abrupt, sarcastic, funny and grumpy all at the same time. His supervisors thought Gagne's abruptness and sarcasm made him difficult to manage. But I found him supportive and colorful, and I was glad he took a chance on me.

As I entered Gagne's office on the day of my interview, he rose from his chair, held out his hand and said, "I'm Alan Gagne. Good to meet you. Can you start September 26th?"

Dumbfounded, and regretting the hours of study I had put in, I responded, "That's only a week's notice."

"To hell with Oakland County. That's all the notice they need. We need you now."

And so I became a State employee with the Department of Corrections on September 26, 1977.

33

PART 2

YDN Northeast Correction Center

I

September, 1977

The elevator was not working on my first day at the YDN Center. So eager was I to get started, I ran up the four flights of stairs. I entered the floor by the officers' station, quickly introduced myself, and hustled off to my office, a refurbished bedroom which I shared with an extended family of cockroaches. I was the first female agent assigned to that unit. Two male officers were on duty. The younger one later told me that he thought I appeared gullible and naive, and confessed, "I told Officer Greason you wouldn't last three weeks."

My office and the Male Correction Center, a halfway house known as YDN (the "Y" standing for YMCA, the "D" for Detroit and the "N" for Northeast), were located on the fourth floor of a deteriorating five story, red brick YMCA. The other floors were still used as a YMCA. The building covered most of the block and towered over the ragtag neighborhood. It was made up of duplexes and bungalows, and small businesses like Onasis' Coney Island (a.k.a. O'Nasty's—a favorite spot for purchasing drugs), Elmo's Family Restaurant, a couple of bars, Churches Fried Chicken, and the Better Made Potato Chip Factory. A Detroit Police "Mini" Station and a Department of Social Services office building were located across the street.

YDN was located in what is considered one of the worst Detroit neighborhoods, desperately impoverished, crime infested and plagued by drugs and gangs. Political leaders in Detroit at that time, however, denied the existence of gang activity. It was a neighborhood that looked bombed out and forgotten. Shells of burned buildings, targets of arson, or boarded up and vacant buildings dotted the streets. The streets and vacant lots were strewn with broken bottles, empty cans, pieces of furniture and old mattresses.

The main floor of the YMCA consisted of a reception area surrounded by protective glass with a small slit for speaking to the receptionist or for passing papers. The glass did not, however, prevent robberies of the meager sums collected from the male residents who lived on the four floors.

Also occupying the main floor were the YMCA administrative offices, gym and visiting area. Visitors were not allowed beyond the lobby except to use the gym. The entire main floor seemed to be without light, artificial or otherwise. This darkness was enhanced by the cracked, dark green vinyl and wood furniture, well marked and carved by previous users.

O'Nasty's and Elmo's were contracted by the Michigan Department of Corrections to feed prisoners housed at YDN. Surveillance of these places by center employees was not enhanced by the smoke and grease-covered windows. I could always tell by the odor of fried food hovering around him if a prisoner had just come from one of the two. Only once was I foolish enough to be persuaded to have a cup of coffee from O'Nasty's. The coffee glistened with cleaning oil and tasted like bacon.

On Mondays, Wednesdays and Fridays, I ran two miles in the Y's gym during my lunch break. I played floor hockey or volley ball with all male teams on Tuesdays and Thursdays, and started a weight lifting program. These activities seemed to be important to the prisoners who respected brawn, not brains.

Each morning when I arrived at YDN, approximately twenty prisoners stood in the sign-out line. Prisoners would receive day passes to job hunt, which often translated as rendezvousing with their street pals and main squeeze rather than seeking employment. Each day they left with pass and job verification sheet in hand, and returned by the 5 p.m. curfew—at least most did—with signatures indicating they had searched for work. These signatures were often penned by friends, lovers or family members rather than prospective employers.

One day about a month after I started at YDN, I arrived at work carrying my gym bag and purse. One of the prisoners standing in the pass line asked, "Do you run every day, Mrs. Miller?"

"Just about."

The prisoner looked at my bulging gym bag. "Do you lift weights too?"

Although I had just started weight lifting, and was only at the five pound bar bell range, I answered with a smile, "Yes."

All the other prisoners smiled and nodded their heads in admi-

37

ration. I never had any problems with the prisoners at YDN after that, except for Pringle who missed this exposition. I had to pin him against my office wall with my right arm cocked against his upper body while I lectured him, nose to nose, on who was the boss. He left my office mumbling, "That lady's crazy." After that I never had any problems with him either.

I had volunteered to be a caseworker/agent at this center. The reason no one else wanted a job here was that the last supervisor had been shot at by a disgruntled male corrections officer. The bullet hole was still in the wall behind the supervisor's desk. The replacement supervisor would not appear until three weeks after my arrival. She was a young, African-American female, and the first woman to manage this center. Her name was Denise Quarles.

I denied having prejudices, therefore could not explain my fear of being supervised by a black female. I was just as guilty as those I'd previously admonished for thinking women were more difficult to work for. I'll admit I was concerned about her prejudices as well. She was not my first female supervisor, but Denise Quarles was the first I had in corrections. In no time at all, she proved my fears unfounded. She became my mentor, my best friend, and my toughest supervisor, in the best sense of the word "tough".

Denise, in spite of her own struggles with the department, taught me that adherence to correction's policies would ensure my success. She, too, felt integrity was one of the most important qualities a person could have, and supported me when I was shunned by colleagues and superiors for displaying that very trait.

When I'd requested YDN during my interview, Alan Gagne had told me, "If you think we will not accept someone dumb enough to volunteer for YDN, you are crazy. It's yours." Perhaps I was crazy, but the time I spent at YDN, thanks to Denise, equipped me with a quick and thorough education of not only the Michigan Department of Corrections, but of the prison system as well. It also gave me credibility with my superiors because I had taken a difficult position and succeeded. I believe the latter was part of the reason that I was promoted to center supervisor when Denise left. The other part was Denise's confidence in me and her recommendation that I succeed her.

Denise had the strength to remain my friend through my most

difficult times and never failed to give me encouragement. It is hard to be a supervisor and friend, but because Denise was able to perform both roles admirably, I learned from her and was eager to advance beyond a center supervisor. I became determined to eventually become the warden at Huron Valley Women's Prison.

II

Not very long after I arrived at YDN, I met a prisoner called Jo Jo. He was fond of riding the elevators in the nude and greeted other passengers by hitting them with his feather filled pillow.

Jo Jo was a good friend of Billie's, a retarded African-American man in his mid twenties who was six feet tall and had a voracious appetite. It seemed that no amount of food could fill Billie. Many people in the building fed Billie because he was so childlike and always hungry. He never gained weight, but seemed to grow up out of his clothes. His pant legs barely hung to his ankles, the backs of his shoes were pressed down to the soles to allow room for his enormous feet, and his arms didn't end. To my knowledge, he had no family in the area.

Jo Jo and Billie did not represent the normal prisoner population, but increasingly, emotionally and intellectually impaired offenders were being incarcerated in Michigan. This was due not only to the deinstitutionalization of the mentally ill, but also because of the public's growing fear of crime. Offenders like Jo Jo and Billie were imprisoned rather than placed in an alternative community based program that would have met their needs better and would have cost far less. The trend toward locking up such people continues today, but corrections officials know this is not the answer and are researching alternatives.

Each day, Jo Jo and Billie were heard exchanging their incomprehensible dialogue. Jo Jo would say, "Hey man, Allah told me that the true state is the naked one and that I have been chosen to right the world."

Billie's reply would be something like, "I saw the green men again. I know they're from Mars. They told me so."

"Yeah, I know. Allah said they were coming and not to be

39

scared."

"Hey, Jo Jo, I'm glad we know."

And so their conversations went, day after day.

Billie often came into my office to talk. He was unable to work because a special program had not been found to train him. "Hey, Mrs. Miller," Billie called as he entered my office carrying a newspaper in his right hand and wearing white socks, new black prison issued high top shoes and khaki pants cut off below the knees with threads hanging all around each calf.

"Yes, Billie. What can I do for you?"

"I want you to help me with the crossword puzzle."

"Billie, you can't read. Even some people who can read can't do crossword puzzles."

"Yeah, but you can. So, let's do one," Billie pleaded, with the expression of a dog begging for food.

"Okay, let's try."

We did the crossword puzzle at least once a week. He could not read, but did have some good ideas about the words that fit.

Billie stayed at the center for about six months and then was furloughed to a group home. About a week after his release, I received a telephone call. "Mrs. Miller, this is Officer Riley from Wayne County Jail. We got one of your prisoners here. He says his name is Billie."

"Why is he there?"

"He was caught inside a super market. It was a B & E (breaking and entering)."

"I can't believe that. I'll be right down."

I read the police report at the Wayne County Jail. Billie was found sitting on the floor of the supermarket eating cookies and ice cream. When asked by the arresting officer, "What are you doing?", Billie replied, "I'm hungry, man. Don't get enough to eat at the home."

Center employees pleaded with the judge not to sentence Billie to prison on a new charge, but he did anyway. We were not able to convince the judge that Billie meant no harm and probably was hungry. To my delight, though, Billie wrote to me several times. The letters were unintelligible, but appreciated. Judging from the contents of the letters, he apparently worked in the prison kitchen because the letters consisted of lists of ingredients and other items copied from labels on cans and boxes of food.

Orientations for new arrivals from Jackson Prison took place on Thursdays. Jackson's technical name was Southern Michigan Prison (SMP). Among other things, SMP was the men's reception center for newly sentenced felons, and the staging area for transfers to correction centers throughout the state.

As the Center Supervisor, I rarely gave the orientations. This was handled by one of the two male agents I supervised, except on those occasions when I arrived at YDN while the prisoners were unloading from the state bus. Unless they were returning to the center, the prisoners didn't know me, and they would approach me using phrases of endearment and making references to various parts of my anatomy. In these instances I would disappear and get to the fourth floor before them to warn Officer Greason, "The bus is here."

Officer Greason chuckled in response. He knew I would handle orientation that day, and assembled the newly arrived prisoners in the dayroom in preparation. The prisoners, dressed in khaki prison dress-out uniforms, slumped in their chairs to wait for yet another litany of rules. Once they were assembled, Officer Greason would come get me from my office.

I introduced myself as I entered the dayroom. "Hello, I am the Babe (or whatever they called me that day) that runs this joint. You will call me Mrs. Miller."

I enjoyed the startled looks on their faces as they probably thought, "Oh shit. What did I say to her in the lobby?"

Occasionally a group attempted to cover their mistake by verbal intimidation. Once, while I was reviewing the rules for weekend furloughs, a prisoner interrupted me. He was annoyed that he could not stay overnight with his girlfriend. One of a very few Caucasians ever assigned to that center, his apparent need to establish his virility and ensure his power base was not strengthened by his appearance. He looked like a vulnerable young boy with his shoulder length, mouse colored hair and pale complexion. His state dress-out khakis could not hide the scars from previous battles in which I guessed he was not the victor.

"After all," he asserted, "I've been locked up a long time and

41

have the need to fornicate." He actually used the word "fornicate," a dead give away that he was not comfortable in his effort at being macho.

"The rules don't say anything about fornicating. You just can't stay overnight," I explained.

All the prisoners chuckled.

For a long time there had been thefts in the building on YMCA floors. The victims were generally non-prisoner residents and building employees, but an investigation revealed, with near certainty, that a prisoner was committing the thefts. No one would expose the culprit, so I held a meeting with all the prisoners and informed them that they would be on a thirty day restriction unless someone confessed to the crime.

Among the prisoners in this group was Bernard Cole, one of the most colorful prisoners I've ever known. He was heavy set and built like a fire plug. Cole had a large mustache that covered his upper lip. He always wore a white karate jacket, a black belt signifying his alleged ability, and a black felt homburg. During this meeting, he thundered, "While I'm here, there'll be no thefts! I will not permit them!"

The staff and I thanked Mr. Cole for his offer of help. The other prisoners snickered.

The prisoners remained on restriction for thirty days because they would not snitch on a fellow inmate. It wasn't until much later that I learned a prisoner known as Pimp was the thief.

Usually I knew prisoners by their nicknames (Cool Breeze, Chocolate, Shark, Stiletto, Little Bit) before I knew their given names. The nicknames reflected their images and personalities, especially Pimp's. It was not a complimentary name, but one that fit.

Pimp slithered into my office on the day he arrived at YDN. At the close of our interview, he asked me out for a drink at the Ren Cen, a large and expensive hotel complex in downtown Detroit.

I declined immediately.

"Is that because I'm a prisoner?"

"That's one reason. Are you sure you want to know the others? For instance, you're not allowed to drink; you have no money and I'm not paying for you; you have no transportation and I'm not driving you; you're on a curfew; you have no job; you're unreliable."

These other reasons, numerous and ego deflating as they were, did not deter Pimp. Months later, on his last day at the center, he strutted into my office unannounced, dressed in a three piece pink suit that hung in loose folds on his skinny frame, and threw his telephone number on my desk. "This is just in case you want to get a hold of me."

Some people never learn.

Ham, another center prisoner, got his nickname because he was a comedian. He was also difficult, volatile and physically strong. Ham picked fights with other prisoners, broke curfew on a regular basis, returned to the center drunk on most days, and failed to seek employment. He had not adjusted well to the center, so on the Fourth of July I decided to place Ham in custody and return him to a higher security level.

Ham was over 6'5" tall, about twice the size of either of the two officers on duty July Fourth. He was muscular from regular workouts during the many years spent in prison weight rooms, and he was assaultive whether provoked or not.

It was routine to have the police arrest prisoners who were going back to higher custody and had to be housed at the county jail until transported. I knew that taking him into custody under normal circumstances would take the entire Detroit police force. It was therefore decided to make the arrest after he returned to the center from a day of partying in hopes he would be tired, if not drunk.

We chose the midnight shift for the arrest. The police were summoned once the two center officers were sure Ham was sleeping soundly. The two Detroit police officers responding to the call planned to enter Ham's room quietly and catch him off guard.

Not planned for was the condition of one of the two Corrections Officers, Mr. Barkman, who had apparently enjoyed the holiday to its fullest and had been drinking.

Barkman greeted the police at the door and led the way to Ham's room. Weaving down the narrow, dark, green corridor, he shouted, slurring his words, "Take all of them! Take the whole damn lot of them!" Barkman pounded on the doors of the prisoners' rooms as if to emphasize his command.

Officer Barkman not only woke up Ham, but the entire facility. Prisoners scrambled into the hall wearing boxer shorts or sweat pants or robes, belts hanging at the sides. Many had plastic caps on their heads to hold their hair in place. All tried to out-shout one another, and jeered at the police for being so sneaky.

After the bodies were sorted out and Officer Barkman was pacified, Ham sauntered from his room, unruffled and cool. "I knew this day was coming." He held his arms out to be cuffed by the police.

Ham was escorted from the Center by the police to the grumblings of Officer Barkman: "These assholes are all alike. None of em should be here. Worthless. That's what they are."

The two Detroit police officers just looked at each other and shrugged. As they grabbed Ham by the arms, one remarked, "This is some tough guy. More like a pussy cat." He then turned to Barkman. "Maybe you better go home. Wanna ride?"

Barkman took the ride, he and Ham in the back seat of the police car. Ham went to the county jail, Barkman to his house.

III

I received a telephone call from a Wayne County Deputy Sheriff one beautiful summer day in my third year at YDN. It was the kind of day you dream about during those long, grey, winter months, temperature in the mid 80's, cloudless, blue skies, soft breeze.

The deputy sheriff reported that a Center escapee had been picked up and was at the Wayne County Jail. I had to place a detainer on him so the sheriff would not release him. The only jail for Wayne County at that time was old, dingy, crowded and reeked of dirt and urine. Worse yet, I had to go to the windowless basement to file the detainer.

I decided to enjoy this perfect day and get away from the persistent smell of grease from Church's Fried Chicken and the Better Made Potato Chip Factory. My office window was always open because there was no air conditioning in the summer and uncontrollable furnace heat in the winter. Since I knew that leaving the detainer at the county jail should only take a few minutes, I telephoned my friend, John, and asked him to have lunch with me. We agreed to meet at his office.

John managed the Downtown Center which was within walking distance of the jail. We walked from the center through Harmony Park, a jewel jammed into a decaying Detroit neighborhood. On this glorious day, many people gathered around the fountain in the center of the park to eat their lunch, listen to a live jazz band and savor the unusually warm weather.

We were about to follow the lead of those walking in front of us and step over an obstruction jutting out from the bushes and blocking most of the sidewalk when, to our surprise, we saw the obstruction was a shabbily dressed, middle aged man. Blood ran from his mouth and judging from the grey shade of his skin, he was dead.

As luck would have it, a police car drove by. We chased it for about a block waving our arms and shouting, "Stop! Stop!"

The police officer stopped the car and waited. Out of breath, John and I explained the problem, pointing in the direction of the body. The officer told us, "I can't help. I'm transporting a prisoner. I'll send someone over pronto."

Pronto seemed an eternity. While we waited, it was horrifying yet funny in a morbid way how passers-by ignored the dead man. They continued to step over him and even looked in another direction as if that made him disappear. No one questioned us as we stood protectively by the body.

After the police arrived, we continued our trek to the jail and lunch, although the thought of food was beginning to be less appealing. The employees at the jail, mostly male deputy sheriffs, displayed an indifferent attitude toward my request to place a detainer on someone being held there. Their caustic remarks and extensive, inexcusable delays were all part of their indifference. While I waited, I thought about the reasons for their behavior. Perhaps it was boredom or exhaustion or maybe they were just jaded from working with prisoners. Or perhaps the employees simply had an aversion to working in such an unpleasant environment, stuffed as they were into an ancient, six story building with no air conditioning, few windows, crowded unclean cells, and narrow, dimly lit corridors, and assaulted by the continual hum of prisoner chatter and clanging cell doors.

I was asked, as usual, "Is the prisoner a juvenile?"

"No," I responded.

"Is the prisoner a female, then?"

"No." I tried not to snap, knowing that the deputies, police, detectives, and even some clerks (male and female) assumed women worked with juveniles or women offenders, never with men.

The detainer was finally accepted and we were able to leave. John was beginning to exhibit signs of regret for having accepted a lunch date with me. We walked up the flight of stairs to the main floor, grateful to be heading out into the sunlight and the breeze after suffocating in the bowels of the county jail. As luck would have it, I recognized a prisoner named Joe Williams in the visitors' line. He had escaped from YDN a few months earlier after writing "Miller is a hoe" on the wall outside my office door. It was his retaliation for being placed on disciplinary restriction for thirty days because he violated center rules. Officer Greason was incensed by Williams' insult to my womanhood, and I was incensed that he couldn't spell whore.

I pretended I didn't recognize Williams when John and I passed him as we walked toward the exit, our shoes sticking to the clammy floors. Lunch would have to wait, I thought. I leaned toward John and whispered, "Don't draw any attention to us and don't look at the line, but the fifth man in line is another escapee from YDN. He's black with close cropped hair and a hare lip, wearing baggies held up with black suspenders and no shirt. Stop at the deputy's desk as I pretend to leave and tell the deputy to arrest him."

John went over to the deputy sheriff on duty and explained the situation. After he heard John's tale, the deputy raced toward Williams and grabbed the escapee's arm. When the deputy explained to him why he was being detained, Williams shouted, "She's mistaken! I'm not an escapee! She's got me mixed up with somebody else."

Williams pointed his finger at me as I approached him. The deputy tightened his grip on the escapee's arm to prevent him from leaving or taking a swing at me.

"Hard to mistake you with your attitude," I blurted out.

While all this was going on, several people who had been waiting in line left the jail. I guessed they were also fugitives, and no doubt thought John and I were some crack investigative team. They weren't going to wait around to see if our job had been completed.

The deputy restrained Williams and removed all items from his pockets, including a Marine ID with a blurred picture, which he insisted was of him. Once finger prints and other LEIN information confirmed his true identity as Joe Williams, the escapee, we could finally leave.

John never had lunch with me again.

IV

My secretary was away from her desk on a quiet day during that same summer, so I answered her telephone. "Northeast Corrections Center, Tekla Miller speaking."

"Do not start your car after work if you wish to live," warned the male voice.

"Who is this? Is this a joke?"

There was no response, just a click, and then a dial tone.

It was the first time I had ever received such a threat. I was scared even though my head told me that it was probably a hoax. I telephoned the police who said they would send the bomb squad. The center staff—there were five of us—waited on the front steps outside the building for the bomb squad to arrive. The parking lot security guard could not be found. Perhaps he had once again been bribed away with a couple of bottles of Ripple.

The media arrived first, in vans emblazoned with their respective channels' logos. News reporters listen to radios that monitor police calls, and I suppose they pick only those calls that seem most promising or, more accurately, sensational.

As the personnel jumped out of the vans, one after the other, they looked like the circus clowns who all pour out of a small car. The reporters stepped from the vans carrying steno pads and pens. They were followed by camera men and their assistants carrying the large TV cameras and related paraphenelia. And, finally, came the sound men who ran back and forth from the vans to the reporters and their entourages carrying microphones on long booms and small handheld mikes. They readied their equipment, hoping the explosion would occur in time to be aired on the 6 o'clock news.

While holding microphones to our mouths, the reporters asked their persistent questions:

"What is your name?"

"How do you spell Tekla?"

"What kind of name is that?"

"How old are you?"

"What is your job?"

"Any suspects?"

"Who's the one that got the phone call?"

"Has anything ever happened like this to you before?"

"How do you feel right now?" How do I feel? Are they kidding?

About five minutes later, Detective Hardy arrived with the bomb squad in an unmarked van.

I told Detective Hardy that the corrections officer who had been suspended for shooting the center supervisor was on trial at that time. Hardy agreed with me that it was a perfect motive for the bomb threat, and was convinced of the strong possibility that there was a bomb in one of our cars.

"Well, the way I see it, you've got three choices," Detective Hardy said, facing the five of us. "One. We can absolutely guarantee there is no bomb. We'll strip the cars down to almost bare metal, but we won't put them back together again."

"Two. We can be reasonably sure there's no bomb and will not strip the cars, but will do a thorough search. However, you'll have to start the cars yourselves when we are finished."

"And three. We can explode the cars."

All five of us opted for number two.

By this time, the crowd had grown to about a hundred people, most of whom came from the Social Services building across the street from the YMCA. The event drew a bigger crowd than the vendors who sold purses, jewelry, watches and other specialty items outside the DSS building on the days welfare checks were picked up. Traffic was obstructed by gawkers, horns honked and obscenities were hurled in New York City cab driver style.

Although a number of drug busts had taken place on the streets outside the YMCA, entailing the use of force by undercover cops, none attracted the media unless a death occurred. Drug busts and related shootings had become a regular part of life in that area.

Crowds gathered on that day, not so much out of curiosity, but because of the possibility they might be seen on the news or even interviewed. People seeking the fifteen minutes of fame Andy Warhol predicted stood behind reporters or the person being interviewed, giggling, pushing and waving their hands at the camera, yelling, "Hi Mom!"

My car was the last to be searched because it was parked on the street and I was the one who took the telephone call. The other employees' cars were parked in the employee parking lot. When the search was completed, my four employees and I started our cars, palms wet, hearts racing, news cameras focused on our faces. And, of course, just before turning the key in the ignition, the reporters asked again, "How are you feeling at this moment?"

I responded with an icy stare and the thought, how do they think I feel? Excited by the challenge of being blown apart on TV? I don't think this is what Andy Warhol had in mind.

One by one, the suspected vehicles started. There were no explosions. I almost felt sorry for the newsfolk and the crowd that had gathered. They appeared disappointed; an audible moan arose from the onlookers, and the media's departure was rapid. They dismantled their equipment, loaded their vans, and drove off hoping to find another story of human tragedy and pain.

People in the crowd began to talk, make jokes, laugh and walk away. The bomb squad returned the equipment to their van and left. At least they, unlike the media, said "Good-bye."

Standing alone on the corner near my car, the four members of my staff and I stared at the fleeing vans and groups of people wandering off in different directions. Finally, Andy, one of the center caseworkers sighed, "Well, I guess I'll go home."

We all responded in sort of a dazed unison, "Yeah, see yah tomorrow," got into our cars and went our independent ways.

There was no mention of the incident on the news. This was my first encounter with the media, but future experiences with news reporters only reinforced my original perception that they were in search of the gruesome and the negative when they reported on corrections, and often described only that side of the story.

V

Bernard Cole's mother lived in a primarily black, poor Detroit neighborhood where unkempt and abandoned homes were side by side with a few well maintained ones. I had become accustomed to such settings after six years as a probation officer and my work at YDN.

Bernard, the big prisoner with the homburg and the booming voice, described his relationship with his mother as, "Real close. We depend on each other. She needs me at home with her, not here. She's awful sick and has no one to care for her but me."

He used this relationship every chance he could as an excuse for his rule violations. He described his mother as "on her death bed." Of course, his presence was always immediately needed, no matter what time of day or night and in spite of the center curfew. I was never quite sure what kind of support he could give her after years of absence due to imprisonment.

Though I never gave into these tales of woe, this did not deter him. I guess he felt he would eventually get through to me. After numerous pathetic pleadings and sometimes even tears, he found it hard to keep a straight face when begging for a furlough so he could attend one of his mother's brushes with death.

I met Bernard Cole's mother on a Monday morning in February.

"Good morning. Are you Mrs. Cole?" I asked the woman who met me at the door. She appeared hesitant as she nodded her head in response.

"I'm Ms. Miller, your son's agent," I explained as if she didn't know. Who else would be at her home at the crack of dawn, and a white woman at that. "I'm here to speak with you, and see your son."

Mrs. Cole was a robust woman, living on welfare in a modest but tidy, one story, white clapboard home that smelled of fried chicken. She showed no signs of near death, let alone illness. In fact, her well endowed frame, bright eyes, and glowing complexion seemed to exude good health.

Mrs. Cole wiped her hands on her apron and smiled. "Oh, you're that nice lady Bernard has told me about. Come in, come in. Want some coffee?"

"No, thank you. I just need to know where your son is. He didn't return to the center last night."

"Oh, well he was here for dinner. Tried to get him to go to church, but he wouldn't go. You must of forgotten. He's on one of them furlough things. Anyways, he stays across the street." She pointed toward a house identical to hers, except in bad repair, and continued, "He's probly still there. Bernard doesn't report for work 'til ten o'clock, but you know that."

I gathered that Mrs. Cole knew nothing or didn't want to know anything about her son's activities. He had no furlough or job and was not supposed to be at her home, or the home to which she directed me. He was AWOL. I thanked Mrs. Cole for her help and went across the street.

The house across the street was grey from the lack of paint. The screen door was nearly off its hinges and banged against the house when the wind blew. Many of the windows were cracked; some were broken. The drapes and shades were drawn as was often the case at houses where I made home calls. I always thought the occupants felt that daylight would force them to confront their miserable existence, or perhaps darkness would protect them from the decay threatening their environment.

As I walked onto a porch that slanted alarmingly to the right, music blared from within, and I saw there was no door bell. I had to pound on the door. After several forceful knocks, a large, heavy set, unattractive woman in her late twenties, with a puffy, tear streaked face and dressed in a torn white blouse greeted me carrying a shotgun. "I forgot to get the ammunition. I thought the bullets come with the gun. I would of kilt him this time if it was loaded."

I was relieved to discover the shotgun was not loaded, and that it was not meant for me. It didn't seem to matter that she had no idea who I was, and for that fact, I had no idea who she was.

"Who are you?" I asked, all the while wondering why Mrs. Cole had sent me here.

She replied as if everyone should know, "I am Ms. Funderberg."

Sorting through the profanity gushing from Ms. Funderberg's mouth, I learned she was Bernard Cole's girlfriend. Ms. Funderberg explained that Bernard had left just before my arrival on this not so blissful scene. During a heated argument, an event I later found was quite common with them, he had torn up most of her clothing with a huge butcher knife. Ms. Funderberg produced the knife as evidence by flashing it in front of my face. She, in turn, had tried to shoot Bernard. Fortunately for Mr. Cole, she knew very little about the shotgun she'd purchased the day before. Clearly Ms. Funderberg was agitated about failing to do great bodily harm to Mr. Cole, but she was not the least bit upset about him leaving.

After explaining who I was and determining that Ms. Funderberg was okay, I left. I felt fairly confident I would not be returning to her house to look for Cole, and that their relationship was over.

Bernard Cole found a job at a record store and was paroled about three months after that incident. Several months later while at Wayne County Jail, I saw him. His right foot was in a cast, and he was on crutches.

"What happened to your foot?" I asked, just to make conversation.

"It's broken."

"How did you break it?"

"Ms. Funderberg hit it with a hammer after I threw a knife at her." I pictured the same butcher knife Ms. Funderberg had waved in front of me being hurled across the room.

"Why are you in jail this time?"

"Ms. Funderberg's pressin' charges. Attempt murder! She never done this before!" Cole always thundered her name, using only the last one.

Bernard Cole was returned to prison on a new charge, Assault to do Great Bodily Harm Less than Murder. When he was later considered for parole, he told the parole board members that he and Ms. Funderberg had been married in the prison visiting room a few weeks earlier. Love is truly blind.

The day I saw Bernard Cole in the Wayne County Jail, I had gone there to speak with Reginald Cloaker, a 53 year old, soft spoken, grey haired, dignified looking man who, after two weeks at YDN, had been arrested for breaking and entering an unoccupied dwelling. He had spent thirty-six years in and out of prison for non assaultive crimes and was considered an industrious, dependable prison worker who had made it to the coveted status of clerk.

Troubled by his immediate re-arrest, I questioned him. "Why did you do this, Mr. Cloaker? You have such potential. How could you have been so stupid?"

We sat opposite each other in the attorney's booth, I leaning on the stainless steel table, and he leaning against the graffiti marked, mint green walls, his head resting just under the words, "fuck you." His eyes narrowed as he looked at me through his prison issued, black rimmed glasses. "Well, it's like this. All's I know is clerkin' and I'm good at it. Clerk's job in prison is respectable, even for a man. On the streets, it's a joke. It's too late for me to do anythin' else 'n I have no family to speak of. I want to be where I'm respected."

He was returned to prison, died seven years later at age sixty and was buried on Boot Hill with other unclaimed prisoners' bodies.

Shortly after my visit with Cloaker, I received a telephone call from a Detroit police detective. He reported having arrested Smith, one of the corrections officers from my Center.

"Is this some kind of a joke?" I seemed to ask that a lot.

Though I had warned Corrections Officer Smith many times about preaching to the prisoners who lived in the Correction Center, I couldn't imagine what he had done to get himself arrested. He adamantly professed to be involved in and convinced of the benefit and righteousness of the religious life he preached. He had also tried to enlist prisoners like Bernard Cole as disciples, though he knew such proselytizing was not condoned by the department.

Smith sang in his church choir and had hopes of making singing, not corrections, his career. "After all," he commented, "many Mo-Town greats like Aretha Franklin started that way."

He repeated almost daily the ways in which he would spend his fortune: "Buy a house, get married, buy a new car, maybe a Cadillac."

Smith hung posters on the walls of the center that encouraged positive behavior by following the path of Jesus. These posters were promptly torn down by me or the other prisoners. Officer Smith wrote many misconduct tickets on prisoners to prove their need for enlightenment, which did not seem to persuade them to lead the better life he preached.

His arrest made the headlines. As I read the newspaper article about Smith's activities, I thought of all the good officers whose caring deeds never made the news. Like the one who, while on his way home from work, saved a victim from an armed robber. I also thought about prisoner Cloaker who wanted to be respected, but had to stay in prison to achieve it. He and his plight never made the news either.

According to the police report, Officer Smith was running a gang of juveniles and was the mastermind behind elaborate extortion schemes. He sent juveniles to banks with a note addressed to the manager informing him that Smith was holding the manager's wife and/or children hostage. Large sums of money were demanded in return for their release. Fortunately, no one was ever injured, a fact that did not win Smith many points in court.

Officer Smith was sentenced to a federal prison because he had been an employee in the state system. It was feared that if he were sentenced to a state prison, he would become a victim of prisoner retaliation. "Preacher" Smith's case seriously impaired my ability to ever fully trust appearances again.

Two and a half years after I'd started at YDN, I was asked to take a lateral transfer into the prison camp program for minimum security women prisoners. Tradition in Michigan dictated that a woman manage prisons for women.

I was not inspired by the thought of making a lateral transfer, but accepted the position because I was excited about developing and opening the first prison camp for women in Michigan and one of the first in the United States. I also felt that if I were successful in that program I would be closer to my ultimate goal, which was to be the warden at Huron Valley Women's Prison.

PART 3

Camp Pontiac and Camp Gilman

March, 1980

"Oh my God, this is Camp Pontiac? What have I gotten myself into this time?" I muttered under my breath, as I sat in my car staring at the place with disbelief. I immediately had second thoughts about accepting the transfer into the prison camp program. The five white-washed, one story stucco barrack buildings looked like a movie set for "Cool Hand Luke". The only thing missing was the "Boss Man" with his shotgun, mirrored sunglasses and a few hounds yapping at his heels. It was rumored that this Prison Camp had been built to house prisoners of World War II. I believed it.

Taking a deep breath, I turned off the ignition and prepared to face the staff. I was determined to get out of my car looking the picture of confidence and authority. My outfit had been painstakingly chosen to project a conservative and professional image: I wore a charcoal grey pinstriped suit, white tailored blouse and not too much jewelry. Unfortunately, as soon as I stepped out of my car, I sank up to my ankles in mud, new black pumps and all. It was the beginning of the spring thaw, and Camp Pontiac was located in a swamp a quarter of a mile off a dirt road.

Camp Pontiac, recently a men's prison camp, was being renovated to house women prisoners. I fought off the urge to turn tail and run by reminding myself of the reason I was here. My hope was that by working in the prison camp with women offenders, I could help bring them programs equal to those the men had.

I was sure both staff and prisoners were watching me, so I stomped out of the mud and into the building designated "Main Office". On my way to the entrance, I noticed a late model Continental parked on the grass alongside the building.

Inside the main office, I found a young white man behind the only desk, feet propped up on an opened drawer. He shouted into the P.A. system, "Who's in the gym?"

I assumed that the voices I heard answering him came from the gym. Every time a name was shouted out over the P.A., the man checked it on a count sheet.

"Are you the officer on duty?" I asked.

He was dressed in expensive designer jeans and a silk floral print shirt, unbuttoned to show off several gold chains, and his sandy colored hair was perfectly coiffed. From his appearance I assumed he owned the Continental. "Yeah," he replied. "Be with you when I finish count."

He was out of uniform and doing a prisoner count which was supposed to be done face to face with prisoners who should produce pictured IDs to ensure positive identification. My eyes roamed around the small, beige painted office as I stood listening to him. The dusty P.A. system was placed on top of a floor safe directly behind the desk. On the desk stood a manual typewriter, well used by the look of the almost transparent ribbon, a desk calendar covered with notes, and a wire in-basket filled with official looking papers, some yellowing at the edges. Two four-drawer filing cabinets stood to the side of the desk, one grey and one black, with broken locks and drawers.

Across the narrow room was an eight foot long counter. Behind the counter hung a peg board filled with keys, each tagged with a number, and a bulletin board covered with memos and notices, many several years old. To get behind the counter you had to squeeze between the end of the counter and the wall. Directly across from the entrance was the locked door to the prisoners' living areas.

Every counter top was coated with dust, except where coffee cups had rested. The linoleum floor of an unidentifiable color was caked with a blend of wax and dirt, layered to a grey-green muck in the corners and along the floorboards. Again I fought the urge to run.

"Now, can I help you?" the officer questioned.

I was angered by his manner and announced, "I am Ms. Miller, the new camp supervisor. Get your feet off the desk and put your car in the parking lot, now!"

He stood up and his eyes roamed over my body, starting at my head and ending at my muddied ankles and shoes. It was not the kind of first impression I had wanted to make. He gave me a know-it-all smile and answered with a barely audible "hmm!" However, he did move his car. When he returned, I barked a few more orders.

"Although you'll only work for me for the next two months while the camp is being renovated, you will work in a uniform and you will follow departmental policy. By the way, what's your name?"

"Bierce, Officer Bierce, ma'am." That was the beginning of an eternity chained to the title of "ma'am".

Bierce took me on a tour of the Camp, introducing me to the sixteen male prisoners who had remained behind to renovate it. Apparently some attention had been given to equal opportunity since the sixteen men were a mix of Caucasians, African-Americans and Hispanics. None, however, seemed enamored of my presence. I thought it was because I was a woman, but later learned they were afraid I would change the leniency with which the camp had been managed for the past several months. My predecessor, who had retired, had been on a lengthy medical leave and rules had been relaxed.

It was apparent from the rundown condition of the buildings that having 140 males crowded into two dormitories had taken its toll on the camp. The sixteen remaining prisoners lived in a very small dorm attached to the chow hall–living quarters normally reserved for prisoners assigned to the kitchen. Because of a court order mandating program parity for prisoners, seventy-one women prisoners would be housed here when the renovations were completed, until a new camp could be built across the street. Camp Pontiac would become the first prison camp in Michigan for women. I could hardly wait for the women's reactions when they got a look at it. They were being transferred from the only other women's prison in the state at that time, Huron Valley Women's, a.k.a. "Valley of the Dolls" or "The Valley", a prison that was three years old and resembled a college, and where prisoners were housed mostly in single rooms.

Bierce described the remaining staff as we were touring. "The lieutenant has already transferred, so the afternoon shift is run by the sergeant. He likes to drink." I took the latter to mean that he was not always at work. I was right.

"The day shift has you, the counselor and an officer, me or Donalson. And the midnight shift has two officers. Usually, the Lieutenant works days, but like I said, he's transferred."

All the camp employees were men. Women were still not allowed to work in male housing units. A class action suit had been filed, however, by women officers who had not been considered for promotion because they lacked experience which could only be obtained by working in housing units—a neat "Catch 22". Two years later they won their case.

A man appeared as we returned to the main office. Bierce introduced him. "This is the prisoners' counselor, Nate Thomas. He'll transfer with the men."

Mr. Thomas' bony six foot two inch frame appeared to be all legs. He scowled at me during our introduction, which made me feel that he blamed me for his involuntary transfer. I shared my office with Mr. Thomas during the two month renovation, but rarely saw him.

My office was in a perfectly square building separated from the rest of the camp structures. The front door faced the visiting area, but all areas of the camp could be viewed through my office windows, parking lot to the east, visiting center to the south, prisoner and visiting yards to the north, and all the remaining buildings to the west. I had my own bathroom, which was an advantage, but only after it was disinfected. Apparently, cleaning the bathroom had not been a priority of my male predecessor.

An oil space heater sat in the center of the office. After the third time it blew up, belching greasy soot and smoke over me and the entire room, I no longer thought it was a charming accent. I complained about its potential health and fire hazards, but the space heater was not replaced until a year and a half later when the women prisoners left and the men returned to Camp Pontiac.

Each morning, during the time the male prisoners were refurbishing the camp, my car followed Nate Thomas' car into the parking lot at Camp Pontiac. That was the last I would see of him during the day. More mysterious was the fact that his car would be gone from the parking lot at the end of his shift, because no one ever saw him leave.

My newly hired female lieutenant, Renee Jacobs, and I were baffled by his elusiveness. After a couple of weeks of his disappearing act, I finally decided I was going to find out where he went. "Lt. Jacobs, I'm determined to find Thomas. He can't just leave the clerk, a prisoner, alone to type the confidential reports and schedules. The prisoner is making up the reports, for God's sake."

Lt. Jacobs nodded her head in agreement. She and I stalked the camp searching for Mr. Thomas.

We looked for him in all five buildings on more than one occasion, but never did find him. We finally gave up the search because of more pressing concerns, like organizing the camp.

I spent much of my time weeding through the six four-drawer filing cabinets in my office. My predecessor had filled them with pink copies of major misconduct tickets issued to male prisoners during the prior ten years. These tickets should have been in the counselor's prisoner files that accompanied prisoners whenever they transferred. The misconducts were filed neither alphabetically, nor chronologically, and could serve no purpose in that condition. There must have been hundreds of them, so I packed them into cardboard boxes and shipped them to the main warehouse. The staff there could decide what to do with them.

No complete copies of the mandated Michigan Department of Corrections Policy Directives, Procedures and State Administrative Rules could be located anywhere in the camp; no wonder no one cared whether Officer Bierce wore a uniform or took count. Also missing were up-to-date state forms. There wasn't even a list of the forms that were available in the camp program, which meant I had to go to another camp and hand list all the ones they used. It took over a month just to pull all that together.

Camp Pontiac officially became a women's camp on Saturday, June 8, 1980 at midnight. However, the male prisoners would not be transferred until Monday morning. I was left with only the newly hired women employees, because all the male officers had been transferred to other prisons.

At a meeting with the male prisoners, I told them about this change. "As of tonight, all the officers will be women. They'll take all counts. If you choose to flash them, it'll be your choice. It may make the officers laugh, but it will not scare them."

For the next two days, the men tried everything possible to intimidate me and the women officers—exposing their penises; interjecting the word "fuck" every chance they could; and challenging every decision in the hope that we did not know the correct regulations.

On that last Sunday, visits were held in the yard because of the warm spring weather. When the prisoners and guests became rowdy and refused to listen to the officer on duty, I announced, "If you do not control yourselves, I will terminate visits."

"You can't do that! I want to call my attorney," Jake shouted. He was a twenty-two year old prisoner with a slight build and big mouth. Jake had been particularly difficult throughout the camp renovation. He instigated a strike because he felt that the sixteen men chosen to remain at Camp Pontiac were privileged and should not be subjected to working overtime.

"We were hand picked to renovate the camp," Jake informed me. "If it weren't for us, the work would never get done." Obviously, he had forgotten that there were at least another 2000 men in the camp program in twelve camps throughout the state from which another sixteen could be hand picked.

Now I explained, "If you wish to end your visit, you may call your attorney. You know the rules. You can't leave a visit and return."

Jake did know the rules; but was not about to accept my answer and continued his harangue.

I knew I could not back down or I'd loose my credibility with both the prisoners and officers. I warned, "If you don't quiet down, Jake, I'll have no choice but to end everybody's visits."

Afraid he would have to face the wrath of the other prisoners, Jake decided not to pursue the issue. But he left shouting, "My attorney will hear about this."

Jake came to my office when visiting time was over, demanding, "I want to call my attorney."

"Can't you use the prisoner phone?"

"He won't accept a collect call at home, only at his office."

I handed him my phone. "Here, make it short. I want to go home."

He fumbled with a piece of paper and then looked up at me. "I don't have the right number. I can't call, but you'll hear from him."

He seemed smaller than he had when surrounded by an audience in the yard, and I was becoming impatient with his game. "I can hardly wait to hear from him, Jake." The attorney, of course, never called.

II

I looked forward to the change of camp employees and to working with female prisoners even if they were considered the "dreaded beasts" of corrections with whom no one wanted to work. Women prisoners are described as selfish, exhausting, needing immediate gratification, having no social conscience, lacking social skills, and being constant complainers. I believed that these characteristics described all prisoners, men and women alike. In any case, I felt positive about the change and believed I would no longer be challenged by prisoners purely because I was a woman. Above all, I was fulfilling a goal that I had set myself when I worked as a probation officer: to work with women offenders and develop more and better in-prison training programs for them.

Once I became a deputy warden, however, I discovered the real reason men preferred not to work with women offenders. It was because the central office administrators placed little worth on the skills needed to work in a women's prison. Perhaps the reason for their attitude was simply that the male prisoner population far outnumbered the women's, and therefore took most of the time and money. Or perhaps it was lodged in the tradition that women and their needs were unimportant because they were not perceived as breadwinners, but only as caregivers, a position of little esteem. Then, too, male employees seemed to equate a worthwhile prison job with aggression; it was manly and even heroic to engage in combat with male prisoners.

Whatever the reason, I was being paid the same salary to work with women prisoners and preferred it.

"Here they come!" shouted Officer Terri Albright, a robust woman with flaming red curly hair that reached to the middle of her back.

The bus from Huron Valley Women's Prison pulled into the driveway carrying the first twelve women prisoners, all of whom were volunteers. The department had learned its lesson previously when it had transferred a group of women prisoners "against their will" to a special program. On that occasion, the women prisoners had to be gassed before they kicked all the windows out of the bus taking them to the program. So much for the gentler sex.

While the bus carrying our women prisoners bumped up the quarter mile dirt driveway and parked in front of the visiting center, the male prisoners boarded a bus in the rear of the complex. We had planned to sneak the men out, but our planning hadn't worked. The women were still outside the visiting center when the bus carrying the men passed by, so there was a lot of noise. Male prisoners whistled and hooted, "Hey honey! We left you a few surprises. Be sure to look for them."

"Yeah, okay, baby. Too bad you aren't staying. We sure could have a good time."

Nothing untoward happened, however, and orientation was held as soon as the women prisoners were in the building and seated. The session went well at first, but eventually an attractive female prostitute turned murderer raised her hand and commented, "This is more like a maximum, not a minimum security prison. It's worse than 'The Women of Cell Block H'."

"This is the easy part. You ain't seen nothing yet," I replied. "Time for a tour and your bunk assignments. We'll make job assignments after lunch."

The prisoners shuffled out of the visiting center, chattering about what they saw. They stopped talking when they entered the dormitories. There before them were two rows of fifteen double bunks with two lockers between the bunks. The two cinder block dorms, both painted blue, were separated by a community bathroom, painted yellow, and included a cubicle where four prisoners showered at the same time. Women officers had attempted to make the bathroom homey by planting flowers in the six foot long urinal which had not been removed and was located against the back wall. "You gotta be kidden! This place sucks. Where're our desks and chairs?" The first brave prisoner had spoken.

It didn't take long before there was a chorus of questions and complaints:

"Do you really think we'll shower together?"

"Only them that wants somethin' other than clean bodies."

Others snickered in agreement, shaking their heads.

I smiled at the group, saying, "Don't worry, you'll get used to it. Besides, you'll be gone most of the day on your work detail." This met with a lot of groans and a few laughs.

"Get unpacked and be in the chow hall in forty-five minutes for lunch and your work assignments."

A new group of women was transferred to the camp weekly, each more reluctant than the last. Volunteers had ended with the first busload.

Most of the women were assigned to public works crews, the reason prison camps had been developed in Michigan. An eight to twelve prisoner crew worked with a male supervisor who drove them in a van to state parks or other public works areas. The prisoners maintained and cleaned those areas, constructed new and refurbished existing buildings. It wasn't unusual to see a work gang, dressed in two piece navy prison outfits and orange day glo vests, along roadways, in parks or in public buildings.

The male crew supervisors assigned to Camp Pontiac had only worked with male prisoners. Most had worked for the Michigan Department of Natural Resources for several years without much supervision or accountability. And, typical of their age group—largely men in their 50's—they held sexist views. Working for the Department of Corrections made them feel as if they had been demoted, because they would be supervised by a woman and forced to work with women prisoners. Some of them transferred to other prison camps as soon as they could. Those that stayed became dedicated employees and were euphoric when clients demanded women crews because they soon realized the women worked better than the men and were usually less threatening.

About two weeks after women prisoners had started arriving at camp, the first crew of eight prisoners left for their assignment in the green state van which was dubbed the "Green Dog". I heard singing from the dorms on that day. As the crew of six black and two white prisoners came closer, I saw with amusement that they had formed into one long line strung together with clothes line, and were singing, "Working on the Chain Gang".

The prisoners marched by in step to the rhythm of the song wearing the blue two piece male uniforms (no women's models were available yet) pressed to perfection, including a crease in the pant legs. The state issued red bandannas were tied in perfect knots around their necks, their blue baseball caps rested on their heads in just the right spots so as not to disturb their impeccable hairdos, and all wore makeup. I watched as they climbed into the Green Dog and left for their first day on a public works crew.

When the Green Dog returned at 3:30 that afternoon, the prisoners exited the van, dirt smudged and sweaty. There was no singing. Creases were no longer visible in the pant legs which were rolled up, exposing black high top work boots and once white work socks. The red bandannas had been removed from the prisoners' necks and used as rags to wipe the grit and make-up from their faces.

One prisoner passed by me groaning, "Man, that was the hardest day I ever spent in my life."

Another prisoner commented with amazement on the various animals they had seen. She showed me the red welt blossoming on her forehead as she explained, "I almos' got kilt by this huge creature when I got outta Green Dog this mornin'. If I wasn't afraid of doin' more time, I woulda split." The creature was later identified as a buffalo. Most of these women had never seen deer, geese, the great Blue Heron, let alone miles of dirt roads and countryside.

On normal days, prisoners were awakened at 5:45 a.m. By 7:30 count had been taken, prisoners were dressed, beds were made military style, breakfast eaten, sick call completed, and those prisoners assigned to off-ground work crews had boarded the Green Dogs. Others went to their on-grounds assignments as porters, grounds keepers, painters, laundry workers, or as kitchen helpers and cooks. Few, if any, had ever seen the sun rise before this. Daily routines in the summer were often interrupted by thunder storms which meant power outages and flooded dorms. Women prisoners became used to swabbing dorm floors by flashlight.

Green Dogs driven by male crew supervisors passed me each morning as I drove to camp. In each passing van, I could see heads bouncing with every jarring contact between the tires and the washboard road. On one summer morning, straining to see through the sun's glare on the van windows, I noticed there were only a few bouncing heads, one or two in each van when eight was the norm. I knew something was up, something I didn't think I would like. I went straight to the main office to find out what was going on. "Officer Albright, what's up? All the vans are nearly empty."

"It's the 'Green Dog Flu'. Yah know, like the 'Blue Flu' when cops call in sick as a form of protest. The prisoners don't want to work on the crews because they say it's hard. So most of them said they're too sick to work. Yah know, officers aren't trained to be doctors. We can't tell who's really sick and don't want to take a chance. So we laid them in for the day."

Albright was right; custody staff were not trained to be doctors and nurses. A nurse, Jan Schultz, had been hired to run daily sick calls, issue meds, and schedule and assist in the weekly visits by the doctor or physician's assistant. Unfortunately, she was still in training for another two weeks.

"Get all those assigned to off-ground crews and assemble them in the Day Room," I directed Officer Albright. Thirty-eight women were assembled, some still wearing nightgowns, hair rollers, shower shoes and face cream.

Once everyone was seated, I announced, "This may take a while. I'm going to examine each of you for visible signs of illness. If I find that you're ill, you'll receive a one day lay-in. If you're not ill, I have jobs for you. Cramps, headaches, sniffles don't cut it for a lay-in. If women used them for excuses not to work, there would be no labor force in the U. S."

The prisoners fell silent and watched each other as they approached me for the exam. Some admitted that they were not ill. Three prisoners were laid-in, and the other thirty-five were assigned to "G.I." the entire camp, toothbrush style. Sick call was never a problem again. One prisoner even cautioned a new arrival, "Ms. Miller wouldn't lay you in if you were dyin'."

I intervened and said, "No, only if you'd died already."

"Yeah," said the prisoner. "And don't cry around here either. It don't work. She says women are weakened each time they cry to get their way, and that's where men want us."

The nurse, Jan Schultz, arrived in camp two weeks later. Her angelic face was crowned by a mass of blond Shirley Temple curls, and her petite frame gave a false impression. One prisoner commented,

"Schultz looks like a pushover. Lay-ins will be back."

Schultz was no pushover. She refused to coddle the prisoners as other staff had, believing that this encouraged the women to behave like irresponsible children. Schultz was perfect for the camp, because she took the time to listen to and counsel the prisoners, but was firm and conservative when doling out remedies for ailments. Prisoners' hopes for lay-ins died fast, and I thought maybe they would learn a little responsibility along with good health habits.

III

We had all settled into the daily routine by the time the women prisoners had been at Camp Pontiac for two months. One morning I was writing a report at my desk, as usual, when an odd movement outside my office window distracted me. I glanced at my watch. It was only ten o'clock. July's oppressive and exhausting heat made me feel as though I had been at my desk much longer. The movement caught my attention again. I looked out the window facing the parking lot and with amazement watched the graceful descent of a red, yellow, blue and green striped hot air balloon. I ran from my office up the walk to the main building and told the officer, "I think Washington's ride is here."

Carla Washington was the first woman prisoner to be discharged from the camp, and we were waiting for the transporting officers. Before I could let Officer Albright know that I was kidding, she announced over the P. A., "Washington, your ride's here. Report up front."

Washington raced to the main office dressed in a new blue uniform, dragging one of the green military duffle bags in which prisoners transported all their personal property. Seeing her off were all the other prisoners who had remained in camp that day. The scene was like a carnival. Prisoners danced around Washington offering advice, telephone numbers, and crying because they were happy for her, and envious.

Washington assured them, "Don't worry. I ain't never comin' back here again. I sure learnt my lesson this time. I'm gonna git me a good job and take care a my kids. No mo' dope."

The band of dancing women came to an abrupt halt and everyone was silent as they spotted the balloon making its final descent. The basket holding one male passenger bounced twice along the gravel before it came to a complete stop in front of the visiting center. Then the balloon deflated in great colorful folds to the ground.

Washington surveyed the parking lot suspiciously. Her eyes widened and her mouth dropped open as the focused on the balloon. "Where's my ride, Mrs. Miller? I don't see the van."

"That's it," I said, pointing to the balloon. "It's a treat for the prisoners who have done well in camp."

Washington placed her hands on her abundant hips and shook her head, "Ooooh no! I ain't gittin' in that thing. Yah made me do a lotta things, but not this!"

Just as I started to explain the joke, the blue state transportation van turned into the driveway. Washington sighed and all of us laughed. Then the twenty or so prisoners who had accompanied Washington rushed the balloon and surrounded it, just as the pilot was climbing out of the basket. He stopped in mid motion, one leg hanging over the edge of the basket, at the sight of a gang of screaming women, and climbed back into the balloon. His eyes darted around the area searching the dirt road for help.

"Ladies!" I called, as I approached the balloon. "Ladies! Calm down and leave the man alone." (Jean Harris was correct when she reported in her book, "They always call us ladies.")

"Where am I?" the pilot asked in a panicky screech.

"You have landed in a women's prison camp," I responded, enjoying the look of disbelief on his face.

The pilot stood without moving for a few moments, mouth slightly open, staring at the prisoners, then me, and back to the prisoners, who by now were asking one question after another. He answered none. He seemed unable to get his thoughts together or formulate any words, until finally he said, "You gotta be kidding."

Just as the officer and I were beginning to move the prisoners away from him, his transportation team arrived in a van and pick up truck. Pilot and crew disassembled and packed the balloon with such speed, it seemed only minutes before we saw the dust trailing behind the vehicles fleeing the camp grounds.

Washington loaded her gear into the waiting state van. Her task was interrupted over and over by prisoners crying, hugging and kissing her and expressing their farewells. Finally, the van moved down the dirt driveway followed by swirling dust and the band of shouting, waving women prisoners.

As I watched Washington leave, I thought of my final conversation with her just the day before. She told me her parole officer was Darlene Schmidt, a midget physically, a giant intellectually, and a woman whose size never stood in the way of her command and powerful presence. Washington said she had written a letter to Ms. Schmidt, her agent the first time she was paroled, asking, "How can I get off your caseload?"

Ms Schmidt's response was, "Move!"

Washington did move. She also returned to prison for a third time as a parole violator because of drugs, breaking her promise about never returning because she had learned her lesson. Unfortunately, she was only one of a majority who returned and returned and returned.

IV

Rumors ran wild in the department after the women employees at Camp Pontiac were in place. Many employees, men and women, were convinced that the only reason women wanted to be officers in women's prisons was that they were lesbians. I was curious as to why this kind of nonsense did not seem to hold true for men who worked in men's prisons. Emotional involvement between prisoners and employees did occasionally occur, whatever the sexual orientation, but was only one of many employee problems.

Officer Renee Jacks' problem was a particularly disruptive one. I met Jacks during an employment interview shortly after she graduated from the corrections officers' training academy. Officer Jacks gave a convincing interview. She remained soft spoken when delivering her well prepared, deliberate responses and revealed an exceptional knowledge of department policies and procedures.

Officer Jacks, whose professional appearance also impressed me, was hired for Camp Pontiac. Her uniform blouses were whiter than most, starched and ironed with military creases running down each side of the front. Although she was a large woman, her officer's black slacks and green jacket had been tailored perfectly to fit her large breasts and broad back. Hair length was not dictated by a dress code, and Jacks' auburn curls hung to her shoulders, softening her sharp features. I never dreamed she would become the "Officer from Hell".

One day, about a month after Officer Jacks came aboard, I arrived at Camp Pontiac at lunch time to hear yelling coming from the chow hall. As I watched, several prisoners ran from the hall screaming, "Ms. Miller! Ms. Miller!"

"Do something quick before she gets any worse."

"She won't let us have margarine for our bread."

I knew the "she" was Jacks. This type of misunderstanding only happened when she was on duty. I held up my hand. "Hold it. One at a time. What happened?"

One prisoner stepped forward and explained, "Officer Jacks said that the menu allowed each prisoner one pat of butter for their bread. There's no butter, only margarine, but she won't let us use the margarine because the menu doesn't say margarine. She ain't right."

"Okay, okay, go back to the chow hall. I'll check into this."

A discussion with Officer Jacks, held later that day, proved the prisoners' account was correct. I explained to her that we were allowed to make reasonable substitutions in the menu if we ran out of or didn't receive an item in the monthly supply delivery. She appeared to understand, but I knew it would happen again. Her ability to make logical judgements was limited, to say the least.

Lt. Jacobs and I never knew where to assign Officer Jacks. Wherever she went, black clouds seemed to follow. We decided to assign her to accompany the women who were attending a vocational training program at Schoolcraft College in Wayne County. We felt she wouldn't be able to create her usual havoc because the women were in classes most of the day and monitored by faculty. Basically, her duty was to make sure the women remained at school and to monitor them during lunch and while they were being transported.

Pat Gugle, the coordinator of the program, who was generous, concerned, intelligent and had the patience to work with anyone, called me several times threatening, "I'm going to kill Officer Jacks."

Once calmed, Mrs. Gugle regaled us with tales of Jacks' bizarre behavior. For a short time I was able to convince her that Jacks' behavior was due to her newness. But then Jacks began handing out religious pamphlets at both the school and camp, as well as telling the prisoners, faculty at Schoolcraft College, and camp officers that she was an ex-offender and ex-drug abuser who had become a Born Again Christian.

Jack's last hurrah occurred when she ran through the halls of the school screaming that one of the prisoner students was attempting to escape. She stopped long enough to point her out to Mrs. Gugle, shouting, "There she is! Look out the window. In the out of bounds area heading for the auditorium, no doubt to meet a ride."

Mrs. Gugle responded, "That's not a prisoner. That's the nursing instructor, Ms. Judi."

Gugle's explanation fell on deaf ears because Officer Jacks was already out the door. She tackled Ms. Judi and brought her crashing to the ground. Officer Jacks apologized, but was removed from her assignment and placed on a conditional service rating, which ultimately ended in her being fired.

That, I thought, would be the end of Officer Jacks, but it was not. She telephoned me the day she received her termination papers, stating in a very clear, steady voice, "You were wrong to have me fired. I will see that you die."

Jacks hung up before I could respond. I didn't take her threat seriously until a few days later when I discovered that personnel had never run a mandatory LEIN check on her. Then I had a conversation with a police detective who revealed the unnerving information that Jacks was a suspect in a murder.

The detective told me that Jacks was not unknown to police, and, in fact, had been a suspect in another murder/kidnapping. Allegedly, she had kidnapped a man, removed all his clothes, driven him around town and then, with a male co-defendant, killed him. Because she turned state's witness, she was not charged with murder. For months after that, when I drove anywhere I checked for cars that could be tailing me, and I often became anxious when I saw a woman who looked like her. Fortunately, I never saw or heard from her again, but I didn't stop worrying for a long time.

V

No one in Camp Control, the name given to the central office for the state camp program, knew what to do with women prisoners. My boss, Warden John Mills, and those who worked for him were quite happy to leave Camp Pontiac in my hands. That would have been fine, except all our supplies were warehoused at Camp Control, seventy miles away. I was forced to bring the issue to a head during our first summer, over the sanitary napkin allotment.

"Look, Mr. Davis," I said to the warehouse supervisor, pressing the palms of my hands against the top of his desk and leaning my body forward, "you don't seem to understand. Women don't enjoy wearing sanitaries. They aren't a useless luxury item, like perfume."

Mr. Davis wore a state-issued, khaki uniform with his name printed on his left breast pocket. A vinyl pouch containing five pens of different colors were tucked into that pocket, revealing that he didn't adhere to the strict pen quota forced on other camp employees. Sitting behind a desk piled high with procurements, Davis spoke through teeth clenching a toothpick. "Mrs. Miller, you don't understand. I'm responsible for the inventory in this warehouse. The warden reviews it every month, and I don't want nothin' funny on it. I sent all the sanitaries you need for the month."

I rose to an upright position and placed my hands on my hips. "I hardly consider sanitary napkins funny. Besides, unless there are some real kinky men in this program, you could send me every sanitary napkin you have, and no one would miss them." I spat out the words, turned my back to him, and left the warehouse.

When the next monthly shipment of supplies arrived two weeks later, Officer Albright called my office, mystified. "Ms. Miller, you better come look at this. We got two instead of one truck load of supplies."

That seemed a good sign to me. Usually, by the time the supply truck reached Camp Pontiac, it had been picked clean of coveted items such as duffle bags, sheets, floor wax and stripper, by employees at other camps on the route. Even the swing set destined for Camp Pontiac was swiped. The swings had been made by the prisoners at

Camp Cusino especially for the women prisoners' children to use during their visits. Thanks to the great sleuthing of Cusino's supervisor, the thieves, Camp Lehman officers, were discovered, and the swing set was finally erected in Pontiac's yard. Of course, the theft was explained by all as "an honest mistake".

"Hey, maybe we got more than six leaky state pens this time," I laughed. "I'll be right there, Albright."

Prisoners were already unloading one truck when I got to the camp warehouse. It was filled with the usual: food, office and cleaning supplies, linens, and prisoner clothing. The doors to the other truck were open. I didn't have to inspect it closely to discover that the entire semi was filled with boxes of state issued one-size-fits-all sanitary napkins.

I looked at Albright and shrugged my shoulders. "I can't complain. I did tell Davis we were the only ones in the camp program who would use them. I wonder why these weren't pilfered?"

The one-size-fits-all sanitary napkins were issued without any means to secure them—no belt or pins—as part of correctional procedure to prevent weapons from getting into the hands of prisoners. That was before sanitary napkins came with adhesive to attach them to the wearer's underpants. Women prisoners had to walk while holding these napkins in place between tightened thighs. Male corrections administrators in central office (there were no women at that time) eventually gave in, several years later, and allowed belts.

Camp Pontiac was at full count by mid summer. Little separated one day from another. Things were relatively calm, until the last bus load of prisoners that brought the camp to full count arrived from Huron Valley Women's Prison. These were not happy campers.

Anna Carson leapt from the bus. She was the prisoner chosen as the spokesperson, and she greeted us with an unlit cigarette dangling from the corner of her mouth. "We don't wanna be here. We didn't volunteer for camp. Yah can't force us ta stay."

Carson, a 5'2" thirty-year-old booster (shoplifter), was built like a wrestler. Her muscular arms seemed to burst from under her rolled t-shirt sleeves, the right sleeve holding the obligatory pack of Kools.

"You obviously haven't heard of prisoner classification. Choice is not a factor. If you were sent here today, you belong here," I informed the scruffy group of twelve prisoners glaring at me through narrowed eyes.

Anna Carson refused to go on her public works assignment the next day. "All new prisoners start there and work their way into other jobs once they prove themselves," I told her.

"I ain't goin'. The only place I'm goin' is back to the Valley," she declared. "It's nothin' personal, Ms. Miller. It's just not my time."

"I guess you didn't hear what I said the day you arrived. You don't pick your time."

Anna Carson did not go to her assignment that morning. In fact, she started a sit down strike in her dormitory shortly before the Green Dogs were scheduled to leave at 7:30. The eleven women who had arrived at camp with Carson joined her.

Albright, the duty officer, was the only other employee in camp besides me. She ordered the strikers to their assignments. The prisoners responded by grabbing chairs, curtain rods, brooms and whatever was handy and began swinging. One of them hit Officer Albright with a curtain rod. I made it to the main office and telephoned the State Police for backup.

By the time I returned to the dorm, all but two prisoners were quiet. I announced, "Police are on the way."

Carson—one of the two—would not give up, but the other hold-out prisoner did. As Officer Albright hand-cuffed her, Carson chided, "You're chicken shit. Who's side yah on anyways?" Albright took the other prisoner to the county jail section, while I waited alone for state police to arrive.

The police car siren was heard within minutes of Albright's departure, so I returned to the main office to meet the trooper. The police car jumped the curb around the parking lot and came to a halt on the sidewalk directly in front of the main office. The car door flew open and one very young, rather small white male officer vaulted from the car. It was obvious to me that he was a brand new graduate from the academy.

"A fish. They sent me a fish. Look at the shine on his shoes. Up all night, no doubt, polishing," I moaned to myself.

Convinced he couldn't handle the job alone, because of his

stature and my perception that he was a fish, I greeted him without enthusiasm. "I'm the camp supervisor, Ms. Miller. Do you think you'll need my assistance?"

"No, Ma'am. Just lead me to the prisoner."

In the dorm, we found Carson standing on top of her foot locker swinging a curtain rod and yelling, "These Motha fuckas can't make us do shit. Git off your sweet asses and fight, yah bitches."

The State Trooper walked toward Carson, stopped within a few feet of her, and looked up at her face. "Get down. Hand me that rod. Don't force me to hurt you."

Carson stopped swinging her arms, and as she started to form the words, "Get fucked," the trooper lowered his right hand to his gun and unbuckled the holster. Carson climbed down from the foot locker. "You've got me at a disadvantage."

"Carson. That's your name, right? Well, Carson, put your hands behind your back."

Carson obeyed the trooper's order. He cuffed and escorted her to his car. As the trooper put her in the rear seat he threatened in a soft, deliberate voice, "If you make one wrong move, I will break both your legs."

Carson's eyes widened and tears began to fall down her cheeks. She looked at me as though she hoped I would intercede, but I didn't. Watching the car drive away, I thought, "Okay, so I was wrong about the trooper." I was pretty upset with myself for not being able to defuse this minor insurrection without getting outside help.

Another confrontation, a few weeks later, was less threatening. A group of about fifteen prisoners headed by Caroline Smith, a scrawny, toothless woman, surrounded me as I entered the dayroom. Caroline, placing her hands on her hips, put her face in mine and blurted out, "Yah know, Ms. Miller, we need sexual relief just like anybody else."

"What?" I asked. "What brought this on. Never mind, I really don't want to know the details."

"We're serious, Ms. Miller."

"Okay, what's the problem?"

"At the Valley, they let us buy battery operated dildos to relieve ourselves. You won't let us have them. Why?"

"Well, mainly because this is a work camp and you must go

manual."

I will never know what possessed me to say that, but Caroline and her group of sex starved maidens silently accepted my explanation. The subject was never brought up again.

VI

Prisoners look forward to visits more than anything else. Visits break up the monotony of prison life. Other than mail, they provide the only contact with the "real world". In the camp program, prisoners received visits on either Saturday or Sunday, and holidays.

Some of these visitors displayed unusual behavior. One such visitor was Mr. Taylor who claimed to be a Baptist minister, but unlike other ministers who visited, he never applied to be a volunteer or wished to help the camp as a whole. He visited one prisoner, Carmen Jones, every Sunday during regular visiting hours, and was the first visitor to arrive and the last to leave. Taylor was white and in his mid sixties. Prisoner Jones was black and in her twenties. Her major occupation, to date, was prostitution. When prisoner Jones was found in possession of marijuana after one of Taylor's visits, officers monitored his next visit closely. The visiting room officer caught him passing marijuana to Jones in a zip-lock sandwich bag which she attempted to conceal in her bra. Their actions were so quick that the pass was almost missed by the officer who circulated around the room. The state police were called, and they arrested Mr. Taylor before the visit ended. He was later prosecuted for bringing illegal contraband onto prison grounds, a felony.

Drugs were sneaked by prisoners in a variety of ways. Women prisoners hid drugs in any and all body cavities, including vagina, rectum, mouth and ears. A body cavity search was not permitted without absolute proof, that is seeing the prisoner concealing the drugs. Once the search was approved by the warden, the body cavities were probed by healthcare staff to retrieve what was concealed.

We were not always lucky enough, as in the Taylor case, to catch the visitor bringing the drugs into camp or to find the drugs once they were hidden on prison grounds. Several measures were taken to help in this battle. All visiting areas and fields adjacent to the camp were searched and trash was burned after weekend visits. Officers on duty in the visiting areas noted any suspicious behavior, including excessive use of the bathroom by visitors; they could hide drugs there to be picked up later by a prisoner. Other suspicious behavior included gestures made by a visitor that looked like a pass of contraband, or a long kiss—permitted at the beginning and end of visits—which could allow the passing of a balloon filled with drugs. If there appeared to be enough evidence that drugs had entered the camp, but they were not found, the state police were asked to bring a drug sniffing dog to the camp.

On a Monday following a rather busy visiting weekend, I requested the dog. The lieutenant in charge reported, "That dog is out on another job. All we have is the tracking dog. You know, the one that's used to track escapees."

I thought about what he said, and replied, "Bring the tracker. The prisoners won't know the difference. We just want to get rid of the drugs before the Fourth of July weekend coming up."

"Okay, whatever you say. We'll be there tomorrow morning."

The lieutenant and his tracking dog, a German Shepherd, appeared at the camp at seven o'clock the following morning, before the prisoner crews left for the day. All the prisoners were ordered to their rooms while the Shepherd energetically went from room to room and area to area, sniffing every inch.

The ploy worked. The prisoners didn't guess that it was not a drug dog. Soon toilets began to flush, and plastic bags were thrown from windows as the dog made its rounds. The retrieved plastic bags were filled with marijuana and valium. All in all, we thought the event quite successful. The Fourth of July was peaceful for employees, but less festive and more sober for the prisoners.

If summer holidays brought the threat of drugs and home made alcohol, fall brought the problems of hunters in the woods surrounding the camp. One Saturday in October, I was at home enjoying the warmth of an Indian Summer evening when Officer Pam Rhodes called. I sighed, "What's the problem, Officer Rhodes?"

"Well, I had to call the state police because of an assault. They just arrived."

"Oh no. Which ones were at it tonight and over what this time?"

Officer Rhodes hesitated for a minute, and then responded, "It's not what you think. I don't know quite how to tell you. Two guys, or rather hunters, wandered into the camp through Dorm A's back door, the one facing the woods. They were drunk, or at least had been drinking. I'm not sure they knew where they were."

She stopped for a minute, and I urged, "Go on. What else happened?"

"Well, the ladies, I mean prisoners, jumped them. I heard the screaming, so I ran back toward the dorm. I got as far as the dayroom. Every prisoner from both dorms was on the hunters who, by the way, were carrying loaded shot guns. The prisoners were yelling all sorts of stuff, like 'We'll make sure you'll never use your peckers again!' and 'Who'd you think you were going to scare?', all the while slugging and kicking them and pulling their hair. It's a miracle the guns didn't go off."

Rhodes chuckled, "But, when I think about it, it was a pretty funny scene, a heap of women in prison seersucker nighties piled on top of these two stupid white guys."

"Where are the hunters now?" Envisioning sixty women of all sizes and colors in prison issued night gowns chasing these men, I had to laugh, too.

"They're with the police in your office. Me and officer Tobey just got the prisoners back into their dorms."

"Transfer me to the police."

State Trooper Stanley Whittaker answered the telephone, and I said, "This is Ms. Miller, camp supervisor. What condition are the two hunters in, and what do you plan to do?"

"Well, Ma'am, the two hunters wanted to press charges for assault and battery, but after I explained a few things to them, they changed their minds. I think their egos are bruised more than their bodies. They'll survive the blows."

"What exactly did you explain to them, Officer Whittaker?"

"That they're trespassing on posted prison property in an inebriated state with loaded shotguns, which is a felony. I told them that the prosecutor may not think kindly of them. They agreed to leave, not press charges and never to return."

I've often wondered how those two hunters explained the events of that evening to their wives.

VII

One and a half years had passed at Camp Pontiac. During that time, Camp Gilman was being built across White Lake Road. We moved from Pontiac to Gilman two days before Thanksgiving Day, despite my appeals to camp control administrators. I reminded them that neither staff, nor prisoners had been trained to use the unfamiliar wood burning stove that heated the camp and its water, or the state-of-the-art kitchen equipment, which included a potato masher large enough to serve the U.S. Army. Also, no one had keyed the 120 doors in the place. But schedules are schedules.

Camp Gilman's grey cinder block building contained four housing units on two floors. The main floor contained the furnace/utility room, warehouse, kitchen, library, nurses station, laundry, mud room, class room, administrative offices and visiting room. These and the housing units surrounded a multi-purpose room used as a gym and dining room. Stainless steel tables and benches stored in the walls of the multi-purpose room were brought down for each meal. Basketball hoops were mounted at each end of that room, even though no basketball was played by the women who made up the prison population. The building, as are most prisons, was designed to accommodate men.

Each of the four housing units had a dayroom with a pool table, a television mounted on the wall, a few small square tables, and several multi-colored, plastic stacking chairs. The dayrooms became dormitories when the prison camp was crowded. Bathrooms and showers, one to each housing unit, were shared.

The officers' station (control center) was located at the end of the multi-purpose room, just outside of the administrative offices and visiting room. The control center was a square of waist high cinder blocks topped by plexiglass, with an "OFF LIMITS" sign hung over its entrance gate.

Warden Mills conducted a contest to name the new camp. Contests, always big with women prisoners, were held for any and all reasons, such as decorating the dorms and trees at Christmas, talent shows, naming buildings, and art and essays for Black History Month. Prisoners usually requested that prizes be catered food from local fast food places like McDonald's.

The women prisoners submitted numerous names, among them: Beaver Valley, Our Lady of St. Pontiac, Camp Miller, and Valley Annex. The humorless Warden Mills chose Camp Gilman, often called Camp Gilmore by visitors and letter writers. Everybody asked, "Who is Gilman, anyway?"

The late Mr. Gilman, it turned out, was the first, and long serving, prison camp warden. He was a traditionalist known for his dictatorial approach to management. Since no prize was ever announced, the prisoners didn't care that they'd lost the contest, but some asked, "Why a man's name?" They then began calling the camp "Our Lady of St. Gilmore".

The day before we moved, the keys for all the doors in Camp Gilman were delivered to me in a cardboard shoe box by Warren Twomey, the Physical Plant Superintendent for the camp program. Warren and I had had earlier disagreements over septic and smoke/fire alarm systems at Camp Pontiac, which I had won.

When I had reported problems with the septic system at Camp Pontiac, Warren had ignored me, stating, "What do women know about septics?"

Eventually, Warren conceded that the system needed repairs after an acre was flooded with odorous sludge. He discovered that the field had been improperly wired, which meant that when the main pump stopped working, neither the backup pump, nor the trouble alarm worked. Thus the flood. It took two days to complete the repairs.

Warren also defended the fire alarm system by insisting, "You women don't know how to use the damn thing. You aren't resetting it right. That's why it continues to go off."

The fire alarm/smoke detection system had been installed by Warren's electrician brother. Neither he nor Warren could reset the alarm either. They tried to find the problem by digging up the entire underground cable system with a back hoe, only to discover that an electrical wire going to the alarm had been sliced.

I knew Warren was paying me back for my wins when he handed me a Nike shoe box filled with untagged keys. Not one key was marked, and there was no list identifying them by number. When he handed me the box, he was smiling. "I guess you can't go to lunch with us today."

I looked into the box and then at Warren. I felt the heat rise in my face. "They aren't marked."

"Yeah," he agreed and left the camp.

I was angry, but could do nothing except force exhausted camp employees to work through the night making a master key list and a keyboard with pegs and tags to identify each key. This was accomplished by trying all 120 keys in the doors one by one until the correct key was found for each. The task was completed before the first women prisoners arrived the next day. They came in green state school buses, bumping down the quarter mile driveway from Camp Pontiac and across the dirt road into the paved parking lot of Camp Gilman. It was a cold, drizzling, grey November day.

Each woman prisoner was strip searched. Her personal property, carried in the ubiquitous green duffle bag, was inventoried upon leaving and entering the camps. Our painstaking Gilman shake down was to make sure that no contraband would be moved. Dinner that night was on time and everyone fell into the new routine fairly smoothly.

My patience, however, met the ultimate test the next day over the wood burning stove—imported from France without English directions—that heated the building and water. Camp Gilman was the second camp in Michigan to use this system.

Several prisoners on the first busload were assigned to the wood pile. This was considered the least desirable job in camp because of the amount of physical exertion required. The most important responsibility was maintaining the fire around the clock in the wood burner itself. Three shifts were needed to accomplish this.

Other prisoners were assigned to unload, from a flatbed truck, the eight foot logs that arrived each week from a northern camp, to stack the logs into five foot high piles, and then to cut the eight foot logs into four foot logs so they would fit into the wood burner. The ultimate goal of all this was to make sure the fire never went out. If it did, it meant facing the wrath of eighty cold and unbathed women.

The prisoners assigned to fill the wood burning stove on the first full day at Camp Gilman set upon their task with gusto. They were going to be sure they would not get blamed for any lack of hot water. As a result, the multi-purpose room was filled with smoke within an hour, setting off the fire alarm which we couldn't turn off because Warren had not given us that key.

In the midst of opening all the windows and doors to air out the building, and shouting to each other over the alarm, we saw a prisoner running from the latrine on the main floor, pulling up her blue prison pants and shouting, "All the showers went on, all the showers went on!"

"What are you talking about?" I shouted back.

"When I flushed the toilet, nothin' happened so I flushed it again and all the showers went on. I can't turn them off. I didn't mean it."

The showers were supposed to work on a five minute timer, but they didn't stop. I yelled to the maintenance foreman on temporary assignment to Gilman, "O'Brien!"

Unflustered, O'Brien walked over to me and answered in his usual quiet, reserved voice, "Yes ma'am."

"Forget the smoke. Turn those damn showers off and get them fixed. We've got an open house and dedication next week with T.V. cameras, Warden, Director, Corrections Commission and Mrs. Gilman! This can't be happening."

"Yes, ma'am."

"And O'Brien, show a little excitement here. It will make me feel better."

"Yes, Ma'am."

He sauntered off to the showers, and I went to my office to call Camp Control.

"Is the Warden there?" I asked the receptionist.

"No." She replied.

"Is the Deputy there?"

"No."

"Is Warren there?"

"No."

"Is the business manager there?"

"No."

"Who is there?"

"Me." The receptionist chuckled.

"Can you fix a wood burning stove and turn off our showers?"

"What!?"

"Never mind. I want you to give the warden a message: 'Your decision to open Camp Gilman before we were trained on the new equipment nearly caused its demise by fire.' Make sure he gets it and calls me."

"Well, I think they're all up north huntin'," the receptionist stated in a "gotcha" tone.

I received a tongue lashing from Warden Mills in response to my message. I also got a surly Warren Twomey on the camp doorstep. He and O'Brien spent several days training us to use the wood burning stove.

Eventually, O'Brien was permanently assigned as the full time maintenance man at Camp Gilman, but that was later. On the Monday morning following our move, he arrived with an eight man prisoner crew from Camp Brighton, forty miles away. O'Brien explained, "These men are in the crew that works with me at Camp Brighton. I've been told they're on temporary assignment here to complete construction on the prisoner store."

"O'Brien, when were you told about this?"

"Friday night when I was clockin' out. Orders came from Deputy Johnson at Camp Control."

The prisoner store stocked such desirable merchandise as potato and corn chips, candies, cookies of all kinds, shampoos, conditioners, ice cream, bread, sandwich meat, gum, as well as Avon make-up.

As O'Brien and his crew went to the store, I telephoned Deputy Johnson. "Why wasn't I told to expect this male crew from Brighton, and why couldn't our women prisoners complete the construction?"

"First of all," the deputy responded. "The women will steal everything from the store. Anyway, women can't do this kind of work. And what male maintenance foreman would work with an all female crew? Especially after that incident with that prisoner, Jean, at Pontiac."

He was right about the women, but wrong about the men. The men also stole merchandise from the store, even Avon cosmetics; he replaced them with a female maintenance crew within a month.

The incident Deputy Johnson was referring to involving the prisoner named Jean happened while we were still at Camp Pontiac. Jean attempted to persuade us that she had been raped by a male public works crew foreman to whom she was assigned. He was proven innocent, but went on a stress leave and later retired. After three grueling hours, the police detective who administered the lie detector test to Jean reported to me, "She was a tough nut to crack, very convincing. But she is lying about the rape."

Jean, later diagnosed as a pathological liar and a sociopath, set about destroying other male employees. Some of these employees were fired after being caught in clandestine sexual romps with her. Her five foot, ninety pound frame, pouting mouth, large, ingenue brown eyes, and porcelain complexion captivated her victims.

Jean, like many prisoners, was an opportunist and a manipulator. It was her first prison term—for larceny from a building (felony shoplifting). She was paroled from the camp program about six months later, but returned to prison on a second felony, charged as an accomplice in the murder of her boyfriend. Her male co-defendant filmed her in sex acts with his dismembered body parts.

Jean made me realize that women aren't the only victims in our society. Her behavior also made it clear that, contrary to the stereotype envisioned by male correctional employees, women prisoners can be dangerous.

VIII

Workpass was another parity program for women prisoners mandated by court order. A group of prisoners who met stringent qualifications were employed off prison grounds in community business jobs, such as waitressing at The Hamburger Palace, and were paid minimum wage or higher. These jobs were also bargains for employers since they often received tax breaks and had a guaranteed, dependable workforce. One enthusiastic employer couldn't be convinced not to hire a prisoner as a bookkeeper; she was later incarcerated for embezzlement.

We had no workpass coordinator to find jobs for the women, unlike in the men's camps, so the task fell to me. We had a vocational program at Schoolcraft College, but there were no vocational programs for job training, academic programming or therapeutic counseling. I eventually convinced corrections administrators to hire teachers for GED classes in the evenings. I was also able to find volunteers to counsel the women in all areas. One special program, administered by Haven in Pontiac, helped battered women. The many exhausting hours I spent in developing these programs were worth it, I felt, even if only a few women prisoners were positively affected.

The job of workpass driver was a coveted assignment. It was the driver's responsibility to transport prisoners to their off ground jobs.

The first workpass driver was Carolyn Pollick. Her vision of this assignment was not quite the same as the job description. Hers included joy riding an additional hundred miles on three out of five days a week. There are only so many accidents, road construction detours and delays a driver can use as excuses for failing to pick up workpass prisoners on time and for additional miles on the odometer. Officers kept a log of the mileage and knew when there was an excess.

Our suspicions about Pollick were reinforced when she changed the way she dressed for the job. Drivers were allowed to wear civilian clothes in order to look non-threatening to the public, but Pollick wore clothes that looked as though she was going to a cocktail party or to hustle a trick.

Another clue was the odd telephone calls we received from men asking, "May I speak to Ms. Pollick?"

The officer on duty receiving the call would reply, "Prisoners can't receive calls, only make them collect."

Undaunted, the caller would ask, "Do you know where she is?", or "Can I leave a message?"

"No. This is not a hotel."

Pollick was fired just before a warrant from the Detroit Police Department was issued for her. Apparently she had been delivering drugs for her boyfriend on those days filled with detours, accidents and wrong turns. What better cover than driving a Michigan Department of Corrections van?

A second driver resigned because she admitted the temptations encountered on her route were too much for her. "It's tough to ignore the party stores, drugs, and men. I'm gonna quit before it catches up to me."

Connie McGowan was the third work pass driver for Camp Gilman. She was reliable, but a bit stressed by the responsibility. She had to follow strict rules, as well as resist prisoner pressures to leave them at places other than work, pick up drugs, and stop at liquor stores.

One summer afternoon, after the prisoners had been dropped off, the workpass van collided with a car in front of it that made a sudden stop at a railroad crossing. The car following McGowan hit the state van's rear bumper.

After a few minutes of walking around each car, kicking tires, pressing and pulling fenders and bumpers, and exchanging drivers' licenses, the lead man said he didn't feel there was enough damage to warrant a police report. McGowan said that because of her job she would have to report it, and asked both drivers to wait until she could make a call to the police. She also made a call to me, explaining the situation.

McGowan returned to the scene of the accident and assured the two men that the police would be right over. This seemed reasonable since the Pike Street Police Station was less than a mile away. Fifteen minutes passed and no cops showed. The lead man left, saying he couldn't wait any longer. After another ten minutes and no cops, McGowan turned to the second man. "Look, man, I gotta go. I'm in enough trouble."

The man grabbed her arm as she started for the van, spun her around to face him, and threatened, "If you go, you're leaving the scene of an accident and can be arrested. You'll probably go to jail."

McGowan pulled her arm away, smiled, showed her prison ID to the man and said, "I'm already in prison for killing my boyfriend. I'll take my chances."

She got in the van and drove away, watching the man in the rear view mirror stare, dumbfounded, at the escaping vehicle. When

McGowen arrived in camp, she burst into my office shouting, "Hi, Mom! I'm home." When McGowan finished detailing the encounter, she said in a worried tone, "He's a boy who seen dollars in the state emblem on the vehicle. Thought I was an easy mark. I think I might be in trouble."

"Nah," I said. "I don't think we'll hear from that guy." We never did.

Sadie, like Connie McGowan, was in prison for committing a murder. She arrived with the first group of prisoner volunteers from Huron Valley Women's Prison when Camp Pontiac opened. She had served twelve years of a life sentence for killing a Detroit Police Officer who arrested her and her boyfriend for drunk driving. The police officer searched Sadie's boyfriend, but not her. He cuffed Sadie's boyfriend, but not her. She had a gun and simply blew the officer away.

By the time I met Sadie, her wild days at the Valley filled with assaults on staff and prisoners, insolence, refusing orders, and being segregated were almost forgotten. She carried her six foot frame with an air of serenity, as though she resided in a monastery, not a prison. Prisoners consulted her as one would a guru. Her patient counselling to the women, most of whom were forgotten by their friends and families, gained her their respect. She was what staff hoped for, an "old timer" who knew how to do time and fostered calm among the prisoners.

Sadie converted to the Muslim religion and married. The wedding, held in Camp Gilman's visiting room, was attended by two prisoner bride's maids and five carefully selected visitors, including the groom. Following the wedding, cake and coffee were provided by the prison kitchen, and pictures were taken by a prisoner photographer with a Polaroid camera. The bride's dress was brought in and taken out of the prison on the same day by one of the visitors. There was no honeymoon.

Thanks to Sadie, Camp Gilman boasted the finest vegetable and flower gardens in the camp system. The garden, tilled with my rototiller which I hauled to camp each spring, was Sadie's unchallenged domain. Every fall she took on the task of extracting the seeds from each plant, packaging and labeling them for the following season. A surprising number of prisoners volunteered to help Sadie with this tedious task. They sat on picnic tables in the shade of the oak trees at the edge of the camp near the road.

Eventually, we discovered that the enticement for prisoner volunteers was not the tranquility of the surroundings, but the noon ritual of salutes from the men who drove by and sounded their horns as they passed. Some of the horns played tunes such as "Dixie", "Hail to the Victors" and "Yellow Rose of Texas". Camp Gilman was built about a hundred feet from the dirt road, and by the spring following our move, traffic had tripled, much to the chagrin of the local farmers. Evidently word had got out that women prisoners whose rooms faced the road rewarded passersby with a peep show, bare breasts, bare buttocks and all. I ordered drapes for all windows, but, alas, could not enforce their use.

Sadie saw the parole board at intervals prescribed by law. Each time she was denied parole in spite of her exemplary conduct, though such conduct had allowed the release of others with more heinous criminal behavior. It was her misfortune to have chosen a cop as her victim, which made parole for her unattainable. Sadie also expressed fear about leaving the protected prison environment. "They (cops) will pay me back somehow. I wouldn't last long in the real world."

Sadie is still in prison. She never attempted escape or shirked her duties. She's a good prisoner.

At Christmas, Sadie played Santa. She dressed in a costume donated by a local Jaycee group, which she enhanced with her red and green striped knee highs and black prison-issue rubber boots.

Christmas in prison was a roller coaster ride for most of the prisoners, whether they were practicing Christians or not. The holiday is supposed to be one of sharing, caring, loving and family.

Prisoners raced from one heart wrenching emotion to another— loneliness, guilt, sadness, excitement, exhilaration, confusion. On the one hand, they were thrilled with the many special programs sponsored by both employees and volunteers. Prisoners received gifts from various organizations and consumed foods unattainable during the year, mostly fresh fruit, cheeses, smoked sausages, and chocolates. The prisoner choir sang traditional and gospel favorites at most gatherings.

The children's Christmas party was, however, the best part of

Christmas at Camp Gilman. It was built around the arrival of Santa who gave out gifts, provided by the Salvation Army and wrapped by prisoner moms, to the prisoners' children.

The most difficult part of Christmas visits at Camp was that the men absented themselves, just as they did during regular visiting hours; some were in prison, too, others had found a new woman or were dead. But that first year at camp Gilman something special did happen. A prisoner whose husband and children visited her regularly made arrangements for them to bring the three children of another prisoner to the party. These children had not seen their mom during the seven years she had been incarcerated because their caregiver had no transportation. The joy on the prisoner's face when her children walked into the visiting room almost reduced me to tears.

In preparation for that first year's Christmas festivities, the prisoners assigned to the kitchen were to bake cookies from the special recipe collection of the Food Service Supervisor, Sherry Lyon.

Three days before the party, Ms. Lyon arrived on the scene wearing a blue lab coat, and carrying the promised metal box of special recipes. When she entered the kitchen prep area, Ms. Lyon found ten prisoners, outfitted in new kitchen whites and hair nets, standing around the stainless steel prep table, eager to get the baking underway.

She set her metal recipe box down and then watched, wide eyed, as the box slid to the other side of the table and crashed to the floor. It exploded on impact, scattering her alphabetized recipes everywhere. The ten prisoners' heads moved in choreographed unison from the placement of the box to its demise on the kitchen floor. Ms. Lyon and the ten prisoners stood for several seconds without uttering a word, staring at the heap on the floor. Ms. Lyon looked up with a hint of tears in her eyes. "What on earth is on the prep table?"

All ten prisoners, heads bent, continued staring at the floor in silence. The prisoner assigned to be head cook finally looked up. A small, feeble smile appeared on her face as she confessed, "We know how important Christmas is, and we wanna have the camp lookin' good, so we special cleaned all the stainless steel so's it would really shine."

"It shines alright. What did you clean it with?"

The cook waved her hand around the kitchen. "Well, we cleaned like always, but polished it with vegetable oil. It leaves a nice shine."

Looking around the kitchen, Ms. Lyon saw that a gloss of vegetable oil covered the ovens, refrigerator, stoves, giant potato masher, freezer, and pots and pans. "Oh, my God! Well, you're right, the shine is great, but it's not sanitary. Sorry, you'll have to start from scratch after you pick up and refile the recipe cards. I'll go across the street to the men's camp and see you in a couple of hours. We'll talk Christmas then."

The prisoners responded, some in tears, with a chorus of groans.
"Oh no. We'll never finish."
"And to think, we busted our asses for nothin'."
"No one appreciates our hard work."
"Yeah. What about these clean uniforms?"

Fortunately, their ranting and sobbing didn't interrupt the alphabetizing of the recipe cards or prevent them from re-cleaning and un-polishing the furnishings. Everything was completed in time for Santa's arrival at the Christmas Party.

Depression soon replaced the Christmas excitement, because prisoners were forced to confront the reality of spending yet another year in the confines of prison, and of once more becoming strangers to loved ones and children. The happy memories of Christmas were further clouded by the loneliness that New Year's Eve seemed to bring with it. That year, New Year's Eve Day started as most prison holidays, with a reduced staff, prisoners sleeping in until nine, and a brunch served at ten. There was nothing else for the prisoners to look forward to, except a special evening meal of ham with all the traditional trimmings.

Prisoners slouched through the brunch of pancakes, sausages, omelettes, toast, assorted dry cereals and cinnamon rolls. When brunch was finished, they scuffed their way back across the multi-purpose room to their housing units to watch TV. The quiet was interrupted by occasional arguments among the prisoners over which channel to watch or whose turn it was to break the balls at the pool table.

Officer Littlefield was on duty the afternoon of New Years Day. She went to Housing Unit Three to take count, and noticed the hand written sign taped to the entrance door: "Don't even think of coming in here with dirty boots on."

Unit Three housed the worst of Camp Gilman prisoners, the ones with the most misconduct tickets, the biggest mouths, and the most talent for making trouble.

Instead of ignoring the amusing sign, Littlefield walked into the dayroom and shouted, "Who's the moron that hung the hand written sign on the unit door? You know all signs must be sanctioned by administration and made at the men's prison wood shop."

Littlefield surveyed the room as she spoke. Most of the twenty women were watching television, two others played pool, and none bothered to look at her.

She knew each prisoner, so took count without calling out individual names or checking ID's.

One of the prisoners playing pool was Elly, a petite woman with her hair in corn rolls, who sported white Liz Claiborn jeans. Clenching the pool cue in both hands, Elly asked, "Why do yah wanna go an ruin what's been an otherwise wonderful day here at Our Lady Of Saint Gilmore? Don'tcha have nothin better to do than to bother us, Littlefield?"

Elly was nicknamed "Small Bit" because of her pint size, but no one should have been fooled by that. By the time she was twenty-one, she had had eight children, all by different fathers, had committed two armed robberies and one murder. She had once threatened me, "I'll kick your white ass when you're not lookin', Miller."

Littlefield shot a contemptuous look at Elly who still held the pool cue in both hands. Elly snickered.

Littlefield responded to the challenge by asking, "How many beds did you have to bounce around to buy designer jeans that I can't afford on a good salary and real work?"

Elly stood to her full four feet eleven inches, turned to face Littlefield and retorted, "What'sa matter, Littlefield? Yah jealous cause no one wants your body or that yah can't stuff that ass of yours into a pair of baaad jeans?"

Littlefield's usually pale face turned bright red. She walked toward Elly and stopped directly in front of her. Littlefield extended herself to her full height to emphasize the difference in their sizes, looked down on Elly and grinned. "I can go home at night, that's all that counts. It don't take no designer jeans to do that."

The other women stopped talking, turned off the TV, and were watching to see if Elly would pick up the gauntlet. The audience hoped the encounter would liven up a dull New Years Day. Everyone was already on edge because of the holiday blues.

Littlefield pointed her finger at Elly. "I'm writing you up for insolence, the ticket that will get you returned to the Valley."

The day room was filled with tension. Elly narrowed her eyes at Littlefield. "If I'm goin' back to the Valley, I'm goin' my way."

She then clobbered Littlefield over the head with the pool cue. Littlefield, blood running down her forehead, ran from the day room and out of the unit screaming for help. She was followed by several prisoners throwing pool balls. As the other officer on duty came on the scene, the rebellious prisoners retreated in fear of being identified, except for Elly who threw one more ball. It hit Littlefield in the head and knocked her to the ground.

The afternoon shift had just arrived; with their help, the officers were able to subdue Elly who was still yelling and kicking. As they transported her to the County Jail, she screamed, "I'm goin' to get you, Littlefield, and you, too, Miller, if it's the last thing I do."

Prisoner snitches who feared that all of them would lose privileges because of this fracas, helped identify other prisoners involved in the pool ball throwing. The others thought they were safe, until the next morning when I announced over the P. A. system, "All prisoners are to go to their rooms and remain seated on their beds until otherwise instructed."

The night before, I had arranged for a transportation cadre and additional officers to be at the camp to help restrain and deliver the culprits to Huron Valley Women's Prison. The prisoners would be placed on segregation status until their hearings for Inciting to Riot and Assault were held.

The transportation officers arrived in three vans, two to a van. As we walked the corridor of Unit Three, I pointed out the rooms in which the offenders sat. No words were spoken as the officers entered each room, cuffed and belly chained the alleged assailants, and took them to the waiting vans. The only sounds heard were the squeaking of shoes against the tile floor and the clanking of belly chains and cuffs.

The last prisoner was loaded into the last van, and the vehicles drove out past the entrance of the building. As each van passed, prisoners, hidden behind the van windows and feeling brave, yelled:

"You'll get yours, you yellow haired honky."

"Too chicken shit to deal us yeselfs."

"Yeah, the men had to do the job, chicken shit."

"We'll be back."

We could hear the laughter and muffled sounds as the vans bumped along the dirt road on their way to Huron Valley Women's Prison. The prisoners' jibes were correct. All but one of the officers who answered my SOS were men. The one woman was the transportation lieutenant, the male officers' boss.

As I watched the caravan disappear down the dirt road, I had no idea that in a little over a year I would take the same route to Huron Valley Women's Prison as the new deputy warden. At that moment I felt differently about women prisoners, having gained a new respect for their aggression. I was also glad that not all officers were as petty as Littlefield. There were more like Albright, dependable people who wanted to do their jobs well, and knew how to be both firm and humane.

PART 4

Huron Valley Women's Prison

I

The morning I arrived at the women's prison on my first day as deputy warden, I found myself sitting once again in a parking lot staring at a group of buildings. At least this time the parking lot was paved. I even had my very own parking spot, designated by a state-issued green sign: "Deputy Warden". A rush of emotions confronted me as I stared at the nameplate. The authority and power the title "Deputy Warden" gave me was a little daunting, and I hoped that I was prepared for that role. But I was also excited about being closer to my goal of becoming the warden at the women's prison.

The structures that I stared at were as different from Camp Pontiac as Buckingham Palace is from the projects in the Bronx. The six-year-old buildings, twelve in number, that comprised Huron Valley Women's Prison were one story red brick; four dark brown modular housing units, considered temporary housing, stood nearby. A prisoner industries building was located between the two sets of modular units. Women prisoners manufactured chair cushions and license plate tabs. Those prisoners, I would later discover, also created a more lucrative industry, smuggling license tabs out of the factory in their vaginas. They would mail the inch square tabs from the prison in regular mail (outgoing mail was not searched unless the prisoner was on segregation status), having sold them at high prices to people who could obtain neither drivers' licenses nor auto insurance.

The buildings on the prison grounds were spread across several acres of rolling manicured lawn and formed a circle facing a park-like area that resembled a campus. All the buildings were air conditioned. It was the only prison in Michigan to have air conditioning, and that was due to an undetected architectural error. News reporters often wrote, "The prison is a college campus. What kind of punishment is this?" Despite this perception by outsiders, the prison was surrounded by a twelve foot chain link fence capped by a row of concertina wire known as razor ribbon, a reminder to both prisoners and employees of the environment's purpose.

Huron Valley Women's Prison was the reception center for all women offenders in Michigan. Incoming prisoners were given academic, psychological and physical exams to help determine security level and assignment (job and/or school). The tests were weighed along with the sentence that they were serving and, of course, the crime committed.

The prison housed segregated (severe behavior problems), maximum, close, medium and minimum security level prisoners, the pregnant, and mentally ill. No housing was provided for maximum security, so those who were at that level lucked out and were housed in a close custody unit, the next level down.

Staffing was far leaner at Huron Valley Women's than at men's prisons. When it opened, there was only one captain to manage all three shifts, compared to a captain for each shift in mens' prisons. By the time I arrived, there were three captains, but only one lieutenant per shift compared with men's prisons which had two. There were no yard officers at Women's, let alone a yard sergeant to watch prisoner movement and yard activities. The yards are the favorite areas for prisoner on prisoner assaults. There was also only one Assistant Deputy Warden. Men's prisons were allowed two ADWs, one for security and one for housing, but male central office administration claimed, "Women prisoners pose no security threat. They're just basic pains in the ass and are mostly interested in painting their nails and harassing us for more personal property. They need a housing deputy, not a security deputy."

Much of this changed at my insistence, as I continued to work with the officers' union and central office administration. The staff, however, never equaled that of a similar men's facility, even though none of the men's prisons housed every level of security as did Huron Valley Women's.

The "bubble" at Huron Valley Women's Prison was a prime example of central office's perception than women were not a security risk. The bubble was a bullet proof enclosed area where an officer controlled the opening of three of the four security gates, where visits were monitored and where the arsenal was housed. The arsenal included weapons, restraint equipment and gas. Arsenals in mens' prisons are large rooms with shelves of shotguns, rifles, hand guns, ammunition, gas canisters, and riot equipment. There is enough to outfit at least two platoons, each consisting of four eight-officer squads. Huron Valley Women's arsenal was a small, five feet by two feet closet that held two rifles, eight shotguns, two bull horns, five hand guns, four gas canisters and twenty sets of restraints. Other equipment was kept in a separate metal locker on rollers and included a first aid kit, helmets, vests, and hair nets, enough for one eight-person squad. Attached to each bull horn was a written statement which was to be announced during riots, sit-ins and the like: "In the name of the people of the State of Michigan, you are ordered to disperse immediately." If that order was not given, charges could not be brought against any perpetrator.

Riot squads in men's prisons dressed out in rooms adjacent to the arsenal built for that purpose. In the women's prison, the officers dressed out in the visiting room, after the visitors were asked to leave.

Discrimination in the quality and quantity of arsenal and squad equipment was not only based on central office logic that women prisoners—including those with histories of murder, assault and rioting—were not dangerous. Central office administrators also felt that women officers, who were in the majority at Huron Valley Women's, were not able or eager to handle weapons. Those administrators, however, did not feel that way about women officers assigned to men's prisons.

Central office administrators supported their decision not to enlarge the arsenal, in opposition to the Auditor General's requests, by pointing to a woman officer who accidently shot the perimeter patrol vehicle because she forgot to engage the safety. The accidental discharge of a weapon was not common, but it had occurred to both men and women officers.

Central office did issue a written procedure for obtaining enough weapons to outfit more than one squad in the case of a riot. The shift commander had to call Huron Valley Men's Prison next door and request the weapons and equipment be delivered. That procedure was included in the mandated monthly drills, preparing staff for riots, hostage takings, fires, strikes, etcetera. Only the Women's employees, however, knew about this central office directive. We discovered that the warden at the men's prison apparently never circulated the procedure. Most requests went something like this:

"Huron Valley Men's Facility, Sergeant Jones speaking."

"This is Captain Eddie at Women's. We're having a mobilization drill. The deputy warden has requested weapons and equipment to outfit two squads."

"What weapons and equipment?"

"It's the procedure. You're supposed to send Women's enough equipment and weapons to outfit at least two squads."

"I don't know anything about this. Hold and I'll check."

Captain Eddie waited.

The sergeant returned to the phone. "Captain Eddie, I checked it out. I guess you're right. You can have the equipment, but you'll have to pick it up."

"That's a negative. You are suppose to deliver it. In fact, it's supposed to be delivered within ten minutes. Doesn't anyone communicate central office orders to you people?"

"Don't know about central office, just following orders here. Hold again and I'll check."

The sergeant returned to the phone again. "Okay, Captain. I'll send the equipment, but it's shift change. It'll be another twenty minutes."

"Forget it. The drill will be over. I'll report your cooperation in the critique. Good-bye."

If there had been a riot, the prison could have been burned to the ground by the end of that conversation. Later, when a riot actually did occur at Women's, we were lucky to not need more than one squad. In fairness, the men's prison did place squads on alert to help if necessary that day.

The most frustrating element for me was trying to train officers in the proper use of weapons, and squad and platoon movement, when weapons were not readily available. Training improved over the years because I added weapons and stored them as well as I could in the small closet. Improvement did not come without ridicule from central office administrators, however, who could never understand the correlation between having appropriate equipment and a well trained staff.

In spite of my annual budget requests for an enlarged arsenal and squad room, the only way Huron Valley Women's Prison got a suitable arsenal of its own was by closing its doors and moving to a men's prison.

Once I had an unexpected ally in the ongoing fight for parity. A reporter on the crime beat for the *Ann Arbor News* contacted me after a prisoner had attempted to escape by going over the fence. "How did the prisoner get over the fence? Isn't it topped with razor ribbon?"

"She wore several layers of clothes and used a prison issued blanket to throw over the razor ribbon to prevent injuries. Then she climbed the fence and jumped to the ground on the other side," I answered.

"Isn't the fence alarmed? Didn't the alarm go off? Where were the officers?"

"The fence is alarmed, the alarm went off, the officers were on the scene. That's why she didn't get away."

"How many shots were fired?"

"None."

"None? Not even a warning shot?"

"We aren't allowed to fire a warning shot or shoot at a woman prisoner."

"Isn't it allowed in policy for all prisoners? How else would you stop them from escaping, especially a dangerous one?"

"There's a Director's Memorandum making the women prisoners an exception."

"Well, I think I'll call the director and check this out."

When the telephone conversation ended, I told the warden what had transpired, and we called the director. He was not pleased, nor was he looking forward to being interrogated by the press about his policy exception which made it look as though the department coddled women prisoners.

The director issued a new memorandum rescinding the order. As a result, escaping women prisoners in medium or higher prisons are treated the same way as men. A warning shot is fired. If the prisoner fails to halt and is over the fence, an officer is allowed to shoot to injure. If the officer's life is in danger, the officer can shoot to kill.

II

I arrived at Huron Valley Women's Prison carrying a lot of baggage. I was perceived as: a tough and demanding boss who ran a tight prison; another white administrator unwanted by the blacks; another woman unwanted by the white male supervisors who felt I did not know how to manage a prison. I was also fresh from a recent live television appearance on a popular Detroit talk show. My appearance on the show did not sit well with certain men.

On the show I talked about the many improvements made in counseling battered women in the camp program. The counseling was provided by Haven, a shelter for battered women in Pontiac. Because the focus of the show had been on men battering women, certain male employees perceived a bias. They imagined I would coddle women prisoners because I was sympathetic to the cause of battered women. Things lightened up a little when other staff had business cards printed up in dayglow red on a white background. They announced, "Tekla Miller, AKA, THE STAR." I used every one of those cards.

The usual "honeymoon" given new staff members was short lived, and so was mine. Within three months of my promotion, I was perceived as just another one of the warden's "chosen people"—all of us white. I was lumped in the warden's "chosen" category with the alcoholic female social worker who was a friend of a local judge and who was appointed from outside the Civil Service System by the warden. Another appointed in the same manner as the social worker was a married male principal who was caught by an officer in a school storage closet with his married secretary. After their discovery in the closet, the prison employees watched, with amusement, the lovers' daily ritual. Each day during lunch, they left the prison separately, wandered the parking lot for a few minutes hoping to deceive any onlookers, then got into the same car and drove away.

The warden herself was accused of racism toward the black deputy director by the black female inspector. No one knows all the details, but following the accusations there was a loud discussion in the warden's office between the warden and the director. Not long after that, the warden resigned.

Denise Quarles replaced that warden. She was the woman who had been my first state supervisor, my mentor and my best friend. Since Denise was black, the racist accusations against Huron Valley Women's administration petered out. But this did not endear me to a staff who then saw me as the warden's best friend. Being a woman in a male dominated field didn't help. Because there were so few of us, women didn't have the established success pattern in corrections that men did, which meant that many employees challenged my ability to lead.

One captain, George Snelling, transferred back to a men's prison. Before he left, Snelling filed a sexual harassment grievance against me, the first for a female in the department, because I disciplined him for absenteeism. When annual leave had been denied him due to lack of staff to cover his absence, he had taken sick leave, a policy violation. The sexual harassment charge was withdrawn under the advice of Snelling's attorney, but resurfaced when he was given only a satisfactory rating during his annual review. He didn't win the second grievance either. Snelling's transfer request, however, would not have been honored if not for my intervention. I wanted him removed because of his alleged involvement with female prisoners.

During a lie detector test, a woman prisoner, being interrogated about her accusations that county sheriff's deputies forced her to have sex with them, mentioned his name, too. The lie detector operator called me, saying, "I think you may want to look into something. The prisoner related a story to me that she brought up on her own, but, according to the test, she was telling the truth. I think she felt she had no other way of getting out the information. I was the vehicle, so to speak."

"What exactly did you hear?" I asked.

"Well...this is not easy. You have a captain named Snelling that works at Huron Valley Women's, right?"

"Yes, on the morning shift. Why?"

"She claims that he asks for favors from the prisoners, including her."

"What kind of favors?"

"When he makes rounds, he places a note against the prisoner's window asking them to take off their clothes."

"That seems pretty risky, since he would be in view of an officer most of the time."

"That's why he uses the note. There's no verbal request. He stands at the door like he normally would to talk to or check on a prisoner."

"Why would a prisoner do what he asks?"

"She said he brings them drugs, mostly Valium."

"Thanks for the information, but without corroboration from another staff person, nothing can be done. It's prisoner's word against staff's word."

"You're sure? Even with the lie detector test?"

"I'm sure. We couldn't even win a case against an officer who beat up a retarded prisoner after the prisoner refused to be the officer's drug mule. We had telephone bills showing collect calls from the prisoner's unit phone to the officer's house, as well as other officers who gave evidence, but wouldn't give us written statements. The jury, I believe, made an emotional decision about the prisoner's offense. She had burned her house with her child in it and the child died. That's all the jury needed to hear."

"That's hard to believe. Well, I felt I had to let you know. Good luck."

As soon as I finished the conversation, I telephoned the deputy director who agreed with my conclusions that it would be difficult to discipline Snelling without corroborating evidence. Fortunately, he was as concerned as I was about leaving Captain Snelling in a women's prison, so he agreed to honor his request for transfer.

Renee Jacobs, another of my captains, worried me at first. My trust in her had been shaken when she was the lieutenant at Camp Pontiac, because of her relationship with the Food Service Supervisor, Dan Clarke. I thought they were having an affair, but Ms. Jacobs denied it. She knew I also suspected Clarke of drug trafficking and being too close to the women prisoners. She led me to believe that she shared my suspicions about Clarke. At that time, Clarke filed a grievance against me when I ordered officers to search the state vehicle he drove. I had received a written tip that he was transporting contraband, but nothing was found in the car. Later, I was told that Clarke had confessed to Warden Mills that Jacobs warned him about the search.

Jacobs and Clarke married after she was promoted to Huron Valley Women's Prison as a Captain while I was still a camp supervisor. Our reunion when I was appointed deputy at women's prison was less than happy.

Ms. Jacobs, however, was an intelligent, articulate, no nonsense person, and her managerial potential developed over five years of close supervision. We were able to work through our problems, and she was promoted to inspector at Huron Valley Women's. She also divorced Clarke.

The door to my office was half glass which meant little could be hidden, including me. Employees seemed to believe that I had to be accessible at all times, no matter what I was doing—on the telephone, in a meeting, or in the bathroom. Yes, even in the bathroom!

Lydia Kraas, a social worker and union vice president, tracked me down while I was inside a bathroom stall. She passed a note under the stall door, and demanded that I review and sign a gate pass immediately so that she could take books and supplies into the prison before classes started.

I didn't take the gate pass, but responded, "Are you talking to me? Are you sure you have the right stall?"

I flushed the toilet and left the stall only to find an angry Lydia Kraas still standing there with her hands on her hips. Walking around her to wash my hands, I said, "You know, Lydia, some things are sacred and private. High on that list is going to the bathroom. If you want me to review that gate pass, bring it to my office in about fifteen minutes. I'm on my way to meet with the warden. Oh yes, be sure all those items are on the approved list." I left the bathroom confident that none of the requested items were approved. I was pretty sure Ms. Kraas was hoping to catch me off guard so I would sign the gate pass containing items which were not on the formal list.

The formal list of approved items had been developed at each Michigan prison to prevent contraband from entering the prison and to prevent potentially dangerous items from getting into the hands of the prisoners. It was also an attempt to prevent employees from using such items to pay for a prisoner's favors or silence about the employee's wrongdoing, such as love affairs with prisoners or drug trafficking.

The list was a major topic of discussion at every union meeting. I had to deal with four unions and their versions of approved items, and stay sane. It seemed that we wasted hours at every meeting arguing the validity of requested items, updating the list, and attempting to appear that the administration was not being petty, but concerned about security.

Contraband items were found on employees through mandated random searches (pat searches) in lower security prisons. In maximum security prisons, everyone who went through the security gates had to be searched and pass through a metal detector. All employees, including the warden and deputy warden, were required to submit to searches. Some wardens, whose egos got in the way, exempted themselves, creating an elitist hierarchy.

If there was enough evidence, usually drug related, an employee or visitor could be asked to submit to a strip search and even a urine test. Evidence included seeing the suspected individual hiding something on their person, finding an unknown substance on the person, feeling an unusual bulk under their clothing, or receiving a tip from a credible source. An employee could be suspended pending discipline and visitors turned away if either refused a strip search with probable cause.

The contraband issue also consumed hours at the wardens' quarterly meetings. Wardens debated what should be considered contraband, how and what kind of searches should be conducted and to whom, and how officers should search women who were wearing skirts and bras. Policies and procedures were always being rewritten. Skirt and bra problems were never settled, although one male warden professed to be an authority on bras because he was once in the lingerie business. In his eyes, this gave him more expertise than the women wardens wearing them.

III

Two weeks after my transfer to Huron Valley Women's Prison as the deputy warden, I was clocking in when I heard over the PA: "Deputy Miller report directly to the control center."

I dumped my personal belongings in my office and went

through the third security gate to the control center, where I was quickly briefed by Sergeant Clyde Howe. "The prisoners in Mod One are sitting-in. And guess who's the leader? Carson!"

"What are they worked up about?"

"The poor babies aren't happy about the new rules that were posted last night. They're refusing to go to their assignments."

"I haven't even seen the new rules. I barely know what's in the old ones. Carson pulled the same stunt at camp. She just doesn't like to work. I guess if she did, she wouldn't be in prison."

"The warden's already over there and wants you there pronto," the sergeant instructed.

Prisoner rules were unique to each prison. They concerned everything from the number of prisoners allowed to use the bathroom during count to when the cell door window could be covered; they could never be effectively addressed in state-wide policies.

I walked the quarter mile across the prison grounds to the mod, thinking that I would be glad when spring arrived. When I entered the mod, I found thirty-three prisoners on their bunks, and Carson standing at the officer's desk. The warden, Assistant Deputy Warden Roy Rider, and the warden's administrative assistant, Ray Toombs, were all there. This is a great set-up for a hostage taking, I thought—every prison administrator is here.

As I approached the desk, Carson shouted, "There's the Deputy from Hell. She couldn't wait to change the rules, make them tighter. She's gointa squeeze us dry."

I looked around at all the prisoners who sat on their beds in silence, letting Carson do the work. Then my eyes settled on Carson. She was dressed the way she had been the day she got off the bus at Camp Pontiac, including the pack of Kools tucked up under the rolled sleeve of her t-shirt.

"Carson, why don't you live with the rules for a week. If they don't work, the elected unit reps can discuss the changes at the monthly Warden's Forum. It meets next Thursday. You don't want any trouble, and I'm sure you don't want to make trouble for the other prisoners."

Carson stood silently for a while. I was sure she was remembering that it took her over a year to work her way out of close custody after the Camp Pontiac sit-in; she knew another such violation would

mean returning to higher custody and less privileges, maybe even segregation.

She looked around the room and then at me. "Okay, but if the
rules don't work, there'll be trouble. I promise."

"I know, Carson. Your promises are good."

After Carson's concession, the prisoners shuffled out of the
mod to their assignments. I never admitted that I had nothing to do
with the new rules, since that idea helped establish my credibility. It is
always easier to become softer than harder once rules are established.
In a later meeting with the prisoners, I discovered that one of the main
complaints about the rules was the limits placed on the items they
could take to the yard when they sunbathed. Hard to believe that was
the issue they were willing to risk segregation for.

As the fearsome foursome—warden, deputy warden (me),
assistant deputy warden, and administrative assistant—left the mod,
the telephone rang. The officer who answered it told us, "It's Sergeant
Howe. He wants to talk to the deputy."

I took the phone from the officer. "What's up, Howe?"

"It seems there's a group in the school who don't want to be
outdone by the mod prisoners. They're protesting the rule changes,
too, and won't go into the classrooms."

"I'm on my way."

I explained the situation to the other administrators. The warden ordered all of us to the school. When we heard screams coming
from that building, the four of us ran to investigate and found two
women prisoners in the middle of an all out, no-holds-barred fight.
The prisoners who had been protesting the rule changes were gathered
in a circle around the brawlers, one of whom had lost her blouse and
bra in the battle, exposing her breasts. The other had the beginnings of
a black eye.

Rider and Toombs hesitated. They looked as though they didn't
know how to grab either fighter without entering forbidden territory,
so I grabbed one and the warden grabbed the other. This didn't stop
either of them from kicking, punching and yelling at us: "bitches, motha
fuckas, honky, dyke sluts..." I gathered that these adjectives were directed at the warden and me since neither of the brawling prisoners
were white.

I ordered the officer to get something to cover the bare breasted gladiator, and remove the spectators who, from their laughter and cheers, seemed to enjoy the hands on approach to management that the warden and I used. I never did find out what the two women were fighting about, but it took the other prisoners' minds off the rules protest.

IV

One incident that solidified my credibility with employees and tested my ability to handle a crisis occurred after Denise Quarles became warden at Huron Valley Women's. It was during the July Fourth holiday and I was on call. Denise was to join my husband and me for a barbecue at our home, but before she arrived, I received a call from the shift commander, Lt. Don Israel. He reported that prisoner Cookie Coleman had bolted from the officers who were attempting to transfer her to temporary segregation for a serious rule violation. Yard activity was in progress, so several prisoners witnessed what happened next. Sergeant Howe tackled Cookie to the ground and held her there by forcing his knee into her back. This method was not uncommon when subduing a resisting prisoner, however it was not a tactic with which the women prisoners were familiar. The officers who assisted Howe put Coleman in restraints and carried her to the segregation unit. The prisoners who watched the tackling began yelling, "Howe beat Cookie! Howe beat Cookie!" That shouting drew the attention of more prisoners, until the crowd grew to over a hundred.

Cookie Coleman was a six foot blond who lifted weights and ran three miles every day. She was not a prisoner who could be subdued easily, even when circumstances were on the side of the officers. Before being locked in the segregation unit, Coleman was taken to the infirmary at the men's prison next door for a physical exam to ensure that there were no injuries. On the way there, she kicked out the rear window of the transportation vehicle and bit one of the transporting officers.

While in the infirmary, Cookie confessed, "Nothin' happened to me. I was bored and needed a little excitement before goin' to the hole. You guys deserved the ass kickin'. The women got real pissed,

108

didn't they? It's just a game. Somethin' to put a spark into Fourth of July."

When the yard whistle directing prisoners to return to their units was blown, it was ignored by most of the prisoners. Instead, they rampaged through the yard and pushed through housing unit doors opened by unsuspecting officers, some of whom were trampled to the ground. One woman officer received a severe beating, resulting in several months of sick leave for both physical injuries and emotional trauma. Some prisoners attempted to come to her aid, but they were unable to stop the assaulters who had become a mindless mob. Other prisoners ran through the open doors to the units trying to avoid being a part of the rioting. Some of them were assaulted for "Siden with them honky police."

By the time I arrived at the prison, about a hundred prisoners had assembled on the hill outside of Unit Three, opposite the front entrance of the administration building. I was glad that there was a fence that separated us as they heckled me when I walked by them.

"Hey, you honky bitch. Let's see yah strut your ugly stuff today."

"Where's the media. We ain't comin' in 'til we sees the media."

"Get ridda the honky mutha fuckas that throwed Cookie round."

"You seen your last day here, bitch."

I had telephoned Warden Quarles before I left my home to inform her of the situation, and she agreed to meet me at the prison. I had also instructed the shift commander to request three spokespersons from the offending group. I was determined not to give in to the prisoners' demand that I meet with the entire group alone on their turf, a tactic previous administrators had given in to, but one I perceived as dangerous and conciliatory.

Three prisoners were chosen. They demanded: "Fire both Lt. Israel and Sergeant Howe; amnesty for all the prisoners involved, including those who had assaulted staff; release of Cookie Coleman to general population; and a prisoner committee to rewrite the rules."

Needless to say, we did not come to terms.

Before Warden Quarles arrived at the institution, Jeff Crankshaw, warden of Huron Valley Men's, his deputy and inspector came to Women's to offer their help.

"Why don't you hose the bitches down? That should get them in their units in a hurry," the deputy offered. The other two nodded their heads in affirmation.

"They aren't doing anything but sitting there. I'll wait them out. Either the mosquitoes or the lack of food will persuade them to go into their units," I insisted.

The three snickered at me, and Warden Crankshaw asked, "What do you want to do, coddle the girls?"

"I think I'll just do it my way."

My way worked. The tornado warning I had hoped for didn't materialize, but the food delivery truck and mosquitoes did. By about seven that evening, all the prisoners were in their units. They could not escape identification because we had video taped them sitting on the lawn. To their amazement, misconducts were written for assault, inciting to riot, disobeying a direct order, destruction of prison property, and insolence. Good time was taken away, something rarely done to the women prisoners in the past, and several prisoners were classified to segregation.

No, I thought, there will be no amnesty.

The day after the riot, the warden, assistant deputy warden, Lt. Israel and I reviewed the video of the prisoners sitting-in on the hill next to Unit Three. We were surprised to see a woman in an officer's uniform sitting among the prisoners, crying and periodically hugging one of them. On closer scrutiny, we confirmed that not only was there a uniform, but there was indeed an officer with the prisoners—Julie Cole, a ten-year veteran. Several hours into the sit-in, she had asked to be relieved from duty, crying uncontrollably from what I thought was fear.

After I reviewed the tape, I summoned Officer Cole to my office. She arrived with a union representative, signalling that she knew she'd violated a security rule. She willingly admitted sympathizing with the prisoners. Cole was suspended on the spot and later fired for just cause. Her empathy with the prisoners was potentially dangerous to employees and threatened control of the prison, making her a clear security risk.

Cole appealed her termination several months later. The hearings officer assigned to the appeal sided with Cole and ordered her back to work, stating, "Warden Miller made a technical error. She did not suspend her on the day of the sit-in." What an ingenious decision, I thought, since no staff knew about her support of the prisoner insurrection until the day after the sit-in. Department administrators never appealed this decision, and to this day Cole is an officer in the women's prison.

Women prisoners who were not sent to segregation for their part in the July Fourth sit-in/riot lost good time, which lengthened their stay in prison and lessened their chances for parole. However, I'm convinced that at least two prisoners got their revenge for our actions.

Lydia Kraas, the social worker who had tracked me down in the bathroom, was the counselor in the Vocational Evaluation and Assessment Program. Mary Glover and Melinda LaPorte were prisoner aides in that program. Apparently, Ms. Kraas' relationship with them was more like that of a co-worker than a supervisor. Perhaps she felt intimidated, or felt, as did many prison employees, that prisoners assigned as clerks and aides were less threatening. Whatever the reason, Ms. Kraas left the institutional keys assigned to her on her desk and went about her work monitoring the testing of new prisoners. She didn't notice until she needed to open a locked cabinet that the keys were gone.

Ms. Kraas dismissed the class and searched the room. She couldn't find the keys, and was forced to report their loss to her supervisor, the shift Commander, and me. Her description of events left little doubt that the prisoners had taken the keys. I'm not sure why she let the class go before they were searched. Maybe she thought she would find the keys before anyone else knew they were missing, or perhaps she was afraid to confront the members of the class.

I knew that the key security and the method of assigning keys were in drastic need of improvement. In fact, my staff and I had embarked on that task shortly after my arrival at Huron Valley. I had found that neither the supervisors, nor the locksmith could tell me what each key unlocked or who had which keys on their rings. Straightening out this system took over six months and was nowhere near completion at the time of the Kraas incident.

111

The shift commander telephoned me after he and his officers searched all the students, their cells, and the classroom again. "We haven't found anything and, of course, no one knows anything. I've got more bad news. Ms. Kraas' key ring contains a master key that unlocks all the housing units' outside doors and several interior doors. What should we do?"

"That's a high security key. Why would she ever need that key? Her work should never take her to the housing units or outside of the school building. Do you realize what this means if a prisoner has that key?"

"Yes, ma'am."

"Well, call the locksmith and change all the affected locks."

That night was spent changing over one hundred locks, a tedious and expensive task. I was happy, I'll admit, when Lydia Kraas, a lay-off from the Department of Mental Health, was finally called back there to work.

Prisoners look for weaknesses in the system that can be used to their benefit or to harass the administration. Employees like Cole and Kraas often cannot see that their complicity makes them dangerous and plays right into prisoners' hands.

V

At the beginning of my third year as deputy warden, Denise Quarles transferred to Riverside Correctional Facility, a men's prison, and I was promoted to warden at Huron Valley Women's Prison. Although the move for Warden Quarles was a lateral one, it was seen as a promotion because she would be working with male prisoners. I, on the other hand, was elated that I had finally reached my goal of becoming warden at Huron Valley Women's Prison. I could hardly wait to continue the direction the prison had already taken under Denise's leadership—to make it one of the best prisons in Michigan and to develop constructive programs for women prisoners.

As usual, I was not sure if I was ready for such a powerful position. I no longer had a warden to depend on and to help me with difficult decisions, some life threatening. The buck stopped with me. I hoped that I had the knowledge to make these decisions, and that I was strong enough to carry the burden of their consequences.

Employees from other prisons, where prisoners are housed in open barred cells layered in galleries several floors high, found Huron Valley Women's Prison almost serene by comparison. But the security gates that shut behind me each day as I entered the grounds clanged just as loudly. I never forgot where I was.

Making rounds was another reminder of the responsibilities I had taken on. Most of the women prisoners were housed in general population units in single rooms. Those who were classified as general population mentally ill were all in Unit Three. Those who were medium or lower custody had keys to their rooms, allowing them to come and go at will, except during count, at night and during emergency lock downs.

Making rounds was often confrontational. "Deputy Miller, (or 'Deputy Tekla Miller' since prisoners seemed to like the sound of my first name), how come we can't have microwaves in the day room?"

"Can I move to Unit Two? It's not true that I wanna be next to my girlfriend. I ain't no homo."

"Are you gointa take away our Avon?"

"You know what them midnight police (pronounced with a very long 'o' and meaning corrections officers) did last night? They kept us up all kind of hours cleanin' the bathroom. It ain't right we should hafta clean it when the porter fucks up. What are yah gointa do 'bout it?"

When they weren't on school or job assignments, women prisoners huddled around televisions watching soap operas, putting in their two cents as if the actors could hear them: "Girl, you know he's two timen yah. How much are yah gointa take from this boy?"

I often chided them, "Why do you watch this stuff? Your own lives are soap operas."

"Aaah, we know they get themselves into jams like us, but we never looked as good as them."

Watching soap operas as a leisure time activity was surpassed only by roller skating in the gym. When the gym was converted to a dormitory because of crowding, I allowed the prisoners to roller skate on the paved road that ran along the prisoner yard inside the fence. Roller skating was supplemented with playing whisk in the day rooms, or an occasional bicycle ride on warm days. Although the male prison recreation director taught tennis, few of the women prisoners took advantage of that sport, but they enjoyed leering at him in his shorts.

Men prisoners, on the other hand, played basketball above all else. Weight lifting was a close second, until the weights were removed because of the potential for them to be used as weapons. Free weights were replaced, however, with universal weight machines purchased from profits made at the prisoner store. The women prisoners also had a weight machine, but like the tennis court, few used it.

Sometimes the chatter of prisoners in general population units was so deafening it was difficult to hear. But nothing was like the segregation unit. Segregation was filled with the loud banter of the incorrigible, the babbling of the mentally ill, the screams from those mutilating themselves. There was also the occasional attempted suicide. Officers there were allowed to carry pocket knives with two inch blades to cut down a hanging prisoner—hanging being the preferred method of attempted and successful suicides.

When I first arrived at Huron Valley Women's, segregation (Unit Six) had fifteen cells to house the prisoners there. They were on segregation because of negative behavior, mental illness, or the need for protective custody status, meaning their lives had been threatened by other prisoners. Others housed in Unit Six were waiting for a hearing on a non bondable misconduct, like inciting to riot, assault, sexual assault, and attempted escape.

I made rounds in segregation once or twice a week, and it was never easy. The fifteen cells soon expanded to thirty, taking over the reception center. This forced the newly incarcerated prisoners to be housed dormitory style in the unit's two dayrooms until they were cleared for general population assignment.

The segregation population grew to the point where thirty beds in the next most secure unit were converted to segregation and separated from the other wing by a temporary sliding security gate. That brought the total to sixty segregation beds, an increase attributed to an expanding prisoner population which was also becoming more violent.

Self mutilating prisoners were also housed in segregation. These women had not been officially identified as mutilators until I became warden. In the men's prison, mutilators were housed in a separate unit and assigned a special medical team. Once the needs of women were finally understood, this same team became available to them, but Huron Valley Women's Prison never had a separate wing for them.

As I walked the corridors in segregation, I heard the thumping of Marcia banging her head against the wall. "It calms me," she said. I watched Vicki as she recited a passage from the Bible and washed her feet in a toilet that had not been flushed that day. Glenda stuffed toilet paper in every crevice in her cell and on her body, including nostrils and ears, while Jane Doe smeared feces and her food over the walls, windows and furnishings as she sang some upbeat tune. Rita refused to wear clothes.

I often thought about the officers assigned to Unit Six and wondered how they felt at the end of a day during which they had been targets of thrown feces, urine, and food—missiles lobbed at them through the cell door's slot. They could hardly be blamed for having feelings of animosity toward the prisoners. A prisoner who threw her food, or anything else, through the door slot was placed on a nutra loaf diet. A nutra loaf resembled a meat loaf and contained all the foods on the menu for a specific meal shaped into a loaf so it could be eaten by hand.

Officers in Unit Six had to ensure that each prisoner received one hour out of the cell each day, which often meant forcing them into the shower. Some prisoners in segregation adorned themselves and their cells with fecal material and food; Jane Doe (her files offerd only that name) was one who also refused to bathe. Periodically, officers forced her into the shower and scrubbed her. Her head had to be shaved because the fecal material was so imbedded in her hair that it would not come out. Because she had assaulted several officers in the unit, she stayed on segregation status.

Numerous methods, including Top-of-Bed (placing a prisoner on a bed and securing her arms and legs), were used in the futile attempt to change Jane Doe's behavior. Roy Rider finally came up with a plan.

"Jane Doe came into the institution as a homeless person with

115

her grocery cart filled to the brim, and with $5000. Remember, we don't know how she got the money, but she killed a homeless man who attempted to steal it from her. This money means everything to her. Instead of having the officers or other prisoners clean her cell when she decorates it in feces, let's call in a professional service to do it and make her pay for it."

"Brilliant!" I shouted. "But first, let her know verbally and in writing what we are going to do."

Jane Doe stopped smearing herself and her room after the first bill for over $300 was deducted from her account. It was a relief for the officers and the prisoners when they no longer had to live with the stench of an accumulation of a week's worth of feces, especially during the hot, humid summer months.

There was another colorful character in segregation at that time, Eva Dillard, a wiry Caucasian woman who was only in her mid thirties, but looked sixty. The day she entered segregation, she warned, "I'm gointa kick me some ass." Eva was a woman of her word; Eva kicked ass every chance she got.

Eva was mentally ill, often delusional, and an insomniac who talked incessantly, making no sense. "I remember you Miller back in 1959 on the eastside. You tried to kill me. I know the director's with you. He's afraid to show his face. Hey director! Whatcha 'fraid of? You know Toombs, you're my husband. You're ashamed to admit it because you work here. I gots the babies and the drugs to prove it. You can't deny you lived with me in Italy during the war."

The other prisoners on segregation status filed grievances demanding that Eva be removed from that unit so they could sleep and get away from continual babbling. Needless to say, their grievances were denied.

The day Eva was discharged from prison on her max, meaning she had served her full sentence and had not received any good time because of her negative and assaultive behavior, she had to be forcibly moved from the segregation unit in full restraints (leg irons, black box, and belly chain) by a five officer squad accompanied by the prison psychiatrist. I had given the order to use gas if necessary and the entire move was video taped in case something unique occurred or unusual force was necessary. She was transported to the Northville State Hospital for the mentally ill.

Tours of the units also brought some unexpected situations. After mastering the numbering system of the housing units at Huron Valley Women's, I gave a tour of the prison to local dignitaries— Chiefs of Police, the Sheriff, and the Prosecutor. They were impressed by the industry of the prisoners cleaning in Unit Two, a medium custody unit. So was I until I realized that the prisoners assigned to wash windows were using the one-size-fits-all state-issued sanitary napkins. I hustled the tour group through the unit, hoping that they wouldn't notice. I later questioned the prisoners and officers. "Why are you using the sanitaries for housework? That's not their purpose."

One prisoner stepped forward and stated with great sincerity, "They're real absorbent. Nothin' else do the job as good."

"I can understand their absorbency, that's why they're sanitaries; but you're not to use them for housework any longer."

I don't think the practice ever stopped, though. I discovered prisoners had other uses for the sanitary napkins as well. They became door stops, or were stuffed into the air handling unit located in each room in an attempt to regulate the heating and cooling system. When I made evening rounds, I saw women with their hair rolled, using the sanitaries for rollers. Ah, if they could only use that ingenuity to succeed in the "real world".

VI

When I became deputy warden, Huron Valley Women's Prison was the only prison for women in the state of Michigan other than Camp Gilman. Despite a paucity of programs, we considered ourselves lucky, since many states still housed women prisoners in a section of a men's prison. Lack of program parity with male prisoners was the basis for a precedent setting prisoner class action law suit filed by Mary Glover, a murderer incarcerated in Michigan. The suit became known nationally as "The Glover Suit", and set the rules for women prisoners' classification and programming.

The Glover Suit played a large part in my corrections career. It helped bring positive changes to women's prisons, but it also gave me

117

several major headaches during my tenure.

The final court order in the Glover Suit was issued by Federal Judge Robert Barkus in the spring of 1981. Basically, the Michigan Department of Corrections was ordered to provide academic and vocational programming beyond the GED and to include non-traditional vocations such as carpentry, graphic arts, painting, and building maintenance and repair. The court also ordered a two year college program, and demanded that access to a four year college program be made available for those women who wished to pursue it. Despite the court's ruling, the most popular vocational training with the women prisoners remained office and secretarial skills.

In order to achieve proper program placement for prisoners, the court ordered that a Vocational Assessment and Evaluation center be developed. The skills, abilities, knowledge, and interests of each prisoner were tested and the results were used to create a vocational plan; this followed a woman prisoner through to pre-release counseling which occurred approximately six months prior to her release. If the plan were implemented properly, it would prepare her for community re-entry.

The "Glover Manual" was also developed to standardize all prison assignments and wages for men and women. Before the manual, women prisoners did not receive wages or assignments comparable to those given to male prisoners. For the first time, prison industries assignments, the highest paying assignments in the system, were offered to women.

The court ordered that women prisoners must not only have a current law library, but also, like the male prisoners, be allowed paralegal training so that there would be a pool of women prisoners available to assist other prisoners with court filings. Along with that, women prisoners had to have access to the prison legal services attorneys which had only been offered to men prisoners before.

The opening of the women's prison camp under the court order allowed women prisoners to obtain additional days off their prison sentence—called incentive good time—which had previously been rewarded to only male prisoners. Also, the workpass program was only offered in the prison camps.

In defense of the Glover Suit, women prisoners were and are

second class citizens in corrections. The mostly male corrections administration attributed that to the fact that women comprise "just" 5% of the jailed population; therefore, the male population absorbs the budget. A reasonable fact on the surface, this allowed the administration to ignore women's rehabilitative and social welfare needs.

For instance, at that time approximately 80% of the women prisoners were mothers and 75% of those were single heads of household. Like the male prisoners, the majority of women could not even read at a sixth-grade level and were unemployed when arrested. According to the Bureau of Justice Statistics, an estimated 72% of the women in prison were known drug users and, in fact, there were more women than men arrested for drug crimes from 1980-1989. The women prisoner population was growing at a faster rate than the men's and there was every indication the growth would continue.

Ignoring women prisoners because they were a minor part of the incarcerated population only perpetuated ignorance, substance abuse, and welfare. Those women who returned to the community as uneducated, unemployed welfare recipients would more than likely begin using drugs again and raise their children to be exactly like themselves. The fathers were long gone, having disappeared, died or been incarcerated. The elimination of welfare dependency, if nothing else, should have enticed the corrections administrators to do everything possible to ensure that women returning to the community could support themselves and their children. To my knowledge, these concerns still have not been fully met in most jurisdictions throughout the United States.

I did not always agree with either the judge or the attorneys in the Glover Suit, and felt that many of their decisions were unreasonable. For example, the attorneys' challenges of routine shakedowns of prisoners and their cells made it difficult to limit contraband and to maximize safety.

Judge Barkus made only one tour of Huron Valley Women's Prison during my tenure. That day he confronted me on many issues, including the elimination of picnic visits. He claimed picnic visits helped maintain family ties, and accused me of interfering with family relationships and being too concerned about "a little marijuana" coming into the prison. I in turn replied, "I wonder how that would look in the *Detroit Free Press:* 'Judge Barkus OK's drugs in women's prison'."

The issue was never raised again.

Judge Barkus has threatened to keep the Glover case active as long as he feels that women prisoners are being treated unfairly. He is a man of his word. He is in his mid seventies, semi-retired, and has continued his oversight of this case to the present. According to the plaintiffs' attorneys, the original order has never been completely met in the area of equal vocational training programs. Judge Barkus agrees and has appointed an overseer or monitor of the law suit, Dr. Rosemary Sarri, professor of social work from the University of Michigan.

I'll admit that the good that resulted from the Glover Suit did not always sooth my ruffled feathers, because the mandates also caused a never ending, senseless and time consuming defense to the court of my every decision and action. It often made for long, tedious and non productive days. When faced with court mandates, I frequently had to remind myself and my staff that the Glover Suit gave the women's prison needed funding which would otherwise not be attainable. Whenever we needed or wanted anything, I tried to relate it to the Glover Suit in my annual budget requests, because it usually guaranteed funding. I used to joke that if the Glover Case was ever closed, we would have to find another law suit to take its place to ensure program funding and parity.

As a corrections employee, I had to represent the department in the Glover Suit, which often put me in a awkward position. There were times when I knew that the department had met the intent of the court order, but I also agreed that if the department were not monitored by the court, the value of these mandates would gradually lessen and might even be discontinued in the name of cost cutting. In spite of the inconveniences, I knew its goals were the same as mine, to ensure that women prisoners, upon release from prison, would be drug free and employed in decent paying jobs with benefits, so that they could support themselves and their children.

I won some battles and lost others while implementing the Glover court order. One I lost concerned Melinda LaPorte, a murderer who was taking correspondence courses at the University of Michigan, and being tutored by professors and students. The University of Michigan's generosity, by the way, was limited to just two women prisoners. A third was later added to the program, but it was never open to all qualified prisoners as I requested. The dean claimed such a maneuver would dilute the program. At that very time, Michigan Department of Corrections was being held in contempt of court because they had not made a four year college program available to women prisoners, in spite of my inability to entice a college to provide this.

Back to Melinda LaPorte. A dean and a professor requested that she be allowed to take part in the May graduation ceremonies. I denied their request based on policy at that time; LaPorte's security level made her a high risk. On top of that, she had not yet completed her studies. When I mentioned this, the dean assured me that Melinda's uncompleted work would not be a problem. Puzzled, I asked why. "As I recall, before I graduated I had to complete all course and credit requirements. I don't know of anyone who graduated with less. Why the exception with Ms. LaPorte?"

"This will be her only opportunity to actually participate in a graduation," responded the dean. "She deserves this honor after the work she has completed under the duress of prison."

I still denied the request, but the dean went to the director of the corrections department who overruled me, even after I argued that such a decision gave preferential treatment to one prisoner. I also told him that his decision would set a precedent which I did not think the department was prepared to follow. He disagreed.

The chief and assistant chief of security at the university were friends. As a courtesy, I contacted them to let them know about the Melinda LaPorte decision. I also told them that the decision was made without my support. They issued an order that Melinda LaPorte was to wear cuffs and leg irons and was to be accompanied by two armed uniformed officers during the graduation ceremonies. The dean and plaintiff's attorneys complained to everyone, but campus security stood by its decision. "She graduates with these security measures or she doesn't graduate."

Melinda LaPorte did graduate under the prescribed security conditions. A picture of her appeared in the *Ann Arbor News* to prove it.

Another incident that took me to Judge Barkus' court had to do with a request from plaintiffs' attorneys to meet as a group with the

121

twelve women who had been elected prisoner representatives. By policy, no more than three prisoners could meet with anyone unless an officer were in the room. The attorneys claimed an officer could not be present because of confidentiality. We went to court for a decision.

In court I was joined by the assistant attorney general assigned to the Glover Suit, and the deputy director. We had copies of all the policies pertaining to this issue and had rehearsed for hours in preparation for Judge Barkus' usual tough questioning. We were also prepared to lose because it seemed we always did with this judge.

We were stunned when Judge Barkus asked few questions and ruled in our favor, based on prison security needs and the department's policy. When the judge left the courtroom, I let out a huge sigh of relief. I must admit that the shocked looks on the plaintiffs' attorneys' faces were worth the hours of futile preparation.

Despite the problems, I am fully aware that without the Glover Suit, women prisoners in Michigan and throughout the United States would not have the opportunities that male prisoners do. The struggle for equality continues for women in prison as it does for all women. It's a sad state of affairs that it took such a suit before the State of Michigan changed its policies toward women prisoners, and that a monitor is still necessary to ensure that these policies are upheld.

PART 5

Huron Valley Men's Prison

I

May, 1989

"Good morning, Warden Miller," my administrative assistant, Carol, greeted me as I walked into my office.

"You're on the cheerful side this morning, Carol."

"Welllll, I'm trying to figure out how to best tell you that the reporter from the *Free Press* is coming today and not tomorrow. I don't know who screwed up the appointment—them or me."

"Oh no. How much time do I have?"

"You don't. He's due here any minute. You know how anxious they are to meet the first warden in this state to manage two prisons—one a men's max. Oh, by the way, Betty's not coming in until this afternoon—doctor's appointment. But you can handle it. You're a pro with the media. After all, you're the one who turned down Oprah, and you know how reporters love to write about corrections."

Carol was saying all this on her way out the door. She knew I would be irritated by the revelation that my secretary wouldn't be there to act as the first line of defense. I'd worn pink, too—just what reporters would want.

As Carol disappeared, the front desk officer telephoned to let me know that the reporter and his photographer were in the lobby. I told the officer that I would meet them at the door.

A man stopped me as I was leaving the office. "I'm the reporter from the *Free Press* and this is my photographer. Can you get us some coffee? We were in such a hurry, we didn't have time to buy any."

"Sure, I'll just be a second." Carol, who had returned, looked at me, trying hard not to lift her eyebrows.

I returned to my office in time to watch the photographer set up his equipment and check his light meter. I handed each a cup of coffee. "You didn't say whether you wanted anything in your coffee. Hope black's okay."

Neither answered, but the photographer motioned to me. "Sit in the warden's chair so I can see if the lighting is right."

"Sure," I responded.

I sat in my chair and watched him and the reporter, who was setting up his tape recorder and making notes. The reporter looked around the entire room, taking in every inch. My office was filled with a collection of pig memorabilia that my staff had given me over the years. My favorite one, a picture of a pig with wings flying over a rainbow, has a caption that reads: "Rise above the ordinary." It was hanging behind my desk next to the plaque of the official state seal. Once my staff had discovered that my family raised hogs when I was a child in upstate New York, they couldn't miss the humor in my choosing a career in which employees are often referred to as "pigs." I happened to love pigs because of their intelligence and playfulness, and this gave my employees the incentive they needed to sustain years of pig giving. They even gave me a live one at a Christmas party, which was fortunately returned to his owner.

When both the photographer and the reporter finished their setting-up ritual, the reporter looked at me, still sitting in the warden's chair, and asked, "When is the warden coming in?"

"I believe she's already here," I responded.

"She?" he asked.

I stood up, held out my hand and said, "I am Warden Miller, Warden Tekla Miller. Nice to have you here. Please take a seat."

The reporter, face reddening, fidgeted with his collar and sat in the chair across from my desk. The photographer's mouth dropped open and then he chuckled, "I'll be damned. You sure don't look like a warden."

"Don't let my outfit fool you. Real wardens do wear pink." I smiled at them sweetly.

I thought about my first appearance on a local T.V. show. As I walked on stage, when I was introduced to the studio audience, their gasps indicated they were not expecting a tall, slender, well dressed blond. I guess they expected female wardens to look like the one portrayed in "Women of Cellblock H": severe navy blue suits, orthopedic shoes, hair in a bun at the nape of the neck, and build like a sumo wrestler.

The reporter brought me back to the present when he cleared his throat. "Well then, let's, uh, begin."

At the end of the interview, the reporter turned off his tape recorder and looked at me. "Can I ask you a personal question off the record?"

"You want to know about the pigs, don't you?"

"Yes. What's the story?"

"My staff says that every time they see a pig, they think of me." I smiled again, but gave no further explanation. He didn't pursue it, thanked me for my time and started to leave. When he reached the door, the reporter looked down at the floor at a blue plastic dog's dish. He looked back at me and began to say something, but shook his head. I continued to smile and didn't offer an explanation for the dog dish either. It belonged to B.J., a Golden Retriever who was in puppy training for the Leader Dog School in Rochester. Women prisoners trained the puppies as part of a vocational program, and B.J., our first dog, often visited my office.

After the reporter and photographer left, I sat at my desk and looked out the window, watching a flock of Canada geese land on a pond in front of the prison complex. As I stared out, I recalled the day I learned that I was going to be the warden of two prisons.

My secretary, Betty, had buzzed me one afternoon early in April to say, "Melody Wallace is on the phone. Something about a decision that's needed in a law suit." Melody was a departmental attorney.

"Put her on." I couldn't think of any law suit pending at the women's prison. Besides, it was Friday afternoon and I was anxious to end the day hassle free.

"Hi, Tekla," she said when I answered the telephone. "I need some information on a case pending at the men's prison."

"Sorry, I have no authority over that prison. You'll have to talk to Dr. Houseworth. He's been filling in as warden there."

"But I have a memo right in front of me from the deputy director, dated today, stating that you have been appointed the acting warden of Huron Valley Men's, and will manage both Huron Valley Men's and Huron Valley Women's."

"What? Well, I don't have that memo and until I'm told I'm the warden of both places, I can't make any decisions regarding that institution. It's been hard enough sharing services with them, let alone managing that group of cowboys. You know how they feel about Women's. Shared services means eighty percent for them and twenty percent for us—that's all women need, quote-unquote. Anyway, I can't help you, Melody."

"Well then, I'll talk with the deputy director and see what he wants to do."

Within minutes of that call, I received a call on my direct line, which does not go through the prison switchboard and usually signals trouble. It's the line the warden's boss, the assistant deputy director, generally uses. I picked up the receiver gingerly and answered, "Warden Miller."

"This is the deputy director. Sorry things got screwed up. You know I was supposed to be at Huron Valley Women's today with your boss, Charlie. Did you get the message?"

"Yes. Your secretary notified me you weren't coming after you called to ask me if I knew where Charlie was."

"Yeah, well, by the time I discovered he wasn't around, it was too late for me to drive the hour and half to see you. Anyway, I thought Charlie told you about your new position."

"No. No one spoke to me about it. But from this conversation, I gather it's true. It would have been nice to have had some advance notice."

"Well, Tekla, go to the front of the prisons and take a long look. As far as you can see, it's yours. See yah!"

As soon as I hung up the telephone, my secretary informed me that the acting deputy warden from Huron Valley Men's, Rick Mayer, was on the phone. I suddenly realized the mammoth task that lay before me.

There were no other wardens in Michigan at that time managing two prisons, especially two as volatile and different as Huron Valley Women's and Men's. I knew many people felt that women shouldn't manage a men's prison, much less two prisons, because women are too soft. But that attitude was gradually being changed by the growing number of competent women in corrections who, like me, believed that a safe and secure environment was synonymous with a humane one.

I had become a firm believer in a humane corrections policy. As a Marine officer said to me later, concerning Iraqi POW's during Desert Storm, "Thumbscrews and racks are a thing of the past. You can break anybody and get them to say or do whatever you want, but you get a better response if you treat them humanely."

It would be a daunting struggle, I knew, to convince many employees at the men's prison that a humane approach was also the law. Persuading them to embrace such a philosophy would be especially tough because of prisoners like Paul Larner, a hostage taker and rapist, and Richard Goodard, a prisoner who had murdered a corrections officer.

There was another issue I knew I had to come to grips with. I didn't really want to work with male prisoners. Although I had made tremendous progress with prisoner programs for women, I knew that much more needed to be done, and I enjoyed that aspect of my job. The security level of the Huron Valley Men's Prison limited access to prisoner programs. I also felt that the women's prison was gaining respect from our colleagues throughout the state, making it a credible, rather than an embarrassing place to work. However, the one comforting feature of my new position was that I would be in control of all services for both prisons; for the first time, the women's prison wouldn't get the short end.

Taking a deep breath, I asked myself—Am I prepared for this huge responsibility? Yes, I thought. I'm going to give it all I've got!

II

As I mentioned, I was well aware that many correctional employees, some women included, felt that women should not work in men's prisons, let alone become wardens. But I was not prepared for the negative reception I received at Huron Valley Men's Maximum Security Prison. The fact that I was a woman was only one reason.

My title as warden of the women's prison carried little weight. Furthermore, although past attempts at sharing services had failed miserably, I was now expected to combine many of those services and, in the process, abolish more than a dozen positions. That caused resentment, as one would expect. As if that were not enough, Huron Valley Men's Prison had been without a warden for four months, and most of the supervisory staff positions were either vacant or filled by temporary staff. I knew it would take several months to get the staff up to par.

I didn't have a hard act to follow, however. In fact, several central office personnel commented, "If you just show up for work, you'll surpass your predecessor."

All four of my predecessors were men who had left Huron Valley Men's Prison for other positions under less than desirable circumstances. But none went out the way Travis Jones did.

Jones was the warden immediately before me who made national news for losing the prison keys assigned to him—including the master key. It seems that Mr. Jones was discovered naked in the apartment of a woman sergeant who worked at Southern Michigan Prison, and his keys were in his missing clothes. The lost keys business came to the surface when the woman later attempted to stab him. The keys were never found, and Jones was suspended, then fired; he was rehired at a lower level after a Civil Service Hearing. The woman sergeant was suspended, prosecuted for assault and fired.

Huron Valley Men's Prison had a physical plant similar to Huron Valley Women's, only more modern and spacious. There were five housing units, each housing eighty male prisoners held in single cells. Other buildings included the chow hall and kitchen, program/education, a gym, infirmary and administrative offices which also contained the indoor and outdoor visiting areas. An area of the program/education building had been converted to a dormitory for another one hundred prisoners. The buildings formed a circle facing a park-like area spread across forty-nine acres inside the security fences. The maintenance building and power plant were located outside the fence between the two prisons.

Like Huron Valley Women's, the buildings and grounds looked like a college campus, but Huron Valley Men's was surrounded by a double rather than a single chain link fence, and both fences were topped by razor ribbon. Six gun towers stood at strategic points in the fence, announcing the high security level of the prison. A perimeter road circled the prison; this was patrolled by an officer in a four wheel drive vehicle. When fence security was breached, an alarm sounded through the control center computer, indicating to the monitoring officer where the breach had occurred. The monitor would then notify the officers in the nearest gun tower and in the perimeter vehicle to check that area.

Huron Valley Men's was originally planned to be a medium custody facility for 400 prisoners, with a forty bed segregation unit. In mid construction, the institution was designated maximum security to meet the fast growing maximum security population in Michigan prisons. However, cell furnishings did not meet the standards for that security level. The central office administrators' solution was to send Huron Valley Men's Prison only those maximum security prisoners who supposedly displayed "positive behavior". It didn't take long before everyone realized the plan would not work, because those prisoners demonstrated little respect for their new surroundings and, in fact, demolished much of it.

Instead of reducing the custody level, however, the desperate need for segregation beds in the men's system dictated a second change for Huron Valley Men's. In 1988 it started being used for the segregation and mentally ill population as well. That population was violent, assaultive and destructive—hardly "positive behavior" types.

Those prisoners dismantled the porcelain sinks and toilets, metal beds and lockers, windows, radiators, and wooden desks and chairs, and used the parts as weapons or tools to break out of their cells. As warden, I ordered cement beds installed, stainless steel units containing a toilet and a sink to replace the porcelain sinks and toilets, stainless steel desks bolted to the walls, window glazing replaced with lexan, and foot lockers without lids bolted to the floor. However, a replacement for the radiators was never found.

Three fourths of the five hundred prisoners at Huron Valley Men's Prison at that time were on segregation status and considered among the most dangerous and difficult prisoners in Michigan; many were also mentally ill. Segregated prisoners remained locked in their cells twenty-three hours a day, except on those occasions when a prisoner was able to breach the door locks and leave the cell without authorization. Those excursions often ended in an assault on an officer. The computerized locking system installed during the prison's construction was supposed to be state-of-the-art, but it never functioned, which forced officers to unlock individual doors with keys. The locking system had been installed by the lowest bid company as dictated by law, and that company went out of business shortly after completing the installation. The computers remained on site, but were unusable.

Huron Valley Men's also housed mentally-ill male prisoners on close custody status (the level below maximum security). Those prisoners were allowed out of their cells for job and school assignments, general yard exercise, gym, and therapy. They were locked down during count and after lights out. A small population of approximately 100 medium security prisoners lived in dormitories converted from vocational classrooms located in the program building. That group had been classified to Huron Valley Men's Prison for the sole purpose of maintaining the prison as porters, groundskeepers, kitchen workers and the like. Medium custody prisoners were afforded more freedom of movement than those in close custody.

III

On my third day at Huron Valley Men's Prison, I made my first rounds. Several staff were in the control center including the female shift commander, a male sergeant, a male lieutenant, two officers, and the acting deputy warden, Rick Mayer. The two officers monitored the computers, radio conversations from within the institution, personal body alarms worn by officers and nurses, prisoner movement, and answered the telephones. Personal body alarms, which looked like garage door openers, were used to signal control center when an officer was in danger, and then a "Code Blue" was announced over the prison radio, alerting all available officers to report to the area of the signal.

Before I retrieved my keys, I read the critical log in which all the significant events that occurred during each shift were written. It listed assaults, cell changes, prisoner gassings, attempted suicides, weapons found, problems with visitors, serious security issues, medical issues, maintenance needs, etcetera. Reading the log was a daily habit I had formed at the women's prison to keep me abreast of prison activity, and to ensure that my instructions and departmental policies were being upheld. It was a habit I intended to keep. I signed my name in the log after I finished reading the entries, as anyone making or reading the entries was required to do, and turned to the shift commander. "I'll be making rounds in all the housing units, so I won't be back for a couple of hours."

"Do you need an escort?" Rick Mayer asked.

Everyone in the control center stopped what they were doing, held their breath, and waited for my response.

I turned to face Mayer. He had a smirk on his face and was leaning against the counter, his right hand in his pocket. "I have never had an escort and I don't plan to have one now. I ask to be accompanied only when I think there is a problem in a specific area. The person who accompanies me is the one who'll have to straighten out the problem. I hope you're not accustomed to being escorted, deputy, because it'll give the wrong impression to staff and prisoners—that you're afraid."

Everyone but Mayer chuckled and nodded their heads in agreement.

Mayer responded, " Er uh, great, great. I didn't know how you wanted things done."

Rick Mayer, an ex-offender and a known wife batterer once accused of rape, had greeted me on my first day at Huron Valley Men's with, "You know, women shouldn't run a men's max. It's too dangerous and they don't understand the methods necessary to control this prisoner population."

I knew Mayer would be a difficult employee, but did not think he would start in on me so soon. Perhaps he sensed my uneasiness at being in a prison where I didn't feel accepted, and thought I could be intimidated and manipulated.

I left the control center and made rounds, speaking to both employees and prisoners in each housing unit. Rounds are mandated for wardens by policy; some are as diligent about making them as I, while others do it as little as possible. I believed that I couldn't really know what was happening inside the institution unless I went in there every day.

Unit Two, a segregation unit, was the fourth unit I visited that day. As I entered, a prisoner was being taken to the day room (unit recreation area), which was in view of the officers' station. The room was a large square and had no furnishings, except for one chair and one table, both bolted to the floor. All other furnishings had been removed because the prisoners destroyed them, and, like cell furnishings, used the broken pieces as weapons.

As I passed through the day room, I noticed an officer removing a prisoner's handcuffs through a slot in the door. The prisoner, Ray Phillips, shouted to me as I passed, "Hey Warden!"

I walked to the door where I saw a small, eighteen year old squatting so he could speak through the slot in the door. Phillips had never seen me before, but knew that I was the warden. It amazed me how swift the prisoner grapevine was. It never took them long to find out what was happening in the system.

Phillips asked my age for some reason and, before I replied, announced, "Well, you look as old as my mother and she is fifty-six."

I was forty-six, but I didn't want the prisoner or the officers to think I was offended by his question, so I replied, "No, I'm older."

As I continued on my rounds, the sound of prisoner voices swelled to a roar.

"It's the new warden."

"Here she come now."

"Sure smells better than them men."

"And looks better too."

That was followed by several prisoners yelling, "Hey, Warden, I need to talk to you."

I walked from cell to cell, speaking with each prisoner through narrow windows in the cell door. The cells seemed void of light, even though each had an outside window and interior lights, unless they had been broken.

Some of the prisoners complained about the temperature (it was either too cold or too hot). Some asked about getting "outta the hole", or getting their good time back, or transferring to another prison. Some complained about how they were treated by officers and unit managers, and some just wanted to talk.

When I stopped to talk to one of the prisoners who called out to me, I looked through the cell door window and saw that he was masturbating. I assumed he was doing it to see how I would react. I asked if he had any other skills, and then wrote him up for sexual misconduct and told him that future communications between us would be in writing only.

I continued on rounds, walking between units Two and One,

and the chorus of male voices accompanied me.

"You're sure the sexiest thing we've seen around here in a long time."

"That's the warden. You can't talk to her like that."

"Hey, Warden, baby. You goin to get me outta this hole?"

An African-American woman officer walked by me, diverting the prisoners' attention to her. One voice could be heard above the others, "Look at that fine black ass on Officer Worton. Gonna gimme a piece a yo ass, tramp?"

I couldn't identify the face in the darkened window, but I could identify the cell. I knew prisoners coveted the inside cells so they could watch prisoner, staff and visitor traffic. So I went straight to the Unit One sergeant and told him to move the offending prisoner to an outside cell. I also directed the sergeant to be sure that the prisoner understood the reason for his move and to make the explanation loud enough to be heard by other prisoners.

When I returned to the control center to turn in the keys, the captain asked, "Well, how'd it go?"

"I went from looking like I was someone's fifty-six year old mother to the sexiest thing they've see. Not bad for the first day."

I thought about how different the rounds were at the women's prison. Most of the women were in general population, making conversation easier and more relaxed. Few conversations took place through a slot in a door, since only 60 of the 480 women were on segregation status. Women prisoners were interested in my wardrobe, but confined their remarks to:

"Nice shoes, Warden"

"Where didja get that dress? It's sharp."

"Can't wait to get back to the real world so's I can dress like you, Warden Miller."

The men prisoners, on the other hand, would write long letters, known as "kites", in which they described the cologne I wore and every detail of my outfit. Men prisoners often fantasized about what they saw. Prisoner Schweigert, who first met me while I was on a tour with the Corrections Accreditation Committee, focused on my red dress, though it was a mid-calf, conservative affair. The kite I received from Schweigert following the tour discussed at length my "long sexy legs" and how I "should always wear red." That was followed by, "I saw you walking to the school today. You wore a brown suit and although you were a vision of loveliness, as always, it wasn't the same as the red dress."

My staff had great fun singing to me, "See the warden with the red dress on. She can dance all night long. Well alright ...etcetera." I found it made little difference what I wore. Men prisoners fantasized about it and women prisoners wanted to own it.

A couple of days after my first rounds at Huron Valley Men's Prison, I received a letter from Kohl, the masturbating prisoner. It was filled with dried semen. That ended written as well as verbal communication with him. But it did not stop him from sending me one more letter threatening my life: "Beware, Warden Miller. Either me or my street friends will do the job when you don't expect it."

Although I didn't take such threats seriously, they always left me uneasy—I never knew who just might be crazy enough to carry out such a threat.

Some of the letters I received from prisoners were bizarre and scary, but many made me laugh. An escapee sent me a letter from Juarez, Mexico. "Sorry I disappointed you but don't take my escape personal. I told you that I just needed a vacation and a couple of cold beers. I'll be back in a few weeks and turn myself in." She did!

One letter began, "By now you must know that I am General Colin Powell's nephew and was sentenced to prison to spy." He warned me, "Don't contact General Powell because I'm not supposed to tell anyone about this." But my favorite was from Jimmy Potts.

Dear Warden,

By now you must have read my appeal papers. You know I am not guilty of that ticket and hope you will prove to be as understanding as I have seen you in the past. It's these police in the prison. They always out to get me. I know you will agree with me when you read my side of the story. Call me out so we can discuss this man to woman. I know I can make you understand and see my way. If you don't change your mind and change the guilty finding on the assault, I hope you die of cancer you maggot face bitch.

Sincerely...Jimmy Potts

IV

I felt lucky not to have to deal with the prisoners for eight hour shifts each day, like the officers did, especially those working in the segregation units. In addition to being subjected to prisoners throwing feces, urine and food, segregation officers were always in danger of being assaulted when removing a prisoner from his cell. But the most contemptuous and rage producing prisoner action was spitting Many officers had to be disciplined for reflex actions, slapping or punching a prisoner who'd spit on him.

Assaults on staff came in many forms. One particularly disgusting incident happened to the male deputy warden at Huron Valley Women's Prison. It took place a week or so after the poor fellow's nose had been broken by a mentally ill prisoner. The deputy rushed into my office, shouting, "I want that bitch locked in segregation forever! I intend to write her up for sexual assault. Do you think it will stick?"

"You sound really upset. Who and what are you talking about?"

"Garrison, the eighteen year old that had her mother killed for a twenty thousand dollar life insurance policy."

"That's why you want her locked in segregation forever?"

"No. You know her temper. If she doesn't get her way, she explodes. This time she went too far."

"Well, what on earth happened?"

The deputy warden started to pace, stopped for a moment, then paced again as he recounted his story. "When I told her that she wasn't being released from segregation, she jumped up from her chair, placed her hand down the front of her pants, pulled out her used sanitary napkin and threw it at me. It hit my chest, and if she hadn't run from the room, I might of belted her!"

We agreed that he should write Garrison up on a sexual assault misconduct. To my surprise, Garrison was found guilty. Not to my surprise, she remained on segregation status for a long time.

Forced cell moves were made when a prisoner trashed a cell, set fire to the contents of the cell, demonstrated self mutilating behavior, attempted suicide, flooded the cell, was being transferred to another prison or a higher custody level, was searched for weapons, tampered with door locks, etcetera.

Forced moves were often dangerous and were made with a five officer Emergency Contact Team (ECT). The entire move was video taped to prevent the officers from using excessive force and to have evidence for any litigation that might result if a prisoner claimed abuse.

Officers on ECTs at Huron Valley Women's Prison reflected the over-all officer mix: female, male, black and white. When I arrived at the men's prison, the team members were all males, and came from outside the unit in which the recalcitrant prisoner was locked. The men's teams were referred to as the "Goon Squads".

When I became warden, I ordered that both women and men be on those teams, and that the teams be made up of staff from the unit in which the prisoner was housed. The decision was well received by the women officers and many of the men who made up the "Goon Squads". It was rejected by the male officers from the old school who believed it necessary to: "Gas the prisoner (usually called 'asshole' by the officers), beat him, then talk to him."

My decision to change the Emergency Contact Team at the men's prison came after watching a team dress out while I was in Unit Two on rounds. I saw the male officers enter the unit and change from their uniforms to protective gear, which consisted of vests, gloves and helmets, and a large plexiglass body shield for the lead officer. I asked the unit sergeant, "Why don't you use the officers from this unit?"

The sergeant replied, "We've chosen and trained the biggest guys to extract a prisoner from a cell. Most of them are assigned to the yard so they can be available."

A male unit officer standing nearby chimed in, "Loeb's no bigger'n me, so why's he here? I can take care of business."

I turned to the unit sergeant. "What kind of signal do you think this sends to a prisoner—no one from the unit is big enough? Or maybe they are scared? And no woman can do the job at all? You're setting up the officers in the unit to look unable to handle their jobs by showing that others have to be called in when the going gets tough."

"I can see your point, but this is the way it's always been done," the sergeant replied.

After that discussion with the sergeant, I had a meeting with the deputy, assistant deputies and shift commanders. Except for one woman shift commander, Theresa Dalton, they were all men. I explained that the procedure for a cell extraction would be reversed. "You will talk to the prisoner first—find out what his problem is. Ninety-five percent of the time you can talk him out of the cell. If you can't, you'll have to use gas, but under no circumstances will you use gas without my authorization, or the deputy's in my absence. And I don't want to see any more critical incident reports on my desk that state the injury was due to the prisoner tripping, or falling down the stairs, or hitting his head against the wall while resisting. To a lay person it may sound okay, but to me it's pure brutality. I know the games—you lift a prisoner up by the leg irons and belly chain, bang his head into the wall and claim he resisted. Or you push him so that he loses his balance and trips or falls down the stairs. The games are over, and I intend to discipline abusive staff."

"Yes ma'am," they responded, but I detected a hint of resentment.

It took the employees at the men's prison a long time to realize that my technique, which was also the legal one, worked. At least most employees eventually realized it. I remember one particular officer's union meeting where the all white male union executives argued, "It's just not like it used to be. You've changed everything. We're coddling and begging the prisoners now."

"All I'm asking is that you follow policy," I responded.

"Yeah," the union president retorted, "that's what they said about you at women's prison. They told us you'd say—follow policy."

"Are there far fewer assaults?"

"Yeah."

"Are there far fewer injuries?"

"Yeah."

"Are there far fewer misconducts?"

"Yeah."

"Do you think it might be working?"

"Yeah, but it's not the same."

Assaults may have decreased, but attempted suicides by prisoners remained a constant threat. Facing them was uncomfortable for me because of my mother's suicide, and I felt powerless since suicides were particularly difficult to prevent in a prison setting. If a person wanted to kill themselves, they would do it at a time least expected, and prisoners had all the time in the world to plan. They would often make the attempts right after count or a cell check.

One Sunday morning I was home, making my weekly call to my sister, Alyce, in California. Because I was on stand-by that day, I had to remain at home to be near a telephone and within an hour's drive to the prisons. I was feeling somewhat resentful too, because I had to miss an important event. My youngest stepson, Robert, was competing in a local triathalon, and it was a big accomplishment for him.

The day was perfect for the triathalon, warm, but not hot, and sunny, with a crisp spring wind to keep the athletes alert. As I was telling my sister about the blueberry muffins I'd made for the family celebration—to take place on the boy's triumphant return—our conversation was interrupted by a call-waiting signal. I dreaded answering it, knowing that the caller was probably from one of the prisons. It was the twenty-third call I had received since Friday night. That was a record, one I preferred had not been set.

"Alyce, hang on—I have another call coming through."

"Yes?"

"This is Captain Dalton at Huron Valley Men's Prison. Prisoner Kern, who was recently transferred from the protective environment unit to segregation, has attempted suicide by hanging. He is being transferred to the hospital by ambulance. It left approximately five minutes ago."

"Complete the critical incident report and have it on my desk in the morning, Captain. Be sure you have statements from all those on duty in the unit and the prison medical team. Call me back on the prisoner's status when you hear from the hospital."

"Yes, ma'am."

I switched back to my sister and explained, "A prisoner I don't even know has attempted suicide. This has been a wild weekend."

The call-waiting signal sounded again. "Hold on again, Alyce. I think I'm getting the call from the prison about the attempted suicide's status."

I put her on hold and answered the incoming call.

"Warden Miller, this is Captain Dalton again. Kern was pronounced dead at the hospital."

"Oh." I was silent for a few seconds. "Have the medical staff notify the next of kin, seal off his cell and make sure no one goes in there. Call the Michigan State Police to start the investigation."

"Yes ma'am."

I returned to my sister who was waiting patiently. "I have to go. The prisoner died. I have to contact my boss. This'll cause a big investigation; lawyers think all suicides can be prevented. Talk with you later."

I hung up the telephone and called my boss, one of four assistant deputy directors who supervise the wardens. While waiting for someone to answer, I started to feel the familiar stiffening in my neck, the tightening in my chest and that damnable pain over my right eye. A migraine was coming on.

I thought about the many prisoners, males and females, who had attempted suicide while I had been warden. It came with the territory when one was managing a large population of mentally ill and self-mutilating prisoners. Many suicide attempts were planned as a way to shake up the staff and get attention. Often, several attempts would be made by the same prisoner, and after each, the prisoner would be confined in a suicide observation room in the prison's infirmary.

Some of the attempted suicides were even comical. Lori Kaster, for example, was a woman who regularly repeated the same suicide attempt. She would stand on top of the sink in her cell with one end of a sheet tied around her neck and the other attached to a ceiling fixture, and then wait for an officer to go by her cell door. When the passing officer looked into Lori's cell, she would jump off the sink. However, she always made sure the sheet was long enough to allow her feet to touch the floor.

On one occasion, Lori chose a new suicide method. This time, she was taking a bath. As usual, she waited for an officer to appear. When the officer walked by, Lori sank under the bath water, covering her head in an attempt to drown herself. The officer shouted, "Kaster, you're too heavy to lift out of the tub. You might drown."

Lori sat up like a bolt of lightening and got out of the tub. I understand that after she was released from prison, Lori jumped into the Detroit River from the Belle Isle bridge, but she survived that too.

Cindy was another prisoner who attempted suicide on a regular basis. She would do anything to get attention, including burning herself with a lit cigarette over and over so that her body, especially her arms, were covered with fresh red scabs and aged scars.

One day, officers were helping the medical and psychiatric staff move a prisoner who was kicking, screaming, and foaming at the mouth. She was being taken to the segregation unit in a straight jacket. Cindy, in an attempt to be heard above the commotion caused by the officers and medical staff subduing the prisoner, yelled, "Hey, hey! Look at me. I'm going to kill myself."

An officer running by her cell door saw Cindy standing bare foot in her toilet, holding the ends of two frayed electrical wires together. "You do what you have to do, Cindy. I don't have time now."

Cindy got out of the toilet.

Few prisoners were thought to actually want to end their lives. Kern was the second prisoner at Huron Valley Men's Prison, and the last while I was warden, to fulfill his death wish, or to use the official term, to become a "successful suicide".

A year previously, just one month after I became warden of both Huron Valleys, Thomas Tailor, sentenced to prison for armed robbery, was the first "successful suicide" in my career. He used the same method as Kern, hanging himself with a state-issued bed sheet. Neither he nor Kern were on suicide watch at the time, but both prisoners had attempted suicides in the past, as noted in their medical histories.

I can still see Tailor's body propped against his cell wall after officers cut the sheet tied to his neck and lowered him to the floor. This picture brought back the dreadful memory of my mother's body being lowered in the same manner.

At the monthly Warden's Administrative Staff meeting that took place shortly afterwards, Tailor's suicide was discussed. The meeting was my first since I'd become the warden for both prisons. Supervisors shared what they termed an unusual phenomenon—staff were feeling depressed about the suicide and afraid the suicide would encourage others in a copy cat fashion. The supervisors said the officers were taking the blame for not being able to save the prisoner's life. We all felt that no matter how much we disliked a prisoner, death was a difficult reality to cope with, because it left no alternatives or solutions. But many prisoners, especially those serving life sentences, felt there was little chance for change in their situations and despaired. To them, facing the rest of their life in a bleak cell was not considered a positive alternative, even if they could take advantage of the many programs offered.

The most difficult population in both Huron Valley Men's and Women's Prisons were the self mutilators. Incidents involving them constituted the majority of the calls I received from prison supervisors, both during the work day and when I was on call. Self-mutilating prisoners were diagnosed as not being seriously mentally ill, and lay persons often confused mutilators with suicidal prisoners. Huron Valley Men's Prison had the dubious distinction of having the first unit in the United States devoted to treating self mutilators, setting the precedent for treatment in this area.

Officers assigned to the mutilator unit asked, "How can prisoners do such things to themselves and not be insane? It's gruesome!"

The answer, given by the capable and dedicated medical personnel, was that self mutilating behavior is manipulative, and a technique that had been used by the mutilators since childhood to get the attention and/or item they want. Some mutilators get worse with age.

We questioned how the officers at Huron Valley Men's Prison, trained to work in a maximum security setting where assaults on them were commonplace, would ever be able to offer appropriate help to a population who assaulted themselves. "More training" was the chief psychiatrist's answer. "Training, and wanting to work with these prisoners to change their behavior. Behavioral modification and deprivation is the key. Officers have to stick to the written therapy posted for each prisoner, with no deviations."

The mutilator unit was always filled. Not a day went by without a plethora of telephone calls notifying me about mutilations, which often meant transporting a prisoner to the hospital, followed by the prisoner's placement on "Top Of Bed" (TOB) status once they were returned to prison. Prisoners on TOB were given suicide gowns and blankets to ensure their protection. These could not be torn and, like all prison bedding, were not flammable. Some prisoners also had to wear large leather mittens to prevent them from tearing out stitches.

Many prisoners went back and forth between general population and the self mutilating unit. Simpson was one of these. He liked to push pencils, forks, and other objects in his arm and up his penis. After months of that behavior, he cut off his penis using a piece of metal from the radiator, and then ate it. One day, after he had recovered sufficiently to return to the general population, I received a call from the shift commander. "Simpson won't come in from yard until we give him a new penis."

I had to force myself not to laugh, but I replied, "Call Dr. Gallagan and have him talk to Simpson. I'm sure he will be able to convince Simpson to lock up." I don't know what Gallagan said to convince him, but Simpson did go back to his cell.

Gallagan was the psychiatrist for the out-patient mental health prisoners and the one who had handled the mutilators before a special psychiatric team devoted to the self mutilators was added to the staff. I had many conversations with Dr. Gallagan about prisoners.

One was about Amy Dins, a self mutilator who had been put on finger foods and whose cell was stripped to bare walls. The strip included covering the electrical outlets, removing the lighting fixture (she, as did many mutilators, ate light bulbs), removing the floor tiles (she had peeled some away and used them to cut herself), and removing the bedding so she could not hang herself. She was not allowed any smoking materials because, like Cindy, she burned herself. Her water source was turned off because she flooded her cell, and she was often placed on Top Of Bed restraints.

After one near death incident, Dins was sent to the infirmary at the men's prison (a shared service), and placed on suicide watch. After a couple of days, I received a telephone call from Dr. Gallagan. "I'm on the speaker phone with Dr. Reager. Since he's the medical director, I thought he should be with me when I told you what we decided to do about Dins."

"This has to be a good one with both of you on the phone. What am I in for now?"

"Well," Dr. Gallagan answered, "you know we have had Dins

here for the past three days. We want to send her back to Women's."

"You can't tell me she's cured or even better. Can't you keep her for just a few more days? The women's prison needs a break."

"No. There's no reason for it. She's not responding any differently here than at Women's."

"Where is she now?"

"She's in the ceiling above us. All we can see are her eyes."

"She's in the ceiling?"

"Yeah. She took out a ceiling tile and climbed into the ceiling. She's been roaming around up there for several hours now. She claims she won't come down unless she's sent back to the women's prison."

"Why would any infirmary housing mentally ill prisoners have a drop-in ceiling?" I wondered aloud. "It's good for hiding contraband, and apparently it's good for hiding prisoners. Send her home, gentlemen, but you owe me."

The self mutilators never ceased to amaze me. That they could mentally block out the pain they were inflicting on themselves seemed uncanny. These prisoners tore at their skin with their hands until they caused wounds that needed stitches, and then they would tear the stitches out. They would use anything to cut themselves or reopen old wounds. Their behavior depressed many prison employees, including myself.

Millazo was the king of mutilation. Nothing, and I mean nothing, could keep him from mutilating himself. In fact, the leather mittens we placed on prisoners to prevent them from reopening wounds and tearing stitches out were tested on him before they were given to others. Millazo ate them. He was also fond of eating light bulbs.

Hour after hour, Millazo would fiddle with a new gadget we had found to prevent mutilation, until he was able to conquer it. He was inspired by this game, and it was the only time he was quiet and not injuring himself.

Radiators became our nightmare because there was nothing we could find that would secure them to the walls and prevent prisoners from tearing them apart. A metal strap-like device was developed which attached to the walls with security screws. I told the maintenance men to "give it to Millazo" for testing.

On the day the radiator straps were installed, Millazo was like a child with a new Christmas toy. His face glowed and he rubbed his hands together over and over, giggling, "This will be fun. A challenge, but fun."

It took Millazo a month, but he triumphed, successfully dismantling the straps. The bonus was that during that month, Millazo was quiet, and never once went to the infirmary because of mutilation. Finally, he remarked, "I think I can handle general population. Maybe school, too. I feel real good."

The psychiatric team was persuaded to try him in general population. Gradually the team added property to Millazo's cell, and gave him privileges when he began to respond to rewards for good behavior. Within a few months, Millazo was able to leave the mutilation unit and went on to succeed in general population. Something about that month of concentration had calmed him, and quieted the need for self destruction.

The extremes of mutilating behavior never hit me, however, until a woman prisoner pulled her uterus out through her vagina. These were desperate people, filled with guilt, who had no knowledge of how to get attention through positive behavior.

About a week after the incident with Dins, the commander on first shift reported to me, "Prisoner Burkey cannot be found. He was in an observation room in the infirmary, but he's gone."

"Have you looked in the ceiling?"

"No, Warden, but Dr. Gallagan asked me the same thing."

"Why don't you check it out and call me back before we activate the escape mobilization."

Within a few minutes, the shift commander called back. "We've found Burkey. Not quite in the ceiling, but in the heating duct. He's stuck, but maintenance is on the way."

Burkey had been taken to the infirmary a few days earlier because of injuries inflicted by officers using excessive force during a cell move. Burkey was in a segregated-status cell that still had a porcelain sink and toilet. On the day he was injured, he had become agitated over something simple, perhaps not getting a light for his cigarette when he asked for it. Like many prisoners, he demanded immediate gratification. On that day, he acted out his frustration by trashing his room, and then used the broken porcelain pieces to cut himself. The blood from his wounds seeped under the door, forming small rivers.

To prevent further injury, an Emergency Contact Team was formed. I gave permission to use gas because Burkey was in an highly agitated state and unable to be calmed. Once the gas took effect, the team went into the cell. The lead man carried the plexiglass body shield, and the other four, one woman and three men, followed behind him in pairs. The lead man entered the cell and pushed the plexiglass body shield against prisoner Burkey, forcing him to the ground, but the force of the action caused the lead officer to slip on the blood covered floor. As he fell to the floor, he punctured his legs in several places on the broken porcelain. He was bleeding badly and unable to get up on his own.

While the other four officers on the team restrained Burkey, the officer running the video camera, Franklin, gave the camera to an inexperienced officer, Johnson, so that Franklin could help the lead officer out of the cell. The other officers reacted to their teammate's injuries by carrying Burkey from the cell by the chains on his ankles and wrists, rather than by holding his arms and legs. That caused cuts and bruises on Burkey's wrists and ankles.

Either Johnson's poor camera work was intentional, or it was due to lack of experience, but once Burkey was removed from the cell, the picture became blurred. The sound, however, remained clear. When I viewed the video tape later that day, I could hear slaps, thumps and the prisoner's protests, as well as a staff member yelling, "Get that fucking camera outta here." The voice was identified as the sergeant in charge of the Emergency Contact Team.

Corrections employees are supposed to be above abusing a prisoner, but in the heat of the moment, when one of their colleagues is down, it can be difficult to remember that. The fallen officer was hospitalized and underwent physical therapy for several months, but never returned to corrections. The sergeant in charge of the team received a thirty day suspension without pay. The other team members received various sanctions ranging from written reprimands to suspensions, depending on the role they played in the abuse.

Although sanctions lessened abusive staff behavior, they heightened resentment against me by officers who still harbored the feeling that I was too soft on prisoners. In fact, some went so far as to say that

I took the prisoner's side against employees, rather than supporting them right or wrong. But both the law and state policy were on my side, and I knew that prisoners who are treated humanely are less likely to be a threat.

V

Abuse among prison officers was another constant concern. Two officers, Harold Webster and Joline Anderson, worked the midnight shift at Huron Valley Men's Prison. One night, Officer Webster "slam dunked" Officer Anderson when Anderson rejected his advances. It became apparent during the investigation that unwanted sexual advances and slurs by Webster had been going on for a long time. The night of the assault, Officer Anderson had had enough, and she told Officer Webster, "You can threaten me all you want, but it still won't get me in bed with you. You don't get it. I like the man I'm married to."

As she said this, Webster wrapped his hand around her forearm, and she forced it off. Webster grabbed Anderson again, picked her up and slammed her to the floor, yelling, "Whore. You think you can tease and get away with it. You're wrong."

Although the whole episode was witnessed by the unit sergeant, Bernie Cain, four other officers, and prisoners, Sergeant Cain neither referred to it in the unit's critical log, nor attempted to have Webster disciplined. Sergeant Cain also refused Officer Anderson's request to be relieved from duty because of back pain, nausea and emotional trauma. Anderson left her post anyway and went to the shift commander. But before she got to his office, Sergeant Cain reported to the shift commander that Anderson had left her post without permission and should be suspended. By the time Officer Anderson reached the control center, the shift commander was ready to suspend her. Once he heard her side of the story, however, he ordered a physical exam.

Disciplinary charges were filed against both Sergeant Cain and Officer Webster, but Officer Anderson had the strength to go one step further. She filed criminal charges for assault and battery. Webster was later found guilty of a misdemeanor and returned to work after a thirty day suspension. Officer Anderson, at her own request, was transferred to another prison.

There were many incidents of sexual harassment at Huron Valley Men's Prison. However, unlike Joline Anderson, most of the women employees, especially officers, were afraid to file complaints against colleagues, even when their lives were threatened. Women officers feared that if they complained they would be set up in situations for which they could be disciplined, demoted or fired (like having drugs planted in their locker), or forced to do the most demeaning tasks such as searching rooms where the prisoners had defecated everywhere. Women officers worried that they would not be accepted as credible peers; women who complained were labeled troublemakers—not team players. They were supposed to accept harassment as part of the job.

Of even greater concern to women officers was the fear of getting into dangerous situations where backup would not be available. That is what happened to a rookie officer, Josephine McCullum. Officer McCullum was murdered in 1987 by a prisoner in Southern Michigan Prison, while she was alone on duty in an isolated area. She was assigned to that duty by a male supervisor who had hoped to intimidate her into quitting, because he didn't think women should work inside men's prisons. Her unfortunate, senseless murder gave fuel to those who argued that women should not work with male offenders. The murder of a male officer at Southern Michigan Prison that same year did not alter their opinions or force them to face a more realistic conclusion: prisons can be dangerous places to work, no matter the gender. As of this writing, there have been three officers murdered in the line of duty in Michigan Prisons. Still, that is a remarkably low number considering the number of assaults that take place.

After the extensive investigation into Officer McCullum's murder, Michigan Department of Corrections developed a policy regarding sexual harassment which was implemented along with a thorough training program. The department was ahead of most public and private agencies in the United States in this effort, but it took the death of Officer McCullum to bring it there. Change was slow, especially change that was viewed as threatening to the white male stronghold that has existed for so long in law enforcement and corrections.

Looking back, sexual harassment in corrections should not have surprised me since it reflected the world around us and still does. At Huron Valley Men's Prison, however, I found an unusual amount of it because such behavior had been accepted by prior prison administrations; complaints were ignored and the state policy on sexual harassment was not enforced. My policies represented a welcomed change, both to women who were harassed and to men who wished to not be a part of the harassment. After I earned the trust of women employees, complaints flourished, and the prison began its long, rocky road toward cleansing.

During that period, Rick Mayer, Assistant Deputy Warden, threatened physical harm to a woman sergeant who filed a complaint directly to me. She reported that he warned, "People can get hurt if they don't play the game."

After Mayer made several more threats, the woman sergeant burst into my office and collapsed into a chair, crying, "I can't go inside the prison no more, Warden. I can't. He follows me everywhere and watches me with that shitty smirk on his face. He's just waiting for me to make a mistake. Please, please help me. I know he'll come after me for being in here."

"I know how difficult it is for you, Sergeant," I told her. "But unless you file a formal complaint, I can't do anything. If you file a complaint, I promise to do everything in my power to get him out of here. Maybe your complaint will encourage others to come forward."

"Okay. I'll file one, but I'm going on stress leave. I know I can't work with him if I file a complaint. It's frightening enough to think I may bump into him on the streets."

Mayer also pursued other women for dates, using his position to threaten the loss of their jobs. I helped file two formal complaints of sexual harassment against him and was confident that the women I persuaded to put aside their fears and take that bold step would be rewarded. However, I was devastated to learn that the reports I'd sent to central office charging him with sexual harassment had somehow been lost. I suspected the loss was intentional to protect him, because two other insubordination charges, sent separately to central office, were also lost, forcing me to cancel his suspension and bring him back to the prison.

The sergeant did not return to work, but telephoned me one

day, stating, "You see, Warden; I told you. Mayer's bigger than both of us. What do I do now? I can't come back there."

I was angry, frustrated, and felt as though I had taken a hundred steps backwards in the fight against sexual harassment. I knew it would be difficult, but I tried to comfort the sergeant and to regain her confidence in me. "I'm upset, too, but I refuse to think it's a conspiracy. Otherwise, I couldn't continue here. Central Office gets so much paper, and who knows what happens to it all. I'll try to get you transferred so you won't have to face Mayer. I really appreciate the risk you took. It'll all work out."

"I'm not as confident as you are. I just want out of the Valley."

The women involved in the other complaints against Mayer also asked for transfers, and were accommodated when positions were available. One of his victims transferred out of corrections to another state job.

Sexual harassment at Huron Valley Men's Prison was often carried to extremes. In one case, a black male captain and his subordinate, Lieutenant Reynolds, a white male, did not want to accept the promotion of a black woman sergeant to lieutenant. The woman lieutenant was scheduled to be added to their shift after a mandatory six month probation period.

While the woman lieutenant was on probation, the two men went to the assistant deputy of security and told him she was lazy and not doing her job. They provided the assistant deputy with what was later found to be fabricated evidence to support their claims. The captain denied her legitimate time off, and forced her to work overtime. The two also spread rumors that she was sleeping with them.

The lieutenant reported that when she walked by these two males, they formed their hands into the shape of a gun and stated, "Bang-bang, you're dead." She finally filed a complaint, when she felt her promotion was in jeopardy. As a result of the subsequent investigation, the two offenders received written reprimands and were placed on separate shifts. Again, the woman's only recourse was a transfer to another prison.

It was no wonder, then, that a woman officer was raped by a prisoner who saw, by the treatment they received from their peers and supervisors, that women employees weren't valued. One supervisor sent me a memo, reporting: "I was on the walk between Units Two and One, heading for the administration building, when a female officer passed by me coming from the other direction. A male officer leaving Unit One yelled to the female officer, 'Hey tramp, tramp.' She turned to the caller and made a polite response. Knowing the emphasis you have made on sexual harassment, I thought you should know about this."

When I read that memo, I wondered why that supervisor didn't do something about the male officer's demeaning behavior, and why the female officer accepted being called "tramp". Because of such reactions, prisoners felt free to humiliate women officers without fear of consequences.

When I asked the supervisor why he did nothing about the male officer's behavior, he replied, "I don't know him, and I don't supervise him."

"And just what do you think I can do if you can't identify either party?" I asked. "Whether you are the direct supervisor or not, if you did nothing in that situation, you condoned it. That's why there's such a problem here."

Shortly after that incident, I scheduled all supervisors in both prisons to attend a one day sexual harassment training program. It was a quick fix that slowed the harassment and persuaded more women to come forward, but it didn't stop the behavior.

I usually ate lunch in the employee dining room. It was a territory where titles had no authority and everyone was treated equally. We had great fun during the few lunch breaks we were able to take. During one lunch I noticed two new male officers, in their early twenties, whom I had not met because they had just transferred from another prison. One of the young officers was talking about women. "They shouldn't work after they get married. And all married women should know how to make a decent lunch for their man, let alone a meal."

Everyone who knew me looked at me with anticipation, wondering what I was going to say. I accommodated the stares by asking the young officer, "What makes you think the woman has to cook?"

"That's their role. That's the way it should be. Besides, I can't and don't cook. Why else would I get married?" The officer poked his fork into a meal he had gotten from a vending machine in the prison lobby.

The employees in the lunch room shifted their eyes back to me. "Who told you that a woman comes out of the womb wanting to cook?" I retorted. "And what's wrong with a man cooking—too lazy or maybe too dumb?"

"What are you, a psychiatrist or something?"

The others laughed and someone said, "No, she's the warden."

"Yeah, yeah. I believe that like I believe I'm the president."

I looked down to see that my name tag had been covered by my scarf. Lifting the scarf, I pointed to the name tag, which read: "WAR-DEN MILLER".

"You really are the warden. What are you doing here?"

"I work here."

"I mean in the employee lunch room."

"I repeat, I work here, which means I can eat in this room." I offered my hand to him to shake, "Who are you?"

Officer Jackson yelled out, "Yah better give her an alias, honey. She got you figured out."

He stood up, shook my hand and said, "I'm John Calloway. Maybe I should transfer again. Looks like I blew my chances here."

A male unit manager answered, "Nah. You're just gettin' educated. Wait 'til she starts on your unhealthy eating habits."

We all laughed and he left the lunchroom, but he only transferred to the afternoon shift.

After that, I watched Officer Calloway come to work with the others each day at 1:30, in time for the afternoon shift's roll call. He had long, wavy, blond hair that reached to the top of his collar and was combed straight back. His white officer's shirt was always unbuttoned three buttons to reveal a gold chain around his neck and a perpetual tan. Many times I observed him speaking to women officers, who responded by rolling their eyes upward, shaking their heads, and walking away. He would smile as his eyes followed them until the women were out of sight.

VI

Bobby Hughes, the training lieutenant, stopped at my office door on his way to the conference room and announced, "Warden, the new officers are here. All fifteen of them."

"Take them into the conference room. I'll be right there," I responded.

After completing eight weeks of classroom and physical training and an additional eight weeks of on-the-job training, the new officers spent the remainder of their one year probationary period as trainees at Huron Valley Men's Prison. I greeted each new class on their first day and made sure that I told them exactly what to expect as officers in a prison. It's tough, unglamorous and often dangerous work. Anything short of telling it like it is would have been deceptive and set them up for disappointment and failure.

When I entered the conference room, the officers rose, a formality that rarely lasted through the first year. I looked around the room as they sat down. Each officer was dressed in the standard uniform consisting of black slacks, ties and shoes, white shirts with the green and gold state emblem on the right shoulder, and green blazers. Women were allowed to wear black ascots, but I insisted that all officers wear standard issue clip-on ties, so that if pulled by a prisoner in an attempt to choke an officer, the tie would pop off. Some administrators had pushed to retain the ascots for women officers because they looked more feminine and even went so far as to say that they were "cute". This latter group succumbed to the pressures of both officers and supervisors who argued, "Ascots are potentially dangerous to an employee and should not be retained because they are cute."

The new group of officers consisted of four women and eleven men, ages ranging from the early twenties to the late forties. From their personnel records, I knew that some had been laid off from jobs in the auto industry; that the women were single, three with children; that some of the officers had only GEDs, while others had bachelor's or master's degrees; that two were ex-offenders; and that none was at the top of the class at the Michigan Department of Corrections DeMarse Training Academy.

Ex-offenders were hired to encourage private sector companies to do the same. Corrections administrators believed that we should set the example, and have hired approximately 120 ex-offenders as corrections officers, maintenance workers, teachers and administrators since 1965. Some of the ex-offenders display the same belligerence toward authority as officers that they did as prisoners. On the other hand, many ex-offenders perform well, and some are promoted to supervisory positions.

Bobby Hughes introduced me with a brief background biography and finished by saying, "You can tour the warden's office. It's known for her pig collection. Everyone who visits Huron Valley Men's wants to see it."

I was not sure the teasing about the pigs did anything for my credibility, so I attempted to regroup. "All kidding aside, I want to welcome you to Huron Valley Men's Prison. As you have heard many times during your classes, the Michigan Department of Corrections is in dire need of good officers. I emphasize good, because we don't need officers who are just warm bodies, here to pick up their pay checks. We need officers who want to make corrections their career. Corrections is considered among the top ten fastest growing businesses in the United States. In fact, a recent *Ann Arbor News* editorial cartoon pictured the golden arches like McDonald's with a caption reading, 'McPrisons— millions served'; to the right of the arches, it read: 'The Fastest Growing Chain in Michigan.' The good news is, you have jobs. The bad news is, the United States incarcerates more people than any other country in the world. When I became warden five years ago, there were thirteen prisons in Michigan; now there are thirty-two with a population of over thirty-five thousand prisoners."

I looked around the room at each of the rookies. Most were paying close attention, but a few looked as though they were about to fall asleep. Typical group, I thought to myself, and went on: "Some of you will not make it. That may seem impossible right now, but it's a fact." This woke everyone up.

"We don't know which of you, but we do know it'll be about a third. Some of you will leave of your own free will; others will be fired for a variety of reasons, from abuse of sick leave and substance abuse to improper relationships with a prisoner."

Most of the officers shook their heads in apparent disbelief.

"While you are here, you'll be working with the most difficult prisoners in this state. You will be called every name in the book—whore, mother fucker, bitch, honky, nigger. You will be spit on, and you may even be physically assaulted. But you cannot take out your anger or your frustration on the prisoners, especially those who are mentally ill. You are supposed to be above that."

The room was silent and all eyes were now focused on me as I continued. "You will be 'grieved' and sued for the most frivolous reasons and for unprofessionalism or abuse. All of us are. Your best defense is to follow correctional policies and procedures. If you do that to the best of your ability, the prisoner won't have a case. You will, as we all do, get sick of always having to defend yourself to an attorney during an investigation. Unless you are guilty, the best way to handle this, as difficult as it gets, is not to take these accusations personally. If you're feeling frustrated and angry, talk it out with your supervisor. There's no reason for you to harbor bad feelings or to leave questions unanswered, because there are numerous employees to assist you—from your senior officer and your union representatives to me.

The officers began to fidget from either boredom or anxiety. "I said some tough things to you this morning, because I don't want you to think this job is easy. It's not. It can, however, be rewarding when a prisoner makes it. Most prisoners who have successfully completed parole have reported that the one person who made a positive difference in their lives was an officer. You must deal with prisoners at least eight hours a day. No one else is faced with that awesome task. No one else has the ability to make a difference in a prisoner's life as you do. So the best advice I can give you is to be fair, consistent, firm and know policy and procedure."

I surveyed the room. All the officers were looking at me, except one. He was looking at his watch. I hoped they had heard some of what I said. "And finally, you cannot be a prisoner's friend. That's not your role. The prisoner knows and expects that. If the prisoner thinks you're willing to be his friend, he'll lose respect for you and use you. The prisoner wants you here to ensure his security and protect him from those who don't follow the rules. If you're not doing your job, the prisoner doesn't feel safe. You'll be tested for several weeks until your credibility is established. That's true for all of us when we are hired and each time we are promoted and each time we change prisons."

I paused for a moment before I finished my lecture. "In closing, I would like to paraphrase from the officers' union's public relations tape, 'We do this job so the public doesn't have to.' Good luck!"

"Thank you, Warden Miller." Lieutenant Hughes looked at the officers and asked, "Do you have any questions?"

They all shook their heads. Few ever had questions; either they were afraid to ask or they just wanted to get out of there and on with their jobs.

I wondered if these "fish" officers were ready for prisoners like murderer Richard Goodard and rapist Paul Larner, men who have little chance of leaving prison, and therefore nothing to lose.

VII

For most people, fear in a prison setting is associated with prisoners, but few prison employees will admit it because they don't want to appear weak to their peers and supervisors, or to prisoners. Candid employees admit they fear certain prisoners.

Gene Mallin was one who inspired fear. He made weapons from anything he could extricate from his cell, and then hid the weapon in his anus or in the casts he wore because of his self mutilation. Without an x-ray, the weapon would not be discovered until it was lodged in his victim's chest, back or limb. Whenever custody personnel suspected Mallin had made a weapon and hid it on himself, an x-ray was ordered. That meant suiting up the Emergency Contact Team to force him out of his cell and to the clinic. It was a game Mallin enjoyed. How else would he get so much attention?

Everyone feared Paul Larner, the hostage taker and rapist. Prisoner Larner had been transferred to Huron Valley Men's Prison as an out-patient mental health segregation prisoner, and was serving his sixth prison term when he took Officer Lisa Reynolds hostage and raped her in May, 1990. His other convictions included two assaults on employees, assault less than murder, kidnapping and extortion. There was also a felony case pending against him for taking another female officer hostage in January, 1990, as well as numerous misconduct tickets listed in his file for assaultive behavior while incarcerated.

I was especially troubled by the ease with which Larner had been able to manipulate three separate cell door locks in the most secure unit at Huron Valley Men's Prison, giving him the ability to leave his cell and take hostages twice in less than five months. Even more incredible was the fact that he could do this when his cell door had been fitted with a dead bolt at the bottom, which was supposed to keep him from tampering with it. But we were caught off guard by Larner's awesome control over others and his skill in persuading someone, we assumed a prisoner porter, to slide open the dead bolt on the bottom of his cell door. None of that, of course, excused negligent unit officers who failed to examine Larner's cell door lock when they made their thirty minute rounds. If nothing else, fear of Larner should have made the unit officers perform that simple routine.

Ever since Officer Reynold's rape, I have gone over, obsessively, the reasons for such laxity on the part of employees who were fully aware of Larner's record. There are, I believe, several explanations for their behavior. For one thing, officers become inured to the violence; its daily occurrence at Huron Valley Men's makes it commonplace. Perpetrators of violence, like Larner, become just another prisoner, one among numerous subjects in daily critical incident reports. Weary from the daily battles, officers may perform the minimum duties expected of them, never realizing they are perpetuating a dangerous environment.

I also feel that employee fear of Larner unconsciously lessened because, after the first hostage taking, the deputy director ordered Larner to remain at Huron Valley Men's to accommodate his trial. Other hostage takers before him had always been transferred. Somehow that action trivialized Larner's dangerous image.

We were all afraid of Richard Goodard, the prisoner considered the most dangerous in the Michigan system. As I mentioned, Goodard had stabbed and killed an officer with a home made weapon (shank) in 1974. Earl DeMarse was the first correctional officer in Michigan to die in the line of duty.

157

Goodard's original prison sentence in July, 1967, for breaking and entering and car theft, was not much of an indication of his violent, psychopathic nature, which was nurtured and honed during his incarceration. Two subsequent sentences were for arson and felonious assault. He murdered DeMarse while serving his third sentence.

Goodard was sent to Marion Federal Prison in Illinois after he murdered DeMarse. Shortly after his arrival at that prison, he attempted to murder the associate warden. Goodard was immediately returned to Michigan and placed in a special cell in Unit One at Huron Valley Men's Prison, where he underwent psychiatric evaluation and was placed on psychotropic drugs. Unit One was the same unit in which Larner was housed when he raped Officer Reynolds.

We watched Goodard perform his body building exercises for hours in his cell each day, developing his body into one that could rival Arnold Schwarznegger's. He, like Larner, was allowed out of his cell for a maximum of one hour a day, mostly to shower, in full body restraints: leg irons, belly chain and black box. The only visitor he received was a minister.

Goodard, like all prisoners on segregation status, ate all his meals on trays served through a slot in the door. This was unlocked only when meals were served, medication was distributed, or to place him in arm restraints before removing him from his cell. (Goodard's cell was also fitted with a second slot near the floor through which leg irons could be put on him.) When opening the door slot, officers ordered him to the opposite side of his cell from the door, where he remained in full view. If that procedure was not followed, Goodard or any other segregated prisoner could, and often did, assault the officer when the slot was open.

When Goodard returned from the federal prison system, rumors spread that he was being given extra portions of food in an attempt to change his lean, muscular body into fat. This point became moot, as religious zeal began to replace exercise, and Goodard turned his attention to reading the Bible for hours as he paced his cell. When I made rounds in Unit One, I watched him pace back and forth in his cell, Bible in hand, mumbling. The voices he heard from the Bible were the ones that had previously told him to murder. Goodard never spoke to me, and never acknowledged my presence at his window.

Goodard's body softened over the years, but he never became less dangerous. If he took his medication, he was manageable. When he refused to take his medication, he wrote strange and threatening letters to me, the only form of communication between us. That regression signaled danger and officers were placed on alert. Goodard's long periods of silence, like Larner's, often lulled officers into complacency and a false sense of security, causing officers to be less careful, something Goodard planned on. Like most prisoners with nothing to lose, he was an opportunist, and struck when we were most vulnerable—when we were comfortable.

Goodard's letters were macabre delineations of schemes to rid the prison of "weak officers", in which he offered his help to train them "in the name of Jesus Christ." He defined training by "walking softly and carrying a big stick."

There were women prisoners considered almost as frightening. Wendy Wilder was one. Like Larner and Goodard, she was a permanent resident of the segregation unit because of her volatile behavior. On one occasion, Wilder attacked the prison doctor with a fire extinguisher, and on another she assaulted a hearings officer with his portable typewriter, splitting his head open. It later became procedure to keep all segregation-status prisoners handcuffed during misconduct and security classification hearings and when seeing the doctor, unless it hindered medical treatment. When I left the women's prison, Wilder had been confined to segregation for over two years.

Fear of hepatitis, AIDs and tuberculosis also haunted us. Even instituting universal precautions did not allay those fears. Universal precautions consisted of handling all prisoners as though they had a contagious disease, especially when they were bleeding or when staff administered CPR. Officers carried pouches strapped to their belts containing disposable rubber gloves and mouth pieces for resuscitation. All areas of the prison considered contaminated were cleaned with bleach.

Officers felt especially vulnerable when faced with prisoners like Mary, a prostitute, who displayed with pride the medical papers she received from Detroit General Hospital declaring her to be HIV positive. Her attitude protected her from other prisoners, too. No one came near her.

Prisoners are also feared because they have time to watch every move the employees make. They know employees' habits, strengths and weakness and are adept at using that knowledge against them.

The fear prisoners can inspire in other prisoners, however, is stronger than the fear they engender in prison employees. Prisoners are controlled by prisoner organizations or gangs, some using the disguise of a religious sect. Powerful prisoners and gangs control through intimidation and physical harm. Prisoners know they can die at the hands of another prisoner for refusing to help bring drugs into the prison, for not paying debts, snitching, refusing to be a lover, or not being subservient.

It took Michigan Department of Corrections a long time to acknowledge that there were gangs in prisons, because gangs were not recognized by politicians and law enforcement officials in Detroit. Granted, Michigan does not have the problems that Illinois and California have, but gangs do exist. Gangs existed when I worked at North East Corrections Center and were on the rise.

When the department recognized the existence of gangs in prisons in the late 1980's, training was provided to wardens at a quarterly meeting. The entire session was fascinating, but one speaker stands out in my memory.

Dr. Carl Taylor, Professor at the School of Criminal Justice at Grand Valley State University, studied gang activity in Detroit. In the process, he attempted to change the thinking of young male gang members. Dr. Taylor told the wardens that he took two young boys to the elaborate funeral of a prominent Detroit gang leader. He pointed out to the boys, "Look how young that man is. He's only twenty-one years old. He hardly had a life."

One boy answered, "Yeah, but look at all he had while he was alive."

I asked myself, how do we combat that rationale? Tell the boy to get a job at minimum wage?

Dr. Taylor told us that drug gangs are so sophisticated that they are managed like a large conservative business. The leaders do not draw attention to themselves. It's the street punks used by the gang

160

leaders who are flashy. That makes the real leaders harder to identify; in fact, they could be your neighbors.

More frightening to me were the terrorist gangs that were on the rise and had already become a problem in Illinois prisons. After Dr. Taylor's presentation, we added terrorist attacks on prisons as one of the scenarios for our monthly drills.

VIII

Wardens are fond of saying, "Our jobs wouldn't be so tough if it weren't for the employees." Employees were also capable of inspiring fear, and Anita Brown was an example.

Brown assaulted a prisoner who had refused to continue being her drug mule and dealer inside the prison. Other officers confessed in private that they knew of both the drug trafficking and the assault, and that Brown was harboring a prison escapee who was a known drug trafficker. But when they were asked to put this information into writing and to testify in court, they refused. One stated, "I'm being followed and this same guy watches my house. I know he's one of Brown's civilian friends cause I've seen her with him."

Another officer reported receiving threatening calls, but from a man, not from Brown. The threats were related to the assault, and convinced the officer that Brown was behind them.

The parents of the escapee alleged to be living with Brown had reported both Brown and the escapee to authorities. When asked later to write statements, the parents denied knowing the couple's whereabouts, and confessed to a parole agent they were receiving threats on their lives.

Brown has never been convicted and is still a corrections officer in a men's prison. Her manipulation of others through fear has insured her freedom.

Brown frightened many, but she is not the employee who taught me real terror. The day I learned this, my secretary had buzzed me on the telephone and said, "There's a psychiatrist on the line who wants to talk to you about some officer."

I thought it was about an officer who had been beaten by a

prisoner and was having difficulty returning to work. I was working with the psychiatrist to reintegrate the officer, placing her first in positions with no prisoner interaction and gradually adding more and more contact.

The male voice on the telephone identified himself. "I am Dr. Blake, Penny Hunt's psychiatrist."

I knew at once I would not like this conversation. Hunt was an officer who had been fired because of her outlandish behavior while on the midnight shift. She would wear street clothes under her uniform and remove the uniform on her post. She was also charged with insubordination several times. The last episode ended in an altercation in which she assaulted her male shift commander and knocked him to the ground, inciting several prisoners to join in the fun.

"Dr. Blake, you know she's no longer employed with the department, don't you? I'm not sure how I can help you."

"Actually, it's how I can help you."

"What do you mean?" I asked, not sure I wanted to know the answer.

"Well, I've been Ms. Hunt's psychiatrist for about a year. What I'm about to tell you I strongly believe, and I have cleared the release of this information through our attorney."

I started to feel a prickly sensation across my scalp, and I leaned back in my chair, giving Dr. Blake my full attention.

"Ms. Hunt has threatened to kill you and the midnight shift commander. I have every reason to believe she will carry out the threat. I urge you to take every precaution you can. I have an appointment with her today and will tell her about this conversation. I know this is difficult and I wish you luck. If I can be of further help, please let me know."

"Thank you, Dr. Blake." I knew my voice was barely audible as I hung up the phone.

Supporting my head in my right hand, I rubbed my forehead. Finally I picked up the telephone and called my boss in central office to report the call from Dr. Blake. He authorized a "front gun", an armed officer in the lobby for all three shifts, and permission for the shift commander and me to be armed with handguns while traveling to and from the prison. The shift commander took advantage of this and carried a hand gun; I did not because I did not know how to use one.

Officers in the gun towers and in the perimeter vehicles were ordered to be even more alert to unusual traffic or people in the vicinity of the prison.

I telephoned Sergeant Norman, the state police detective assigned as the liaison to the prison. He informed me that they already had Hunt under surveillance because they suspected she was a drug trafficker. "In fact," the detective reported, "we were about to caution you about her trafficking in the prison when she was fired. We'll let you know if anything changes. We'll try to keep a car in the vicinity of the prison, too."

I sat at my desk for a few moments, not sure what to do next. My training was in prison riots, hostage situations, hunger strikes, and the like. How was I going to combat an intangible threat from an ex-employee who was stalking me?

Armed officers guarded the front lobby and escorted me to and from my car for thirty days. I watched every car that followed me, sometimes changing my route to see if the car behind me would do the same. And I constantly looked over my shoulder. My heart skipped a beat each time I saw a woman that looked like Hunt.

The midnight shift commander was run off the road on his way home, but could not identify the car, and it was never determined if that incident was related to Hunt's threat.

Within a week after Dr. Blake's call, a man came into my secretary's office and demanded a job. She sent him to personnel. Two days later he came back and was more threatening toward my secretary. "I want a job. You promised me a job and don't send me down the hall to personnel. They said they had no jobs. If you don't get me a job now, I'll shoot you. I've got a gun."

I could only see part of the man's left side from where I sat in my office, but I saw something in his left hand that I couldn't identify. I stood up and walked into the conference room through the door behind my desk. I wanted to call the control center for help without the man hearing me, for fear he would start shooting. I knew everyone's anxiety level was high because of Hunt, and we were overreacting to any perceived threat. I also knew innocent people had been shot for less, and I was not going to take any chances.

I made it to the telephone and called control center, explaining to the shift commander what was going on. I told him to call the state police for assistance and to send someone to my office to subdue the man.

Two officers were at my secretary's door within minutes. Their surprise appearance caught the man off guard, and they were able to subdue him. The state police arrived within fifteen minutes and arrested him. The police found a loaded shot gun in the truck the man had driven to the prison. We were later told that he had no connection to Hunt.

About a week after that, I received a surprising telephone call from Hunt herself, claiming, "I know what my psychiatrist said, but I will not hurt anyone."

"I appreciate your call, Ms. Hunt, but we will continue our protection." The call frightened me even more. I felt as though she were watching me. I started keeping the blinds closed in my office.

The front gun was removed after thirty days when the state police detective felt Hunt was no longer a threat, but I was relieved that they were continuing the drug related surveillance of her. We were lucky that time, and we never heard from Hunt again.

Prisoners feared staff and with good cause, albeit only a few deserved that "respect". In one incident, a difficult male prisoner, Redman, was on water restriction, meaning that his water supply was turned off because he kept flooding his cell. Officers on duty had to offer him drinking water whenever they made their thirty minute rounds.

During one of the rounds, an officer who was delivering water to Redman opened the food slot in the door and told Redman to come to the door to get his water. When Redman did, the water was tossed on him. The officer claimed he hit the cup accidently on the door slot, causing the water to splash on Redman. When asked why the water was scalding hot and burned the prisoner, the officer responded, "Redman wanted to make coffee, so I got him hot water."

Redman's room was searched, but there was no coffee found; (prisoners can purchase coffee through the prisoner store). He also denied making the request for hot water, but claimed he requested medical treatment for the burn caused by the scalding water. The unit log showed there was no treatment until the next shift. The offending officer stated, "I forgot to call the infirmary."

Redman asked to be transferred to another prison after reporting he had been threatened by several officers. "They said if I snitch any more on them, it won't be minor scalding next time."

Because there was no other prison to which he could be transferred, supervisors were alerted to possible retaliation. Redman never reported any more attempts, but medical records showed that he had several unusual injuries, like bleeding from his right ear, bruises on his face, and nose bleeds. We could not prove wrong doing by any officer, because Redman was also a self mutilator, and he would no longer snitch.

Physical threats were not the only reason prisoners feared officers. Emotional abuse, too, caused prisoner anxiety. The case of prisoner Renata Anderson is an example.

Officer Robinson was one of two officers who escorted Prisoner Anderson to her mother's funeral in Detroit. It was a short trip that appeared to be uneventful.

About a month after the funeral, the deputy warden came to my office with some paper work from the trip. "Warden, I think we have a problem. Remember Anderson's funeral trip last month?"

"Yes. What's wrong? Her mother didn't really die, and someone screwed up the investigation for the trip's approval?"

"I wish it was that simple. Anderson kited me the other day, saying she needed to see me soon because of a crooked officer; she said she had important information for me."

"And?"

"It seems that while she was on the funeral trip, Anderson made a deal with Officer Robinson. Anderson was going to get some gold jewelry from her family. She knew the rules about no jewelry in prison, so Anderson made a deal where Officer Robinson would get the jewelry from her family, carry it back to the prison and give it to her. In return, she'd give Robinson a gold necklace she claims is worth a couple hundred dollars."

"How much jewelry are we talking about?"

"Since we have no jewelry, it's based on her story only. She claims there's a couple of gold necklaces, a pair of diamond earrings, a pair of gold hoop earrings and a diamond ring."

"If we don't have the jewelry, why are we having this conversation?"

"According to Anderson, Officer Robinson agreed to do as she asked. He picked up the jewelry from Anderson's sister at the funeral, but he never gave Anderson her share. She claims that when she questioned him about the jewelry, he denied having it. She checked with her sister who said she gave it to the officer. Jackson sat on the problem for a while, fearing retaliation if she told on Robinson, like he might set her up for a misconduct, which would put her in segregation. Finally, Anderson decided that she'd lose nothing by telling the story."

"Have you talked to the officer?"

"Yeah, and at first he denied it. Then, he said he did it, but felt guilty so he threw the jewelry away. Jackson's sister called the police about the missing jewelry. After they contacted me, I told Robinson he'd better turn himself in to the police. I think he's on his way there now."

"I want him suspended pending investigation. There's no telling what else he's done if he stooped to that."

Officer Robinson pled guilty to the theft and to fencing the jewelry, not throwing it away. He was fired, but attempted to negotiate a suspension and a transfer to a men's prison. I denied his request because his offense was not gender related—he would be a weak link in prison security if prisoners could use him. He was not rehired.

IX

There are numerous occasions for fear inherent in the supervision of a maximum security prison. One anxiety producing situation I could never have predicted involved a new officer named Ralph.

After the new officers' orientation, he made an appointment to see me before reporting to second shift. I didn't know, when the appointment was made, that it would become a daily routine.

Ralph appeared at my office at 1:30. He paused for a few mo-

166

ments and took a deep breath before closing the office door, and then walked toward my desk. "I hope you don't mind that I closed the door, but what I'm going to tell you is highly confidential. Only you will know."

I felt uneasy, but I was not sure it was because of what he said or how he looked. His immaculate uniform contrasted with his hair and beard, which he wore long. In fact, his appearance bothered me. New male corrections officers were usually clean shaven with closely cropped hair.

"What's troubling you?"

"May I sit down?"

"Of course, sorry."

He sat down in the chair across from me, but did not take off his green outer jacket. He had a large manila envelope in his right hand, which he placed on my desk. Ralph pointed to the envelope as he explained in a soft voice, "In this envelope, I have information for you that'll confirm what I'm about to tell you, as well as the contact person through whom I work and your contact when necessary."

He handed me the envelope and continued. "You can go through the materials at your leisure. I'll give you a brief account of what the material in the envelope says.

"I'm a retired Drug Enforcement Agent in a witness protection program. While I'm assigned here, I'll have to go to court in Miami several times. A women sergeant by the name of Reinart, from intelligence, will contact you when these appearances are necessary. No one can know about this, no one. I'm the only remaining witness in this case. There were five of us. The others have been murdered. I don't want to end up like them."

"Why were you placed in a prison? Isn't that taking a chance someone might know you. Someone who was into drugs?"

"Most of my time was spent in Colombia, five years to be exact. I lived with the Medellin and know everyone there and all their jungle camps. I'm the only one right now who knows this. The people we're prosecuting are from Columbia or are government officials from several Central and South American countries. I don't think anyone would know me here."

"I'm assuming that each time you are needed to testify, I'll be contacted by this Sergeant Reinart?"

"Yes, and you'll have to sign the leave slips so the shift commander won't know."

"I'll have to let them know something. Otherwise it'll appear you're getting preferential treatment. I'll let them know that you were involved in some federal case and the prosecutor contacts me to set up leave, okay?"

"Yeah. I got to go to roll call. I'll stop by tomorrow."

For the next several months, unless he was in court in Miami, Ralph came by each day to share what was happening on the case. It didn't take me long to realize that I was his therapist. He needed someone to talk to about his fears.

"You know, Warden Miller, I think I'm being followed. I see the same black Corvette tailing me and have seen it outside my house."

"Have you reported this to the DEA and prosecutor?"

"Yeah. But there's little they can do without blowing my cover. I've sent my wife and kids away for a while. It's something I was determined I wouldn't do—separate us—and here we are."

"You look like you've lost weight and that you're not getting much sleep."

"I'm okay. Just a little uneasy. I've been getting a few odd telephone calls. Don't know if they're related. But I only have a few more court appearances. If this judge hasn't been threatened or paid off like the others, we should have us a big conviction, and I can get on to a life."

He started to leave my office, but turned toward me. "You know, Warden Miller, I keep having nightmares. Mostly about the assassinations I had to take part in when I was undercover. A lot of people were murdered, some innocent, some my friends."

Tears formed in his eyes and began to slide down his cheeks. He lifted his hand, wiped them away and walked out the door. I wondered how he could be sure that no one would retaliate after the trial. What life could he possibly "get on to" as he wished?

Two days later, about six months into his employment, Ralph rushed into my office and slammed the door shut. He looked scared. "I know I'm being followed now. That Corvette I told you about is just down the street from the prison. Also, last night I worked in Unit

Eight."

"Wait a minute," I interrupted. "I gave strict instructions that you were to work the yard or some other post where you would have little direct prisoner contact."

"I have been, but shift command was in a bind last night, and at the last minute needed an officer in close custody. I didn't think it would hurt, but I'm not so sure now."

"What do you mean?"

"Well, while I was in that unit a woman prisoner approached me and asked, 'Do they know who you are?' I asked her, 'What do you mean?' She repeated, 'Does the administration know who you are?'"

"What did you do?"

"I just looked at her, shook my head, and told her I didn't know what she was talking about."

"Do you know her?"

"Not from the streets, and last night was the first time I've seen her here."

"What's her name?"

"I know her last name is Colby."

My heart began to race, partly for him, but also because I was afraid of becoming an innocent victim, or that someone else in the prison would. "Sit down. The woman you spoke with last night is named Irene Colby. She's the first woman in Michigan to be sentenced to life in prison for drug trafficking. There's no doubt she knows who you are. We've got to get you out of here. I'm calling Sergeant Reinart. You're not going on duty."

Ralph never returned to Huron Valley Women's.

My secretary asked, "Whatever happened to that officer, Ralph, who came here every day? He sure was a pain. Had to see you every day. How did you get rid of him?"

"I had him transferred."

Although I don't know where Ralph is, I still think about him and wonder if he's okay. The most I can hope for is that he has assumed another identity and escaped with his family into another witness protection program.

X

Corrections people are no different from anyone when it comes to love affairs on the job. However, affairs in corrections are too often between employee and prisoner. One affair that took me completely by surprise was that of Jeanie, my secretary when I was deputy warden.

Married with two children, Jeanie often spoke with pride about her family. Before she became my full time secretary, Jeanie had worked part time as a secretary in Unit Three, where mentally ill women prisoners were housed. Her supervisors praised her work with these tough prisoners, especially her ability to listen to them. Of course, what was more important for my needs was having someone who could type, file and take accurate messages. Jeanie filled all those requirements.

One day Jeanie's husband telephoned me sounding distraught. He said, "Jeanie has left me and the kids for a prisoner. She left last week, and I can't talk any sense into her."

"What? Are you sure? Are you sure it's a prisoner?"

"Yeah. Just ask her."

I did not have to ask her because a few minutes after the call, the shift commander came to my office carrying a pair of earrings. He placed the earrings in front of me on my desk. "We just caught your secretary, Jeanie, passing these to prisoner Pam O'Connell in the segregation unit."

"Captain, it's bad enough Jeanie's in trouble, but what's wrong with the officers in segregation? Why are they letting Jeanie in to that unit? She has no authorization to be there." I felt both betrayed by Jeanie and angry at the officers.

"Apparently, she used to go into that unit to visit the mentally ill prisoners from Unit Three. O'Connell's from Unit Three."

"Jeanie was just a part time secretary, for chrissakes. Who gave her permission to go into our most secure unit, or what I thought was our most secure unit?"

"Don't know, but we'll find out."

"Isn't O'Connell the one with all those tattoos of dragons on her arms and chest who gets mail on witchcraft and the occult?"

"Yeah. Must of worked on Jeanie, if yah know what I mean."

"I want a list made of all personnel, shift commanders and up, that are allowed in that unit without prior clearance. All others will have to have permission from the shift commander. Circulate that in a memo with my signature pronto. Meanwhile, where's Jeanie?"

"Sitting on the bench outside of control center where the prisoners usually sit when they are waiting to see the hearings officer. I thought it seemed appropriate."

"Send her here."

Jeanie confessed to the charge shortly after she came to my office. She cried, but did not apologize, and explained, "This is the first time I ever felt really needed and loved for who I am. My husband is always finding something wrong with me. To Pam, I'm beautiful, intelligent, and capable. I've never heard that before. And when she gets out, we want to be together. I didn't mean to hurt you because I care a lot about you and what you did for me, but I need something that's forever. I hope you understand."

"I understand your needs, but I'm not sure I can understand the way in which you are fulfilling them. Perhaps you should see a therapist."

"I know what I'm doing."

"You know you can't work here any more and will more than likely be fired, don't you?"

"Yeah, and I have no one to blame but myself. In the long run, though, it's worth it."

Jeanie was fired, but continued to visit O'Connell every day at the prison. She divorced her husband and lost custody of her children—a high price to pay, I thought. O'Connell was paroled and moved in with Jeanie who claimed she had never been as happy in her life. Jeanie found full time employment and, as far as I know, O'Connell never returned to prison.

I thought I had heard everything once I'd heard Jeanie's story, until the day a man forced his way past my secretary and burst into my office waving several pieces of paper, shouting, "What's the meaning of this? What kind of prison do you run here, lady?"

I stood up and raised my hands, not knowing what else to do. I had no idea what he was talking about or if he had a gun. I only knew that he was angry. "Please, calm down. I can't understand the problem if you're shouting. Besides, I need more information. Sit down so we can talk."

The man sat on the small couch next to my desk. "These are telephone bills totalling over three hundred dollars. These prisoners shouldn't be allowed to make phone calls."

"May I ask who you are?"

"I'm Joe Southerland. My wife, Connie, is an officer here at Men's. This here prisoner, Michels, has been makin' phone calls to our house."

"Mr. Southerland, you do know that prisoners can only make collect calls, don't you?. Someone in your home has to be accepting these."

"Yeah, I know all that. My wife accepts them cause she feels guilty and afraid if she don't accept them, she'll get hurt here at the prison. I told her right from the beginning not to work here. Anyway, I want you to stop him."

"I'm afraid we can't stop the prisoner from placing collect calls, but you do have control over the situation by refusing the calls. I'm sorry we can't do more for you. Perhaps you should discuss this with your wife."

Mr. Southerland left my office, grumbling, "Yeah, yeah. I didn't think you'd help."

I felt there was more to his concerns than the telephone bill, so I explained what happened to Carol, my administrative assistant, and asked her to interview Officer Southerland to find out what was going on between her and prisoner Michels.

Officer Southerland did not admit to Carol that there was any relationship with the prisoner, but instead went on stress leave. Prisoner Michels's cell, including his mail, was searched, and officers found pictures of Officer Southerland in glamorous poses, wearing lingerie. More surprising, however, were the pictures found of another woman officer, Colleen Trombley, in similar attire. Trombley was assigned to the kitchen where prisoner Michels worked. When she was confronted about the pictures, she not only confessed immediately to having an affair with Michels, but admitted being pregnant by him.

Prisoner Michels was transferred to another prison, and Trombley quit her job before disciplinary proceedings could begin, but she continued her relationship with Michels.

Officer Southerland, who appeared to be on the short end of the menage a trois, went into therapy. She ended her involvement with Michels, remained in her marriage, and eventually returned to work. She never did admit to the relationship and claimed her mother, who lived with her, had accepted the calls from Michels. Since her mother backed Southerland's story, it meant that there was not enough evidence to pursue disciplinary charges against her.

Affairs in the department were not confined to officers and prisoners. One warm spring day, a State Police Trooper, on a routine patrol, stopped at the rest area on I 94 near Jackson. Reports of homosexual activities taking place in men's bathrooms at rest stops had added the duty of checking all the rest stops on his route.

The trooper made the required rounds of the bathrooms, but found nothing unusual, so he started to leave. As he walked toward his car, he noticed a state licensed Chrysler station wagon at the rear of the building. It had been parked there when he arrived, but there were no people around. The insignia on the door identified it as a Michigan Department of Corrections vehicle and, from where the Trooper stood, it appeared abandoned. He decided to check the car out, thinking it might have been stolen and left in the parking lot.

The Trooper approached the car with some caution when he noticed it swaying. As he peered into the windows, he saw a man and a woman in the middle of vigorous sexual activity. His mouth dropped opened and he shook his head. The lovers didn't notice the Trooper until he pounded on the window with his flashlight. Once the couple realized they'd been discovered, they scrambled for their clothes and dressed.

That should have been the end of the story, except that the station wagon, generally used to transport prisoners, was locked. Because the rear area where the couple were carrying on was screened off from the driver's area, none of the doors or windows could be opened from the interior, a fact they had forgotten while in the throes of passion. The Trooper had to summon a locksmith. It gave new meaning to the once popular song, "A Prisoner of Love".

The couple suffered some humiliation when they were freed and had to identify themselves. It turned out that the man was a warden of a nearby prison and the woman was someone who worked for him. The state trooper's formal report resulted in the warden being counseled. The story was repeated and embellished, I'm sure, throughout the department for weeks.

XI

The year I became warden, Huron Valley Women's Prison employees held their first evening Christmas party off prison grounds.

"The first door prize goes to Chet Miller. Is Chet Miller here?" asked the officer who was portraying Santa.

As the employees looked from one to the other, I leaned toward my husband. "Chet, I think that's you. They think your last name is Miller."

He would be known from that point on by my colleagues as Chet Miller. In fact, it was not until my retirement party that most people discovered his real name, and then only because he printed "Chet Redford" on his name tag. During the evening, people said, "You mean to tell me that all these years when we called you saying, 'Hello, Mr. Miller, is Warden Miller there?', his name was Redford?"

"Yep."

"Didn't he mind?"

"Nope. Not as long as I kept bringing home the paycheck."

After the Christmas revelers finished their dinners, a disc jockey began the evening's entertainment. Officer Linda Jackson, a tall, willowy woman, wore a black dress trimmed in fringe that covered very little of her body. She was almost unrecognizable out of her uniform. She slinked up to the disc jockey and asked him to play a special tune. She told him that she and five others would be singing, "so give me the mike."

The disc jockey shook his head and rolled his eyes, but handed her the microphone. He put on their request and the women officers began to sing. Gyrating to the music in choreographed movements, the six, all in black sequins, fringe, satin, and crepe, belted out, "We're going riding on the freeway, my love, in a pink Cadillac."

The disc jockey looked at the group in disbelief. He had to

admit they were great, and for the remainder of the evening they performed song after song. On that night, they were christened the "Pointless Sisters".

It wasn't until the following spring that the Pointless Sisters surfaced again as a singing group. Officer Jackson was a member of the committee planning Huron Valley Women's Prison's tenth anniversary celebration. She came to my office one day, plopped down in a chair facing my desk and said, "We all want the anniversary celebration to be something really special. So the Pointless Sisters thought we should have a choir sing at the luncheon ceremony. We have a lotta staff interested in singing. What do yah think?"

"I think it's a terrific idea," I answered. "But how will you be able to rehearse, and what will you sing? You know I can't give you any leave time for this."

"We'll have ta rehearse on our own time the best we can. We've picked out several songs and want you to hear them once we have them worked out. You can help us pick the ones you like the best."

"When do you think you'll be ready for your first audition?"

"Are you free now?" Jackson asked, with a smile. She knew I'd say yes to the idea and had come prepared.

The choir, assembled in the prison employee lunchroom, had grown in number from the original six women officers that sang at the Christmas party to twelve men and women. It was a mix of employees, including a female captain, unit managers (counselors), and officers, and was directed by a male counselor.

After I had listened to several songs, two were selected for the choir to sing accappella at the anniversary ceremony, "The Battle Hymn of the Republic" and "Michigan, My Michigan", a particularly difficult piece. Though their incredible performance at the anniversary luncheon sent chills up my spine and brought tears to my eyes, I had no idea that the Huron Valley Women's Choir would become renowned throughout the state and be in demand to perform at a variety of functions.

During the years that followed, they performed at department academy graduations, community college graduations, the annual day of recognition honoring law enforcement and corrections officers killed in the line of duty, and retirement parties, including mine. They added

175

many songs to their repertoire, picking selections appropriate for each occasion. After I became the warden at Huron Valley Men's and Women's Prisons, the choir grew larger and was comprised of men and women from both facilities, including psychiatrists, psychologists, unit managers and captains. They were known as the Huron Valley Choir, or as one male admirer introduced them, "Tekla Miller's Choir". But we always called the original six the "Pointless Sisters".

At Perry Johnson's (director of the Michigan Department of Corrections for twelve years) retirement party, the choir stole the show. The comical roast was interrupted by one moving moment, when Joann Green, a unit manager, sang "Nobody knows the trouble I've seen." Her vocal range was operatic. The three hundred plus people in attendance were totally silent; not even a cough could be heard, and many in the audience had tears in their eyes. I felt like a proud mother—tears, goose bumps and all. But I felt that way at all their performances, and I attended every one of them.

Many people commented to me, "We never thought of corrections employees as singers. And they are so talented. They make the department seem human."

It was not only the choir members' singing that made life in the prison business more tolerable, but their sense of humor as well. I never knew what they would say or do, especially Linda Jackson. I often think about Linda's daily recounting of weird or funny prisoner behavior. She seemed to have no inhibitions or fears, and could find humor at the most difficult moments. Although Jackson was a handful, I never thought her wit or banter disrespectful.

I found Jackson in my office after one of the annual Officers' Recognition Days, during which I had met with each shift, giving well earned praise to the officers, and serving donuts and coffee. She sat in my chair, feet propped up on the desk top, and asked, "Can we have Churches' chicken next year for Officers' Recognition Day? We're tired of donuts."

"I'll think about it. Can I have my chair?"

"Okay. But I'm taking all the leftover donuts."

She picked up the box of donuts I'd brought into my office and left. "See yah tomorrow, Warden."

On another occasion, after Jackson had become a mother for

the first time, she came to my office, unannounced as usual, and plopped down in the chair across from my desk. "You wanna kid?" she asked.

Before I could answer, she leaned toward me and continued, "Here's the deal. I'll give yah my kid and my next paycheck and I'll take B.J." (B.J. was the leader dog in the puppy training program at that time.)

"Jackson, you don't even like dogs."

"He's gotta be easier to take care of than my kid. Being a workin' mother isn't all that glamorous, and I can't count on baby sitters to work overtime when I have ta."

"Well, you're too late anyway. Dr. Tyson already offered his paycheck to me for B.J., and he earns a hell of a lot more money than you do."

"Well, Warden, you can bet this child will be my last."

"That's good, because you were not a pleasant person when you were pregnant. I'm not sure I could survive another one of your children, either."

We both laughed, and as she left, she called out as usual, "See yah tomorrow, Warden."

Shortly after that, I attended the annual American Correctional Association's Conference. That year it was held in Las Vegas, and many of my employees, including several Pointless Sisters, attended. When I got to my hotel, there was a message for me which read, "Dear Mom, we are in room 602. Call us." It was signed by Jackson.

Gladys Knight and The Pips were performing at the hotel, and I had planned to see one of their shows. On the second evening in town, I was heading across the hotel lobby to the elevators when I heard a woman yell, "Mom, Mom. Wait up!"

I turned to look and saw Jackson and several other Pointless Sisters heading toward me with two men in tow. When they reached me, Jackson motioned toward me with her right hand and said, "This is our Mom."

She looked at me and nodded toward the men, stating, "These are the Pips."

The Pips and I stared at each other for a few seconds, and then awkwardly shook hands. Jackson smiled and led the group away as she shouted, "See yah later, Mom. We'll be home early."

The next day I asked Jackson how she met the Pips. "Well," she explained, "we were leaving the hotel to check out the strip when this stretch limo pulled up, and Gladys Knight and the Pips got out. There was no one else around but the hotel doorman and the driver, so we walked up to them and introduced ourselves."

"How did you manage to meet up with the Pips yesterday?"

Jackson shrugged. "They were wandering around the hotel casino. We just stopped them and asked if they remembered us. We started talking, and then we saw you."

I laughed and asked, "How could they forget you—a group of women all dressed in yellow? You looked like a bouquet of blackeyed susans. Whatever you do, don't tell me what else you do while you're here, okay?"

I was surprised that Jackson and her cohorts didn't talk Gladys Knight into letting them perform with her group, but I'm sure they tried to persuade the Pips.

The last time the Pointless Sisters performed as a group was at my retirement party. They were the original six and all wore black again, as they had at their first performance. They didn't belt out their songs as usual, because they were crying. It was a performance I will never forget.

Shortly after I left the department, the women's prison closed and the prisoners were moved to another facility. Employees were split up and transferred to several locations, which ended the Huron Valley Choir. But recently, I was contacted by a warden who was opening a new prison. She asked if I could help her locate members of the choir so they could sing at the prison dedication. I was happy that the choir was still remembered. It proved something I'd suspected—they not only sang well, but they were the best public relations the department ever had.

XII

Becky Cudia was the only white woman in the original Pointless Sisters. Her skills and professionalism, particularly when handling prisoners, impressed her peers and subordinates as much as her singing. All the policies, procedures, disciplinary actions, and lectures could not teach the staff about proper cell extractions the way Cudia could. Her positive interactions with prisoners made it no longer uncool to talk a prisoner out of a cell. It became uncool to be the idiot who did not have that skill and ended up being assaulted. In fact, when officers were having trouble with a difficult prisoner, they asked for Cudia.

I remember one occasion when I watched Cudia at work. She convinced a prisoner to come out on his own by asking, "What do yah think it's gonna look like being dragged out of a cell by a woman?"

In an attempt to save face, the prisoner answered as he left the cell, "I didn't wanta hurt no woman."

The officers that made up the Pointless Sisters proved that some of my employees were great. There were others who went about their jobs a little more quietly, but just as impressively.

When I was warden, the employees who impressed me as being good on the job were capable of doing what was asked of them and more, while maintaining their composure under any situation and continuing to demonstrate a genuine concern for others' well being. Ron Desbrough was one of these officers.

In the second hostage taking at Huron Valley Men's, he and three other officers were held hostage in the prison kitchen. They were threatened with butcher knives and held for several hours. Fortunately, all the hostages were released unharmed. Officer Desbrough returned to work the next day and never sought any revenge. Prisoners respected, rather than feared him, which meant his and our jobs were made a lot easier. Revenge was not in Desbrough's vocabulary, and I never knew him to raise his voice, use profanity or speak negatively about the prisoners or, for that matter, other employees. We were lucky because he loved being an officer and had no intention of doing anything else. Ron Desbrough was rewarded by being chosen officer of the year at Huron Valley Men's Prison.

Ozzie Hernandez was another of my favorite employees. I first met Hernandez when he was promoted to segregation sergeant at Huron Valley Women's from a segregation officer at the Michigan Reformatory, a men's close custody prison. When he arrived, he bragged to the other custody personnel who were mostly women, "I can teach you a thing or two about running a prison."

I was a little concerned about the reasons for his promotion, because the women who had interviewed candidates for the position remarked, off the record, "Hernandez sure is good looking, and will be a nice change of pace around here. We need more men in this joint anyway, and he's got a great sense of humor, too. And, of course, we can use an Hispanic to meet affirmative action goals."

I agreed with everything they said, but hoped that the final reason he scored so high was because of his merit and positive references from his supervisors, not his handsome face.

Hernandez's startling introduction to working with women prisoners happened his first day on the job in the segregation unit. The unit manager was introducing Hernandez to the other segregation officers when Officer Jackson interrupted them to report, "Coleman won't come out of the shower. She's screwing up the schedule. If we don't get her out, the afternoon shift will hafta finish the showering. Yah know how they hate that."

"Let me talk to her. I've handled tougher than this." Hernandez walked into the bathroom toward the shower stall, arms held out away from his sides, hands twitching. He looked like he was preparing for a gun fight. His walk was deliberate and slow, and he never took his eyes off Coleman.

"Who's this jerk?" Cookie Coleman yelled. She was standing naked in the shower stall. The water was no longer running because it had been turned off by an officer who hoped that would get Coleman out of the stall.

"I'm Sergeant Hernandez. You don't want to get me mad my first day on the job, do yah?"

"Why would I care? I ain't goin' nowhere for a while 'n this stall's better than that yellow peeling paint in my stinkin' cell."

"If I come get you out, you may regret it. I don't like to force nobody, especially a woman. But I will if I hafta. You're makin' alotta other prisoners unhappy, takin' up their shower time."

"Some sweet talker you are. What makes you think I give a fuck about them other bitches. They never do nothin' for me. You'll hafta come in here 'n get me, big boy. Let's see your stuff."

"Okay. Officer Jackson, get the video camera. I'm goin' in after Coleman."

Coleman was about three inches taller than Hernandez and as tough as they come. She'd been confined in segregation for the past six months, but had lost none of the strength she'd demonstrated during the July Fourth incident.

Jackson returned with the camera, after notifying the shift commander what was going down in the segregation unit. Jackson knew this would be a forced move and, by policy, would have to be taped for possible litigation.

Hernandez unlocked the door to the shower stall, and when he started to pull the door open, Coleman pushed it and tackled Hernandez, who tumbled to the floor. The force of the fall knocked the keys from Hernandez's hand. Coleman grabbed the keys, leaving Hernandez on the floor, and ran from the bathroom, naked, toward prisoner Kane's cell door, the first to the right of the bathroom. Officer Jackson, who was filming the whole event to oblige policy, yelled, "Coleman's got the cell door keys from the sergeant. Kane's out. We need help."

The other twelve women locked on that corridor started banging on their cell doors and yelling, "Let me outta here."

"Get that Mexican chile bean."

"Who do he think he is. Show 'em who gots balls."

The unit manager had contacted the captain, and I met her as I entered the segregation unit. She and I got there just in time to watch Hernandez running from the bathroom toward a naked and laughing Coleman, who was cornered at the end of the corridor. The only exit for her was into the yard, which was impossible since the officers controlled that door electronically from their station beyond the security gate.

The look on Hernandez's face as he ran from the bathroom indicated his determination to beat the shit out of Coleman. With eyes ablaze, face reddening and lips tightened, he ran toward his victim. Officer Jackson yelled out, "Careful, this is on tape and the warden's here."

Hernandez did not slow his pace and reached for Coleman with both his hands. "You'll pay for this."

He did not seem to notice that Kane had come out of her cell, and that Coleman had given her keys to her. Kane was about to unlock other cell doors, but stopped when Coleman let out a horrifying screech and ran at Hernandez. This time he was prepared and blocked her. The impact of their bodies forced them both to the ground. In the middle of the tiled floor of the segregation unit, Hernandez and Coleman rolled, punched, pulled and scratched at each other until Kane raced over and sat on them both.

It was quite a picture: Coleman, on the bottom, naked, with her back against the floor; Hernandez lying on top of her, shirt ripped away from his body exposing his bared chest; and Kane, all three hundred pounds of her, sitting on Hernandez's back. It looked like some kinky scene from an X-rated movie.

It took six employees to separate the pile and rescue Hernandez. Once Kane was dragged off his back, she gave up the keys and returned to her cell. Four officers were needed to subdue Coleman—each restraining a limb—as they carried her to her cell and locked her in.

Officer Jackson continued filming until the prisoners were secured. As she turned off the camera, she said, "I guess this means afternoon shift does the showers."

Hernandez walked toward me with head lowered; if he'd had a tail, it would have been between his legs. When he got to me, he confessed, "This sure changes my mind about women prisoners."

"Just think, this is only training." I slapped him on the back and smiled.

Assistant Deputy Rider had also been summoned to the unit, and he later took it upon himself to inform Hernandez's former colleagues at the Michigan Reformatory about his heroic beginnings. Rider told Hernandez, "It's the least I can do to welcome you."

Prisoner Kane had bathed as little as possible before this incident. After it, she demanded showers, did her hair, which had not been out of the matted corn rolls since her arrival in segregation three months earlier, and begged for perfume. She even began wearing her uniform rather than her unusual attire, an unwashed state-issued nightgown, which she refused to send to the laundry. She sent Hernandez love letters, asked him to marry her, and said she would name all of her children after him. Kane changed her name to Elsie Kane Hernandez, although unofficially, and signed all her correspondence that way. She also sent Hernandez anniversary cards each year on the date she chose for their wedding.

We started to notice a change in most of the women prisoners in segregation once Hernandez was assigned. They vied for his attention the best they could with the resources available, including propositioning him with naked bodies, some masturbating as he made rounds. Hernandez can also boast of being the first male at Women's to be sexually assaulted. Kane grabbed his genitals one day when he was escorting her to the yard. She was charged with sexual misconduct.

Although Hernandez took it all in stride, I had to admit that men could be victims of sexual harassment too, and that it was not less offensive if the victim was a man. I realized we could not laugh off Hernandez's encounters any more than we could laugh off harassment involving women victims. In spite of the unwelcomed attention he received, Hernandez managed a tight unit and was respected by his peers and subordinates for his abilities and his sense of humor.

Hernandez had been on the shooting team at Michigan Reformatory, "and, by God, I'll be on one here. It's bad enough to hafta face those guys after the Coleman thing and then tell um there's no shooting team here. Hellava mess."

Huron Valley Women's Prison had never participated in the annual state wide shooting contest, but every men's prison had a team. Even the state police had teams representing each post. No one at the women's prison seemed to think they would get enough people to qualify for the team on all three weapons—handgun, shotgun, and rifle—as well as skeet shooting. No one, that is, until Hernandez arrived.

Huron Valley Women's Prison shooting team emerged during his first year at the prison. Only one woman, Norma, qualified that year, and she was not even an officer. Norma weighed maybe one hundred pounds and, if she stood as straight as possible, was slightly over five feet tall. Her husband had taught her to shoot, to his dismay it turned out, because she was so good that she usually bagged two deer each season, one for her and one for him.

Huron Valley Women's team did not do well the first year, but it did not place last, either. Thanks to Norma, they beat the men's prison next door. What else mattered?

For years, Norma was the only woman in the whole prison system to compete in this last bastion of maleness. Each year the other male competitors vied for the choice spots from which to watch Norma perform.

I admit that we were fashion conscious competitors and purchased team t-shirts. We were the first team to do this, and were teased and called "sissies". But by the following year most of the teams had t-shirts, and the department was entertaining thoughts of official shooting team uniforms.

Roy Rider was another of my favorite employees because of his loyalty and his M*A*S*H like humor. One time he raced into my office, saying, "Look out the window. See that girl? I want her for my secretary."

He was pointing at a striking African-American woman in her mid twenties. "That is a woman, not a girl. Who is she and can she type?" I asked.

"What difference if she can type? She has great legs!"

"I'm not sure whether you're serious, but if you are, you're in trouble. Is she new? I don't know her."

"That's Pelston, the one who killed her baby by putting her into the washing machine. She arrived a couple of weeks ago. She was just classified to general population today and she needs a job. At least I didn't assign her to the laundry."

"Bad joke."

I stood looking out the window, and as the elegant prisoner disappeared into the program building another prisoner emerged. "Come here, Rider. Look at the blond coming out of the program building right now. I know she has good secretarial skills because she's been taking classes. I'll assign her, since you seem desperate for your own secretary."

Rider walked to the window. "Oh no. That's bouncing Barbara. She's gotta be two hundred and fifty pounds. You wouldn't do that to me, would you?"

I did not answer. He studied me. "You would. I think I'll use the same secretaries I do now. He chuckled and left my office. I never knew when he was serious about his wandering eye.

184

Rider was bored one spring weekend when he was the duty administrator, i.e. the most senior person in the prison. He noticed that most of the women prisoners were just lying around and decided, since it was a warm and sunny day, that the prisoners should play a game of soft ball. He announced over the P. A. system, "There'll be a soft ball game in the yard in fifteen minutes. All those interested meet me at the field."

Rider picked up the equipment at the gym and wheeled it on a dolly to the field. No one showed up. Rider was ticked, and he went to each housing unit, again announcing the game, but adding, "You have a choice—the game or you can drop a urine sample."

Within ten minutes, there were enough women on the field for several teams, plus spectators. They played ball until dark that day and every weekend thereafter until it snowed. The prisoners dubbed him "The Rec Director".

On the first day of the Children's Visitation Program (CVP), Officer Larry Atkins was the knight in shining armor to many terrified little people.

Organizing CVP took six months, several intrepid volunteers, ten special prisoners, and four dedicated prison employees. It was a unique visiting program for the children of incarcerated mothers at Huron Valley Women's Prison. The primary motive was to strengthen and foster positive mother-child relations and to offer preventive intervention in the lives of children of women prisoners. As a group, children with a parent in prison are more likely to become delinquents or criminally involved.

Each Saturday morning, children and prisoner moms participated in four hours of constructive visiting, monitored and facilitated by a volunteer Ph.D psychologist, a volunteer social worker, one civilian prison employee, and prisoner caregivers who either had no children or whose children had been taken away from them by the courts. The visits were created to foster intimacy between mother and child and reduce the stress caused by separation. Unlike regular visits, both the mother and child were allowed to move about the visiting room, and there were no uniformed officers present. Our ultimate goal was to have CVP fully funded with a permanent, full time staff.

Children from all over the state were transported by trained volunteer drivers in vans donated by churches for CVP. The more than two hundred children were divided into four groups, one group for each weekend; some had not seen their mothers for two or more years, and some prisoners had not seen their youngest child since giving birth to it while in prison. Many of the children arrived hungry, unbathed, and in need of lots of tender loving care. They got it all, including a change of the court-ordered caregiver, if necessary. This task was handled by volunteers from the Michigan Women Lawyer's Association.

Officers like Larry Atkins, who would come in contact with the children, were chosen carefully to instill a feeling of calm and caring. On the first Saturday, two vans arrived early for the visit. The drivers decided to entertain the children, who ranged in age from four years to ten years, by walking them to the ponds in front of the men's prison to see the geese nesting there. But visitors were not allowed in that area, so Officer Atkins was told to get the band of five children and two drivers and bring them back to the prison.

The next thing I saw was Officer Atkins, all six feet five inches of him, leading a parade of children who were marching in a straight line, followed by the two drivers and a row of geese.

Once the children were back at the prison, they were taken through the security gates. The children jerked around to stare at gate one when it clanged shut, separating them from the familiar outside world. They were enclosed in a small room with this tall, strange man in a green and black uniform, and a woman dressed the same way. Each child was pat searched, and then lined up in front of gate two.

A four year old boy cowered in the corner farthest from where the line was forming. He was whimpering. When it was his turn to be searched, he began to wail. Every inch of his little body shook. Atkins squatted down to face the boy. "What's the problem, my man?"

The little boy softened his wail, but he neither stopped crying, nor answered the question. His nose began to run.

Atkins took some tissue from a box on the table. "Here, let's blow your nose and talk."

The frightened boy quieted as he blew his nose and Atkins wiped his face. The child took several deep, shivering breaths and stopped crying. He looked up at Atkins with wide eyes.

"You know, your mama is waiting for you just on the other side of this gate. And you know what else?"

The little boy shook his head "no", his body quieting.

"Well, we're going to party, my man!"

The other children who had been watching in silence cheered. The little boy looked at them and a large smile spread across his face.

"Can I check you out now before we go in? You know I have to be searched, too."

Atkins motioned to the woman officer, who picked up on the message and searched Atkins. After seeing that, the little boy nodded his head "yes" to Atkins' question. Atkins pat searched him and called out, "Gate two!"

Gate two slid open, and Atkins turned to the other little people. "Let's party!"

The small group of children marched to the visiting room behind Officer Atkins to enjoy the first of many such Saturdays. This time they did not notice the loud bang of the gate closing.

One of the four employees assigned to CVP was Marilyn Marshall who served as a perfect role model for women prisoners. Marilyn was a battered wife who divorced her husband and, as a single mother, raised her twelve children on welfare. While on welfare, Marilyn took advantage of several programs, including furthering her education. She graduated from college, started the first Displaced Homemakers in Michigan's Upper Peninsula, and eventually became a state employee. All of her children are successful and independent. We nominated her for the Miss Clairol award and she won, but in reality, we won because she was such an asset to us.

Marilyn's concern for children not only made CVP, but the Women and Infants at Risk Program, possible. This intensive community based program in Detroit is a three part plan devised to improve the physical, emotional, and social well being of pregnant, substance abusing female offenders and their children.

I think Officer Atkins and Marilyn Marshall would answer the question, "Why do people work in corrections?", by saying they believe that they can make a positive difference in a person's life, and that, given the right materials and support, people can change.

There are those, of course, who work in this field because the pay is competitive with the auto industry in Michigan. Many have been laid off from other jobs; to them, corrections is just another job. Some join corrections with good intentions, but succumb to the notion that success is achieved through the defeat of others and that self esteem is limited to those on top.

Women correctional officers are no longer called matrons and neither women, nor men, are called guards. The change was made in an attempt to soften and upgrade the image. To the public and the media, correctional officers will always be guards, to prisoners, they will be police (long o) or polices. To those of us who have worked with the good ones, they are the people who do the dirty work so the public won't have to.

XIII

Late one afternoon, I sat alone in my office waiting for the shift commander to notify me that the transportation bus had left. We called such trips "ride outs". My staff had already gone for the day, leaving an eerie silence in my office. This exchange of prisoners was the first of its magnitude in my career. Eighteen prisoners classified as severe behavior problems were being transferred to Ionia Maximum Security Prison (I-Max), Michigan's first super maximum security prison. In reality, the prisoners that were transferred to I-Max were the best of the worse, because I-Max did not take the mentally ill or the self mutilators. They stayed at Huron Valley Men's.

I-Max exchanged eighteen prisoners for those we transferred. The exchange took from ten o'clock in the morning until nearly five in the afternoon, when the shift commander finally notified me, "The bus is leaving the prison. Everything went without incident."

I got ready to leave the prison for the day, relieved that this exchange of some of the most dangerous prisoners in the state had gone well. The bus had been parked the entire day outside the garage through which all incoming prisoners are received. That garage had direct access to a row of holding cells and was in view of the control center. The process was long and tedious. Accompanying the prisoners who arrived on the bus were four armed guards, two at each end, two with shotguns. Prisoners were separated from the officers by caging at the front and rear of the bus, which was equipped with tear gas canisters. An armed officer drove a separate state car, known as a chase vehicle, behind the bus.

One officer, armed with a shotgun, stood guard outside the bus while the unloading and loading took place. Armed officers in the two gun towers closest to the loading station were on alert, armed with M14 automatic rifles.

Arriving prisoners, restrained in the most secure equipment, were removed from the bus one by one, processed and assigned to a housing unit. Once the bus was empty, the procedure started in reverse; the prisoners leaving Huron Valley Men's were processed one by one and secured in the bus. The departing prisoners were the greatest concern, since they were being classified to a higher custody level and not by choice. I was especially uneasy because an exchange of such a large number of prisoners was not a normal procedure. Usually only a few were transported at any one time.

Eager to get home, I left my office and made my way toward the lobby of the administration building. When I reached the front door, I saw the transport bus and chase vehicle returning. That damn bus has only been gone fifteen minutes, I thought. What could be the problem? All of a sudden I felt exhausted.

I turned to go back to my office to call the shift commander, but I stopped when I saw Rick Mayer, the acting deputy warden, and Lieutenant Reynolds coming from the security gates toward me. "We were hoping you'd already gone," Reynolds announced as they approached me.

"What does that mean, Lieutenant Reynolds?" I asked.

"Well, what you don't know will protect you. We're here to protect the warden, especially if something doesn't go according to policy. Remember your instructions about protecting the quarterback?"

This was said within earshot of the front desk officer and a few visitors, and I felt it was said to intimidate me. My body grew hot with anger when Reynolds brought up the quarterback reference. It came from one of the first meetings I held with the command staff at Huron

Valley Men's. During that meeting I likened the men's prison employees to a football team in which it is the job of the players to protect the quarterback, in this case the warden.

"Lieutenant Reynolds, you either misunderstood what was intended by the quarterback analogy, or you're deliberately taking it out of context to cover your ass. As I remember, Lieutenant, I explained that the team protects the warden by running a clean prison both physically and emotionally. If that's done, no one has to worry about ass covering. If you recall, I said that, like the quarterback, the warden only looks as good as the team, which can make or break the institution. I have a feeling you were about to break it."

Neither man said anything, so I continued, "Now, gentlemen, please accompany me to my office, where you can tell me what's really happened with the transfer."

Once we were all seated in my office, Mayer began the explanation. "All the loading went well, except Brooks. He gave us trouble right from the beginning, but we got him on the bus, so we didn't say anything to you."

"Isn't he the projectile vomiter? I didn't think he was cleared for I-Max because he's considered a self mutilator."

The two sat silent and then, with a slight smile on his face, Lieutenant Reynolds said, "Well, we got him cleared. But he's the reason the bus came back. He nearly caused a riot on the bus because he was vomiting on the prisoners around him. The officers had to gas him."

"And just what were your plans when the bus returned?"

Reynolds did all the talking in his cocky and confident manner. "Take him off and put him in the chase vehicle and let him ride alone. We felt that without an audience, he would calm down."

"You did say that he was gassed, right?"

Both nodded their heads.

"Have you called any medical staff to check him out for any after effects and wash the gas off him, before transporting him? Did either of you contact the medical staff to see if their records indicated he had any medical problems that precluded the use of gas? And, by the way, who authorized the gas?"

They remained silent. Mayer uncrossed and recrossed his legs, and sat with less of a confident slouch, but said nothing. I picked up the telephone and called the infirmary and spoke with the nurse in charge. "The transportation bus has returned because prisoner Brooks was gassed. Please examine him and make sure he can still be transferred. I'll meet you at the bus."

I hung up the telephone and looked at the two supervisors. "I hope I never have to clean up your messes again. This one was easy and no one was hurt. You had better hope this will be the last time. Now, let's get to that bus."

Brooks was checked and released by the medical staff. He was transferred without further incident in the chase vehicle, which had a plexiglass partition which kept the officer safe from any vomiting. And if Brooks ran true to form, he wouldn't vomit anymore because there was no victim.

A few days later, Brooks was returned to Huron Valley Men's, and I received a chewing out from my supervisor because Brooks had not been cleared from self mutilator's status as Reynolds and Mayer had claimed. It turned out to be a case of trying to dump a nuisance prisoner. From that point on, no transfers were made without my final approval or that of the new deputy, Sam Bentley. It was a duplication of effort, but I could not trust "the team".

XIV

The week after the transfer, I went on grounds to hold my monthly Warden's Forum Meeting at the men's prison. That meeting was designed so that elected prisoner representatives in general population could air complaints and offer ideas to the warden. The prisoners were often confrontational and manipulative, but I felt these airings were better than having them burn the prison down.

As I walked, I slowed my pace in an attempt to delay the unpleasantness, and basked in the warm sunshine. The nice weather was a welcome change from the previous week's chilling rains. My stroll took me alongside the fenced prisoner yard which was filled with men dressed in prison "blues". Some prisoners huddled in small groups, talking and smoking, careful not to exceed the number that would draw the attention of the three yard officers circulating among them, or the armed officers in the gun towers. Other prisoners jogged or walked in two's and three's along the fence, but not close enough to set off the alarm. I could easily identify the leaders, those in control; they were acknowledged with hesitant nods from prisoners who moved quickly out of their paths, anxious to please.

I passed the park-like area that reminded me of a college campus. Several benches sat in a circle among trees, flowers and bushes. To my knowledge, no one ever used the park, and I had no idea of how it was originally intended to be used. It was a serene creation ignored by all, except when the grass was mowed or when the mentally ill prisoners planted flowers each spring as part of their therapy.

Taking a deep breath, I savored the moment, hoping it would sustain me through the Forum. But I wanted to get to the program building before the yard was closed for the afternoon, so I wouldn't be caught amidst the throngs of inquisitive prisoners, and I picked up my pace. I took one last look at the yard, wondering what devious plans were being devised by the prisoners in those clandestine huddles.

Two prisoners leaving the yard area caught my attention. I watched as a corrections officer tucked his hand held radio into a pouch attached to his belt, signed the prisoners' yard passes, and unlocked the gate, allowing them to return to the "house" where they bunked. They were heading in the same direction as I, and I recognized them as Jones and Breeze, both trouble makers. From where I stood, these two men could have passed for brothers. They were close in height and had similar muscular builds, probably developed from daily workouts in the weight room. Their shaved heads were covered with blue wool caps issued as part of prisoner winter clothing.

Neither seemed to notice me, but they were close enough for me to hear them. I watched Jones chase Breeze across the prison yard shouting, "Yo, Breeze! Wait up!"

But Breeze didn't acknowledge the command and kept a steady pace toward his housing unit. Jones caught up to him. "Hey man! Didn't yah hear me? I said, wait up!"

Breeze turned to him, but said nothing. Lowering his voice, Jones continued, "Did yah get the stuff, man? Did she bring it?"

Breeze still did not respond.

"What's the matter with you, man? Did yah get the stuff or not?"

Breeze took a deep breath, "Yeah, I got the stuff, but I...I ain't gonna share it this time. An' I ain't lettin' her bring it no more. I ain't gonna be your mule." He turned his back to Jones and started toward his housing unit again.

Jones lunged after him and grabbed his arm.

Breeze spun around, arms swinging, and pushed Jones' hand away. Breeze's jaw tightened. "Keep your hands off me, man!" He pivoted on his heels and left Jones on the path.

Jones' face reddened. Clenching his fists at his side and barely moving his mouth, he warned Breeze, "You're a dead man, Breeze. Do you hear me—a dead man!"

Breeze paid no attention. Jones put his right hand in his pants pocket and pursued Breeze. Just as they reached the door to the dormitory area, I saw something shine in Jones' right hand.

I rushed to the closest housing unit, cursing myself for not having my radio with me. As soon as I entered the housing unit, I called the dorm. The sergeant answered.

"This is the warden, Sergeant. Watch Jones. I think he may try to assault Breeze. I overheard a conversation between the two—sounded like a drug deal gone bad."

"Okay, Warden Miller, will do."

Before I reached the program building, I was paged by the shift commander. I turned around and walked to the control center. The shift commander reported, "Breeze has been stabbed. It appears it happened right after he signed back into the unit from yard. No one knows nothin' as usual. Medical's on the scene, but it looks bad. He might have to go to the hospital."

"Get prisoner Jones up here. I want to talk to him. Call the State Police, cordon off the scene, and keep me posted. Make sure every employee in that unit at the time of the stabbing writes a report. Don't let anyone, prisoner or employee, leave there. We'll conduct a thorough search when the State Police arrive, so nothing should be touched until then. Monitor prisoner movement closely and only let two at a time use the latrine; shake them down coming and going. All the others are to remain on their bunks. Got it?"

"Yes, Ma'am."

"I'll be in the deputy's office across the hall. Oh, and reschedule the Forum for next week."

"Right."

Within a few minutes, I stood in the deputy's office looking through the large bank of windows which provided a view of the entire prison grounds. Jones strolled to the administration building and disappeared as an alarm sounded, signalling the gate was being opened by a control center officer. The building shook as the gate clanged to a close. It had only been fifteen minutes since I had seen Jones with Breeze on the sidewalk.

The shift commander brought Jones to the deputy's office, and I interrogated him for a couple of hours. I repeated the conversation I'd overheard. He knew and I knew that unless there was some solid evidence, like a weapon or blood stains, something other than a threat, I had no case. Threats are a matter of routine in a prison, and not all are carried out.

No one admitted seeing Jones do anything or even that he was seen with Breeze. The prisoner code of silence, by the way, is not due to respect for one's peers, but engendered by fear of being the next victim. Jones wasn't charged because there was not enough evidence, and Breeze died. I managed to have Jones placed on a "ride out" to another prison, hoping it would slow down his drug trafficking. I kept thinking, these are the medium custody prisoners, the "good guys".

The following week, during the regularly scheduled meeting with the deputy and three assistant deputies, we brainstormed about the drug problem. It was agreed that periodic use of the state police drug dogs was not hindering the introduction of drugs into the institution.

I asked the four men seated around the conference room table, "Well, then, what should we do to at least slow the traffic and the assaults? It's bad enough to have to deal with drug wars on the streets. I'd like to prevent those wars in our prison before they get out of hand."

The deputy responded first. "After you told us what we'd be concentrating on in this meeting, we got together with our staff and talked the problem out. We have listed our ideas."

"Good! Let's hear them."

"Most of the drugs, we feel, come into the prison through the visitors. The first thing to do is not let visitors use the bathrooms in the visiting room. Generally, when the visitors carrying drugs use the bathroom, they either stash the drugs in there or when they leave the bathroom, if the officer is not watching, drop it by the mule."

"That sounds good, but the officer already shakes down the bathroom after a visitor and before a prisoner uses it. Won't the officer find the stash?" I asked.

"Prisoners bank on the fact that the officer is rushed because there are visitors and prisoners arriving all the time. In fact, they plan it that way. The prisoners know that the officers don't shake down the bathroom as thoroughly as they should each time. If any drugs are found, they also know how hard it is to pin a charge on anyone with so many using the bathroom during visits."

I agreed that it seemed like a good approach, but pointed out, "The visitors will pitch a bitch if they can't go to the bathroom. Some of them visit all day. What will we do about them?"

"They'll have to use the bathrooms in the lobby, which means being shaken down again. It might mean more work for officers, but we think it'll slow the drugs."

"Okay. What else did you come up with?"

"The vending machines in the visiting room have to go, too, because prisoners and their visitors transfer drugs through shared food."

"How so?"

"If the visitor buys a pop and has a balloon filled with drugs in his mouth, he can drop it into the pop, and the prisoner can retrieve it when he drinks from the same can. Same thing with a bag of chips, except they use their hands."

"Sounds logical. Those machines are a pain in the butt anyway, always broken or out of their favorite foods. Okay, anything else to add to these?"

All four shook their heads.

"I have one other suggestion, gentlemen. Visitors bringing in babies in diapers will have to change the diaper before they visit. It should be done between security gates one and two, using a diaper issued by an officer. The officer won't touch the baby, and the diaper will be in individual packaging."

The housing deputy sat up straight. "Isn't that going a little overboard?"

"Well, at the women's prison, syringes and drugs have been found in babies' diapers when they were searched. I guess most people think we wouldn't search a baby. I don't find this type of search offensive if the visitor doesn't seem to mind carrying drugs and paraphenelia in that way. It's unfortunate that rules are made for the whole and that innocent people are inconvenienced in order to protect that whole."

"What about changing diapers once the visit begins?" Deputy Bentley asked.

"Like the visitor who has to go to the bathroom, the mother will have to leave the visiting room, get a clean diaper from the officer, and change the diaper between the gates. Can't take the chance that the visitor will hide the stash in a clean diaper."

They all looked at me in disbelief. One even took off his glasses, rubbed his forehead, and muttered, "I can't believe this."

"What can't you believe? That I'm going to this extreme or that visitors would stoop so low? How about the Akin family who used their youngest child as a decoy to disguise their shop lifting? What about prisoners' mothers we have already busted for bringing in drugs in baby diapers. Do you think these people care about placing a baby in danger of being stuck by a syringe?"

"Yeah," the security deputy chimed in. "These guys didn't get to prison because they put others first or they came from the Cosby family. They only think of themselves."

I looked around the table, waiting for other comments, but there were none. I asked Bentley, "Can you get the written notices out within a week? We won't be able to implement this without giving fourteen days notification to the prisoners so they can inform their families and friends of the change. The visiting rules will have to be revised and posted as well. These changes must be read in roll call for three consecutive days."

"We'll manage."

Manage they did, but the prisoners were pretty unhappy. At the rescheduled Forum Meeting, the prisoners complained about being treated unfairly and accused me of "messing with their family ties." I responded, "I thought visits provided time for sharing quality time. The only thing we are stopping are the drugs."

Prisoner drug usage was greatly reduced, but we knew it would be only a matter of time until the prisoners found a new way to beat the system and get the drugs through. I became known as the "Diaper Warden" after several visitors complained to central office. But following a heated discussion at a subsequent wardens' meeting, all institutions had to provide diapers and a changing area between the security gates.

XV

In my second year as the warden of Huron Valley Women's Prison, a twelve foot high berm of earth was constructed between the men's and women's prisons, after a noticeable increase in prisoner on prisoner assaults at both facilities. Before the berm was constructed, the prisoner yards in each facility were in plain view of each other. Prisoners who became lovers through correspondence wore specific colors and items of clothing that set them apart from the others in the yard, and mentioned it in their letters to one another. Once their lover was identified, the two would communicate via hand signals or by shouting.

That was innocent enough until a prisoner would attempt to communicate while on someone else's turf or with someone else's sweetheart. Men prisoners resolved such challenges by knifing the intruder with a shank, women through more traditional combat—hair pulling, eye gouging and biting.

A bargain was struck between the warden of the men's prison and me. I would contribute $15,000 from my budget to build the berm, and he would contribute the same amount to build a platform needed to store the salt used by both prisons during the winter. As luck would have it, new sewers were being installed within a mile of the institutions and the land development company needed a place to haul the unwanted dirt. The owners agreed to deliver the dirt and build the berm for $15,000.

The Michigan Department of Management and Budget (DMB),

however, refused to let me use that company because they had not gone through the bid process. The company DMB chose at low bid, based on legislative requirement, was going to charge $120,000, which no one had in their budgets.

I remember the day I met with the three male engineers from the DMB. I asked, "Can you in good conscience actually recommend the $120,000 bid over the one for $15,000 because of some technicality?"

The head engineer nodded. "It's policy."

"Well, stuff the policy. I just can't accept this. I want to know whose brother-in-law is being paid off?"

No one said anything as I continued. "I'll take full responsibility for my decision and have the company that's charging $15,000 do the job. I don't think there should be too many complaints about saving tax payers $105,000, do you? And perhaps the media and the legislature would like to know about the savings."

As they left, the head engineer gave me a final warning. "We will take no responsibility for this."

"I wouldn't expect you to. Thank you, gentlemen, for your time."

I thought this meeting would be the most difficult aspect of the berm issue, but it was not. Answering the two hundred grievances filed by prisoners from both prisons was more tedious and exhausting. Affairs in prison, however, will endure, no matter what wardens do to halt them.

I was shaken when the medical director told me a woman prisoner was five months pregnant, when her file indicated she had been incarcerated for six months.

"Don't worry, Warden," the medical director tried to console me. "She's only been here a couple of weeks; it didn't happen here. The best we can tell from the exam and her story is that it happened in the county jail. She didn't make bond and was held there all through her trial."

"Don't worry? What makes you think it's any better if it took place in a jail? Who's the prisoner? Who's the father, or don't we know?"

"The prisoner, Glenda Lowell, is the one charged with running a pornographic business with her husband. It seems that the county jail officers thought it would be cute to satisfy the sexual craving of one of the male jail inmates. They didn't think Lowell would mind, since she was used to satisfying anyone's urges—while her husband filmed it, by the way. The officers took away her birth control pills because of jail policy, but they didn't bank on her getting pregnant."

"I still don't understand how this could happen when men and women are locked up in different areas of the jail."

"Glenda and a male prisoner were scheduled for court the same day. The officers placed them in a holding cell together, only the male prisoner was not cuffed and Glenda was, one arm to a chair."

"Has she filed a complaint?"

"No. Just said it was all a part of doing business, whatever that means."

"I want a full report. I'll notify the sheriff in that county. I don't care what her specialty is; this isn't acceptable behavior."

"Okay. One other thing I thought you might like to know. Bolden is back and guess what?"

"She's pregnant. What's this make, three we've delivered."

"Yep. You know her style. Gets pregnant, and then gets arrested so the baby is delivered at the university hospital. She admits she can't get that kind of care on the streets, no money and too busy doing tricks and shooting up. This is another high risk pregnancy. The baby will probably be born addicted."

A few weeks later, Bolden's baby was born addicted to heroin. The baby was born in the prison dormitory. We tried to take Bolden to the hospital three times on the same night. According to the prison nurses, Bolden appeared to be in labor and ready to deliver. But each time they sent the prisoner to the hospital (in a caged prison transport van accompanied by two officers), she was returned with a message from the hospital staff: "False alarm."

Because of crowding, Bolden, a medium custody prisoner, lived in a dormitory located in the gym. Within a half hour of her third return trip, she screamed out for help. "It's coming. The baby's coming out. Help!"

Two officers on duty rushed to assist, while the third notified the shift commander and the infirmary. The shift commander arrived before the nurses and just in time to help deliver a baby girl. The mother and baby were rushed to the hospital and admitted by their embarrassed staff.

The next day when I made rounds, I noticed a large sign painted in black letters on white poster board hanging over the gym/dorm entrance: "OB/GYM".

"That's quite a sign," I chuckled.

An officer responded, "You think that's good, Bolden named her kid Gymma."

Gymma was counted among the lucky ones. She lived in spite of her addiction at birth. So many of them did not.

The number of pregnant prisoners was growing at a steady pace and averaged thirty-two a month. The majority of them were at high risk because of drugs, AIDS, and no prenatal care. The women's prison population in Michigan had more HIV positive and AIDS cases than the men's population because of prostitution and shared needles. Only 1% of all new prisoners in Michigan proved HIV positive, and the majority had been infected by shared needles.

I had to fight for a drug pilot program at the women's prison. It was scheduled to be implemented only in selected men's prisons which meant, once again, women prisoners would be left out. When my staff and I made our presentation to the Michigan State Office of Substance Abuse, we argued that the pilot should be placed at Huron Valley Women's because of the high percentage of substance abusers among women prisoners, the high rate of infant mortality in Michigan, and the fact that these women prisoners would return to the community to teach their children to be exactly like them, addicts. The authorities agreed that the cycle had to be stopped.

The fact that a prisoner gave birth to a child did not always reflect the nature of the prisoner's sexual activity in prison. Officers often complained of "bunk hopping" once the lights went out in the dorm. Prisoners snuck to the bed of their current lover to share intimate moments between bed checks. Officers joked that if it was really quiet in the dorm, groans of ecstasy could be heard, but few of those making the sounds were ever discovered. Often, non-participating prisoners would hold up blankets to hide the activity and to act as look-outs.

The dorm was not the only place lovers rendezvoused. Favorite trysting places were bathroom stalls, showers, and movies, even though the screening room was never completely dark. At the women's prison, there was also the library. It was the perfect place to go when lovers did not live in the same unit. Prisoner couples signed up to use the library at the same time, and studied hard behind the shelves.

Most sexual relationships between women prisoners were by mutual consent. The prisoners even had weddings, though such weddings were not authorized by prison policy.

A prisoner usually mated with a woman who was most like the partner she had on the streets. If she was battered in the real world, she would partner with a batterer in prison.

Colleen Morris, for example, was a petite, twenty year old who mated with Terri Hill, the most powerful prisoner at Huron Valley Women's. Hill was violent in all relationships and was a known homosexual predator and rapist. She saw her women as possessions, not partners.

The first time I saw Hill, she was walking with a pimp roll across prison grounds. When she stood still, her arms and hands were poised at her sides as if ready for combat. Her hair was cut Marine style, her skin was covered with colorful tattoos, and her well-developed arm muscles bulged from under the rolled up sleeves of her uniform shirt. Unlike most of the other women, Hill wanted to wear the state issued black leather, high top prison shoes. I thought she was a man and asked the shift commander, "Who's that guy?"

The shift commander laughed and told me about Terri Hill. She was serving time for the murder of her lover's girlfriend, a classic crime of passion.

Prison did nothing to change Hill. She beat Colleen Morris, her prisoner girlfriend, when she thought Colleen was getting too close to another prisoner. One serious beating was not discovered until the officer taking count found Morris lying in her blood on the floor of her cell. It was later learned that prisoners in the unit acted as decoys while the beating took place, so that Hill was not noticed entering and leaving Morris' cell. The prisoners also made enough noise to muffle the sounds of the beating.

Morris was rushed to the hospital where she underwent hours of surgery to save her spleen and kidney. Interrogating the prisoners in the unit proved futile. Hill, however, was implicated through letters Morris mailed to her from the hospital; in them she asked for Hill's forgiveness and begged Hill to take her back. The letters were the evidence needed to find Hill guilty of assault and classify her to segregation.

My staff could not believe Morris' pleas for forgiveness, but I warned, "You wait. Once Morris is back on grounds and Hill is let out of segregation, they will be a couple again. And, no doubt, Morris will suffer another beating for being so stupid as to write letters to Hill implicating her in the beatings."

I wish I could say I was wrong in my predictions, but I was not.

Morris was not the only one to suffer at the hands of Hill. Although prisoners cannot share visits, the close proximity of the seating in the visitors' room allowed for conversations between visiting groups. Hill and Morris were on separate visits at the same time. Hill apparently felt Morris was becoming too chummy with her woman visitor and raced across the room, picked the visitor up above her head and slammed her to the floor. Then, almost in the same motion, Hill punched Morris in the jaw. By the time an officer was able to get to the scene, Morris and her visitor lay in a heap on the floor, and Hill stood over them, yelling, "Stay away from my woman."

Hill received more segregation time and was placed on non-contact visits, meaning she and her visitors sat in separate booths and could communicate only by a telephone. Morris and Hill remained a couple until Morris was transferred to another prison.

Homosexual behavior in any prison was expected, but rape in a women's prison, at least prisoner on prisoner, was not; but it happened. Some unsuspecting prisoner would enter the bathroom, only to be confronted by the top homosexual predator who would push the victim into a shower stall, remove her clothes, threatening, "Better not yell or you're a dead woman. Maybe not here and now, but I will get you." Paid prisoners acted as lookouts and decoys when a rape took place. Sometimes their pay was to rape the prisoner too.

The victim rarely reported the rape, but it was usually discovered during an unrelated physical exam or when assaults were discussed in therapy by the victims, as well as the lookouts. Such assaults were not admitted to the prison authorities because snitches in general population could get hurt or killed. The gruesome murders committed by prisoners on prisoners during the New Mexico State Prison riots, for instance, were directed at known snitches.

XVI

Prisoners have little difficulty, on the other hand, snitching on prison employees, even when it may not be the whole truth. Noelle, the queen of manipulation, was a prime example. She was demure during first meetings, greeting you with lowered head, wide eyes and soft voice. The real Noelle, however, scrutinized every staff person until she found the most vulnerable, and then ensnared them.

One of Noelle's victims was a ten year veteran, Brad Taylor, the first man to work a housing unit in the women's prison. It happened on the segregation unit where Noelle spent much of her time. Most of us knew her modus operandi and passed the information on, but Taylor ignored the warning and began a sexual relationship with Noelle. Their final rendezvous was discovered by a woman officer taking count. The two lovers got careless, and the officer found them in a storage closet.

Noelle sued Officer Taylor for rape, and named the department administrators, including me, as guilty parties in the suit. The jury agreed with department employees that the sexual relationship was consensual, but they also stated the Michigan Department of Corrections was negligent because it failed to provide a safe environment for the prisoner. The jury felt that Noelle was coerced by Taylor's authority.

Noelle was awarded $10,000 which was all she really wanted. That greed would have been revealed if past criminal behavior, noted in her prison file, had been allowed as evidence. The file showed that she had played the same game while she was a resident in a corrections center in Grand Rapids. That time the victim was a minister.

After Officer Taylor was fired, he made an appointment with me and offered a tearful apology. I struggled with mixed emotions, feeling sorry for him, but disgusted at the same time. The bottom line was that his sexual needs could have been met elsewhere, not in a setting where his uniform alone, according to the courts, was viewed as having coercive authority over a prisoner. His actions almost destroyed the progress we had made in building a positive gender balance among the officers. Fortunately, the department was bound by a previous grievance decision which prevented administrators from removing male officers from housing units at Huron Valley Women's.

Michigan Department of Corrections has never quite recovered from the negative impact of that case. In fact, the women's prisons were under investigation from 1989 to 1992 because of continued complaints about sexual abuse and assaults by male officers. Some of those complaints were true, but most were found to be stories concocted by vengeful prisoners.

Another memorable incident involving Noelle came to my attention almost two years after I retired. The guest speaker at a local annual Equality Day dinner had been a volunteer at Huron Valley Women's Prison. When I was introduced to her, she asked, "You don't remember me, do you?"

"I do remember your name, but can't place from where."

"We never met, but I did volunteer work at Huron Valley Women's. I was the one who exchanged shoes with Noelle. Remember? The officer stopped me between gates one and two as I was leaving after my visit with her. The officer asked how I got the prisoner shoes I was wearing. I'm as ashamed today as I was then to admit that Noelle conned me into trading mine for hers. She said she had no other shoes, and I felt sorry for her."

"She's one of the great manipulators. I wouldn't feel too badly. You weren't her first or her last victim."

She smiled and shook her head. "It's worse than that. Although I was no longer allowed to volunteer after that, I continued my association with her. The bad part is I never learned. She was always so convincing. Even after she was paroled, I was sucked in by her persuasiveness. I kept telling myself it was because of her kids."

"You know she has eight and can't tell who all the fathers are?"

"No, she has nine. Gave birth to one more that I know of after she was paroled and moved to Virginia. I finally saw the light after I'd spent a total of $7000 on her, each time hoping it would make a difference. It never did. I haven't heard from her in a year, and don't expect to, since I told her I will not give her any more money."

"You're lucky. Some of her victims have lost their jobs, their spouses, and have gone to jail."

The woman who fell into Noelle's trap was no dummy. She has a master's degree in social work and is employed full time by the government. As I said, Noelle was very good at manipulating people.

XVII

Most prisoners found ways to spend their prison time with as little pain as possible. Some even took advantage of the numerous programs provided—therapy, volunteer sponsored self-help groups, religious programs, recreational activities, crafts, and vocational and academic education. The latter could result in a four year degree. Other prisoners, who could not cope with confinement, attempted escape. Those who tried to escape did so in a variety of ways and many even made it over the fences, but few got away.

Charles Macklin's escape brought the most notoriety during my tenure. He was serving a life sentence for murdering a sheriff's deputy. He escaped by prying the window off his cell and scrambling over two twelve foot fences covered with razor ribbon. Several shots were fired by officers in the gun towers, but none hit him; the shots went through the administration building. We were thankful that he left after normal business hours so that the building was empty.

Corrections officers from both the men's and women's prisons, County Deputy Sheriffs, Michigan State Police and township police pursued him in the dark. He was fatally wounded by the State Police after being surrounded in the corn fields next to the women's prison.

Two more prisoners at Huron Valley Men's were able to escape by popping out a window in the prison dental office, which at that time was outside the fence. They were recaptured, one in Milwaukee and one in Arizona. It was suspected, but never confirmed, that there was inside help, and that they fled in a car provided by a female attorney representing one of them.

One of the most notable escapes from Huron Valley Women's Prison forced the department to put razor ribbon on the fence there, too. Shortly after the prison opened, Carolyn Keystone leaped over the fence and made it to Pontiac, almost a hundred miles away. She went directly to the Osteopathic Hospital to help her boyfriend escape; he was in custody, but under hospital care. In the attempt to free him, she murdered a police officer, was captured and returned to prison to face new charges.

Some escapes are comical, like the woman who greased her naked, obese body in order to squeeze it through the window bars in her cell. She got stuck half way through and was discovered by an officer during count. She told the officer that she did not yell for help because "there was always hope I'd squeeze through and get outta here." She hadn't thought about what she would do for clothes if she did get through the bars. We had to have a maintenance man saw the bars off in order to free her. The prisoner screamed with each of his motions, and the officers tried not to laugh. She never attempted to escape again.

One male prisoner commandeered a semi truck which was making deliveries to the kitchen inside the fence. He drove it through the first of two salley port gates (entrances for vehicle traffic); the second gate stopped the truck. That time, the truck driver sued the state.

Vehicular escape seems to be favored. One woman prisoner attempted to escape on a large John Deer lawn mower. We never understood why she just didn't walk away; it would have been faster.

A minimum custody male prisoner, working on an off-grounds public works crew assignment, was told to take a state van around to the back of a greenhouse being dismantled for transport to the women's prison. He obeyed the order and drove the state van around to the back of the greenhouse, but did not stop. He kept going. We were happy about losing the state van because it needed replacing, but his departure did little to help public relations. Unfortunately, though the van was found, the escapee was not.

My favorite escape story is one that entailed a naked woman prisoner and Sergeant Hernandez. There was something about him that inspired nakedness. Rita Silverman, serving time for murdering her husband for his insurance money, had been diagnosed as mentally ill. On the day she decided to escape, she said she was meeting her husband in New Hampshire. No one knows why she chose New Hampshire, but since she was the same prisoner who wanted her name changed to KGB Deutch Doll because she was a spy, we didn't try to understand.

Rita did not like wearing clothes, only white socks. All of her clothes had been delivered in garbage bags via cab, but they were not accepted because of their condition. They were filthy, bug infested and showed signs of having been home to rodents. She was offered prison clothing, but I guess she did not feel it met her fashion standards. Just before her escape attempt, she had requested surgery to affix permanent liner around her eyes, claiming that would enhance her dancing career when she was released from prison.

The first time I saw Rita was one February day as I returned to the prison. She was standing in the segregation yard with several other prisoners. I knew there was a problem because that many prisoners were not allowed in the yard at the same time. But that did not explain why Rita was nude. When I inquired about her, Sergeant Hernandez explained, "We had to evacuate the unit because of a fire. Rita refused to put on any clothes, so we gave her a blanket, but she threw it on the floor. We had no choice."

White socks were all Rita had on when she decided to escape. She got over the fence by using blankets to protect her from the razor ribbon. Hernandez and the male manager of the segregation unit caught her about a half mile from the prison. I tried to imagine the reactions of the drivers passing by on the highway, seeing a naked woman, on her knees in the presence of two men, one armed. No motorists stopped.

When the trio returned to the prison, Rita said to the female shift commander, "Some Mexican pulled a gun on me. Can he do that?"

The shift commander replied, "He can shoot your heart out,

honey."

Hernandez was called "Some Mexican" after that escape.

One other attempted escape from women's prison stands out in my mind. Juanita Parks was visited by her mother and during the visit, Juanita exchanged pieces of clothing with her mother to help disguise her. Apparently, they accomplished the switch when duty officers were busy with other prisoners or visitors. Juanita's mother also provided her with a fake driver's license. Juanita hid her prisoner ID under the seat cushion in the visiting room.

The two women waited until there were several visitors leaving at the same time, hoping Juanita would blend in. She managed to get by the visiting room officer to gate two where she showed the fake driver's license. Everything was going well until Juanita was asked to put her hand under the black light. She and her mother had forgotten one very important security measure—visitors' hands are stamped with a symbol that can only be detected under black light; each day the symbol is changed.

Juanita was charged and convicted of attempted escape, and her mother was charged with aiding and abetting an escape, for which she received probation. Juanita was also placed on non-contact visits. Juanita's mother was no different than many parents who visited. Some helped their children escape mentally by smuggling drugs in to them.

Some escapees were not from either prison. A man appeared during one of the hostage takings and presented himself as an FBI agent. He showed me a driver's license, claiming it was his. It had been altered in an attempt to make the picture look like him; glasses were penciled around the eyes. On a hunch, I called the Ypsilanti (mental health) State Hospital located about a half mile away. He was one of their "walk aways", classified not dangerous, but not an FBI agent.

I was getting used to the hospital's walk aways. One had even shown up with her luggage and wanted to move into the prison because she thought it was a prettier place.

John Norman was discovered digging a tunnel to freedom from

the Marquette Branch Prison, also a maximum security prison. He was a serial killer in the late 1960's. His victims were women students in Washtenaw County where Huron Valley Men's Prison is located. He was sentenced to life in prison, but the judge ordered that he could not serve his sentence in Washtenaw county, as its residents feared that if he ever got free, he would create havoc in that community again.

What amazed me about Norman were the women who visited him. During that time, my friend, Denise Quarles, was assistant deputy warden at Marquette Branch Prison, and she watched women by the dozens come to see Norman. Most of the women did not know him, except from what they had read about him in the newspapers or heard on radio and TV—that he murdered women. I never have been able to understand these women, except to charitably assume they thought they could save him.

XVIII

Several prisoners chose to escape their stagnant lives by becoming involved in as many programs and activities as possible. Among the choices were Children's Visitation Program, Black History Month in February, the Christmas decorating contest, prison gospel choir, volley ball, basketball, self help groups, religious groups, and college. Events like Black History Month programs required research to produce authentic historical skits, often accompanied by wonderful prisoner choirs. There was a wealth of talent among the prisoners that was wasted because of their confinement and status in the real world. But while they were incarcerated, their talents brought enjoyment to employees and other prisoners.

The most memorable of all the prison productions was the court scene from *The Caine Mutiny*, acted by the mentally ill male prisoners at Huron Valley Men's. All employees, myself included, were amazed that prisoners who could not get through a day without Thorazine or Elavil performed as well as any professional, especially prisoner Tucker.

The first time I met Tucker, he was in his cell in the protective environment unit, which was the last one of several mental health units, each decreasing in intensity, before a prisoner was returned to general population. Tucker stood next to the cell door, facing the window on the opposite side of the room, throwing his filled laundry bag at the window. Once it landed, Tucker walked across the room, picked up the laundry bag, returned to his position by the cell door and threw it at the window again. He repeated this over and over for several minutes until I asked him what he was doing.

"I can't sit still. I work in the kitchen on second shift. 'Til it's time for me to go, I gotta keep movin'."

All the time he talked to me, he paced back and forth in front of the cell door. I later discussed his case with the psychologist who explained, "Even on medication, Tucker is so hyper he can hardly sleep, let alone sit still."

The woman who was the activities therapist for the mentally ill prisoners at Huron Valley Men's was able to get a local director to help her produce *The Caine Mutiny*. She couldn't convince Tucker, however, that he could not be in the play because he was unable to sit still. Tucker begged and pleaded until she and the director gave in and let him be one of a panel of judges.

I remember her instructions to him on opening night. "Remember, Tucker, if you cannot sit still and must move around, just get up and walk off the stage as if it is part of the play. No one will know the difference."

"I won't hafta do that. I know I can do this. I know I can."

Do it he did. He sat still through the entire play, except for making periodic notes as a judge would. I can still recall the thrill I felt that night, as if I were watching my own child. To this day, I think that somehow corrections and the other agencies have missed the boat. We have not been able to capture whatever inner desire it was that made Tucker calm that night. He wanted to be in that play so much, he did whatever it took to be successful. As I watched him perform, I wondered why he and others like him couldn't succeed in real life. At least for the nights he performed in that play, Tucker was a success and escaped the internal horror that held him. We just hadn't learned how to replicate it.

On special occasions and holidays, entertainment was brought into the prison, including disc jockeys, acting troupes, mimes, singers and bands. Entertainers were investigated for authenticity, and LEIN checks were run to make sure there were no outstanding warrants or arrest histories on them. They were also subjected to complete shake downs before going inside the prison.

An unusually cold summer was heated up by a group of five good looking young men in a singing group. They made it through all the investigations, LEIN checks and shakedowns. Their performance was attended by approximately 150 women.

The five young men sang and gyrated through their first number, to the hoots and hollers of the exuberant audience.

"Shake that thing, honey."

"Let me hear yah sing it, baby."

"Umm umm, you sure look good enough to eat."

It was during the second song that Officer Cramer decided she should call in the shift commander. "I think you need to see this," Cramer explained. "I'm not sure this is what the warden had in mind for entertainment."

"What's wrong, Cramer?"

"Well, Captain, these guys are singing alright, and pretty good too, but they are also taking their clothes off. One's down to a G-string already. These guys are like the Chippendales, not that I have ever seen them, mind you."

"I can hear the whistling and yelling in the background. Sounds like a frenzied crowd. I'm on my way with back up. We'll have to end this party. The ladies aren't going to be too happy."

The captain entered the chapel with a squad of eight officers and announced the show was over. "...And, ladies," he went on, "if you don't want any trouble or write ups, you'll let these performers go without a hassle. And you'll be quiet."

"It's okay, Cap, we seen more than we thought we would've," a prisoner yelled out.

The five singers dressed and left the prison without incident. When I read the log in the morning, I chuckled, but the program staff who had planned it had hell to pay.

XIX

Prisoners, by law, must be afforded access to court for filing appeals, child custody cases, divorces, and the like. In Michigan, this means that prisoners must have law libraries, trained prisoner paralegals, and the assistance of attorneys from Prisoner Legal Services who are not employed by the corrections department. Some of the prison law libraries rival those used by attorneys. Prisoners have become articulate in legalese and often file nuisance suits against the corrections department and individual employees.

When I was the warden of the women's prison, I insisted that if prisoners were to become paralegals, a two year accredited college program should be implemented. This would allow them to be lucratively employed once they were discharged from prison. The prisoners' attorneys in the Mary Glover Suit fought it because the program was different from that in the men's prison, and would take a prisoner longer to finish. Ultimately I won my argument when the judge agreed that the primary goal for women prisoner rehabilitation was to make them self sufficient upon leaving prison, which meant being employed.

The ruling in another suit, filed during my tenure as warden, was less satisfying. The department administrators, including me, and several officers from Huron Valley Men's Prison were sued because of injuries a prisoner sustained in a fire he'd set in his cell, the third that day. He had barricaded his cell door so officers could not rescue him. One of the officers on duty took off his breathing apparatus, shoved it through the cell door slot and placed it on the prisoners face. This action not only helped save the prisoner's life, but jeopardized the officer, who was subsequently sent to the hospital with smoke inhalation. Still, the judge ruled in the prisoner's favor.

The same judge, James R. Giddings, was assigned to hear the class action law suit filed by prisoners to stop the implementation of the department's new policy in which prisoners' personal property would be greatly reduced. The need for the policy arose because too much accumulated property made cell searches difficult, and allowed prisoners to more easily conceal contraband and weapons. Court convened on this law suit in November, 1988, but Judge Giddings has never given a final order, meaning that corrections administrators cannot change anything in the policy. Judge Giddings has virtually held the Michigan Department of Corrections hostage. Like the Glover Suit, the property case could go on forever because there is no statute of limitations for law suits filed by prisoners against the state.

Not all litigation was weighty and some was down right frivolous. There were, for instance, many prisoners who sued me for "holding them against their will". No kidding! The most unusual suit was filed by a woman who berated me for keeping her incarcerated when the judge had only sent her to prison for a psychiatric evaluation. It was Rita Silverman, of the white socks, who was actually serving a life sentence without parole for murdering her husband; one of the judge's recommendations had been that she get psychiatric help.

I have been sued because a prisoner's mail took a week to get to its destination. That law suit actually required hours of investigation and report writing to satisfy the judge before it was dismissed.

I have been sued by families of prisoners who successfully committed suicide, and by the survivors of a woman prisoner who died because of her severe asthma condition. She did not take her medication as directed and, after a vigorous afternoon of roller skating in the gym, had a major asthma attack. She followed that by over-dosing on her prescription medication.

The suit was originally filed by prisoners who claimed they saw the entire episode, including her collapse on the sidewalk outside the gym. These prisoners reported the incident to the American Civil Liberties Union, stating that the prisoner died on the sidewalk between the gym and the infirmary and that numerous officers who walked by her did nothing. Basically, that was true, but important facts were left out. The prisoner, frightened when she realized she was having a negative reaction to the drug, began running toward the infirmary. She collapsed in view of the yard officers who radioed for medical help and began CPR on her. Her collapse happened during shift change which meant officers passed as they came to and from their posts; if they inquired, they were told that there was enough help—three officers and two nurses—attending her already. When the ACLU investigated, they agreed with the results of the institution's investigation, that everything possible had been done before and after the prisoner's collapse.

Sheila came to Huron Valley Women's Prison because of a law suit she filed, but did not win. Her complaint? She wanted the state to

213

pay for the rest of her sex change operation. This was denied because it was considered elective surgery. But central office administrators appeased the court by transferring Sheila to Huron Valley Women's Prison. Sheila arrived at the women's prison with breasts and a penis.

The transfer turned out to be a good decision because Sheila, when she was living with the men, had to be classified to protective custody. But women prisoners accepted her without any problems. In fact, she was considered to be pretty and feminine.

The officers, on the other hand, had difficulty deciding how a strip search was to be conducted on Sheila, since policy dictated that non-emergency strip searches had to be conducted by an officer of the same sex. Strip searches in medium and higher custody prisons are conducted after every visit or when there is suspicion of concealing contraband. Prisoners must take off all their clothes and all body cavities are searched. However, the officer does not touch the body but gives directions to the prisoner:

"Stick your tongue out."

"Open your mouth wide."

"Squat and spread the cheeks of your buttocks."

The solution for Sheila's searches was to have a woman officer search her body from the waist up and a man from the waist down.

Prisoners are not the only ones who come up with unusual reasons to sue. An African-American officer, Colette Johnson, filed a civil rights complaint against me because I did not promote her into a sergeant vacancy. I told Officer Johnson that I did not feel she qualified because of her excessive use of sick leave. I explained, "I cannot use part time custody supervisors." I did, however, promote another black woman officer.

Officer Johnson filed a civil rights complaint, contending, "Warden Miller only hires and promotes dumb blacks so that this makes all blacks look bad."

Black employees were not happy with her conclusions and made her life miserable, but not before her case was investigated by the Department of Civil Rights. Officer Johnson did not win her complaint. Neither did the man who was among ten candidates interviewed for my administrative assistant. He filed an age discrimination complaint before I had announced the person who had been appointed. He filed the complaint in spite of an interview panel that consisted of three members, including a seventy-two year old male.

No law suit will ever surpass the one filed by a male prisoner who was serving a natural life sentence (no parole) for a first degree murder conviction. He had a heart attack and was pronounced dead at the prison. Diligent medical staff in the hospital emergency room continued CPR and brought him back to life. When he found out that he had been pronounced dead, he filed a law suit claiming he had already served his natural life sentence. The judge didn't agree, and he remained at Huron Valley Men's Prison. I thought he should have received an award for creativity.

PART 6

The Hearing

I

Memorial Day Weekend, 1990

"He's got her! Larner's got Officer Reynolds and I think he's got a shank!" the prisoner porter shouted as he ran toward the officers' station.

As Officers Tucker and Wilson raced to Larner's cell at the other end of the block, they saw Larner grab Lisa Reynolds by the hair and drag her into his cell. The cell door slammed shut. They pushed against it but to no avail. Tucker told Wilson, "Forget it, it's too late. Larner's got the door barricaded."

In desperation Wilson pounded on the door and yelled, "Larner, let her go, man. Don't be stupid."

Officer Wilson knew that Larner had nothing to lose and that threats meant little to him; he was already serving a life sentence. Larner liked dangerous games, and he liked being in control.

"I ain't lettin' her go and I ain't talkin' to nobody but the Man. So get the Man here."

Wilson understood who the Man was—the hostage negotiator. He wondered if Larner would bargain for something, or if it would be like the last time he took a female officer hostage. That time, he played out the scenario just long enough to put everyone on edge, and then he let her go, and walked out of his cell. Wilson hoped this would be like the last time—nobody got hurt.

Wilson turned to Tucker, telling him, "Call control center. Let them know what's goin' down."

"Man, we're in big fuckin' trouble." Tucker's voice quivered as he spoke. "Reynold's a rookie and the only woman on duty in this unit. She was doin' our job when Larner grabbed her. What d'ya think the Warden's goin' ta say 'bout that, Wilson?"

"That's not the only thing that's goin' to piss her off. The deadbolt on the bottom of the door was open, and no officer noticed it when they were makin' rounds. For that matter, no one noticed Larner's unlocked door. But that's not the problem right now, Tucker—it's savin' Reynold' ass. So get a move on and call control center!"

Within the hour, Deputy Bentley had formed a command center in the visiting room, and one of the prison's hostage negotiators, Sam Waters, was outside Larner's cell talking with him. Members of the state police swat team had started arriving and suiting up in the squad room. I was sailing on Lake Charlevoix in serene oblivion.

Deputy Bentley received regular communications from the negotiator. Sam Waters felt confident in his role, since over the years he had successfully brought to conclusion four other hostage situations at Huron Valley, including the first one with Larner five months earlier. But he admitted that Larner appeared more agitated this time—he was talking rapidly and banging the walls with a pipe.

Communication between Waters and Larner was also hindered by the noise of other prisoners banging on their cells. Normal procedures to clear the area couldn't be followed here because all the prisoners in that cellblock were dangerous and on segregation status. After a short while the prisoners tired of their game and quieted down.

Waters confirmed to Deputy Bentley that he could see into the cell through the narrow window and that Larner not only had a shank in his hand, but that he had a pipe, and there were several other pieces of metal on the floor. Waters watched as Larner paced his cell and periodically shoved the shank at Lisa Reynolds who cowered in the corner on Larner's bunk. Periodically, Larner would bang the pipe against the wall. Though Officer Reynolds responded to Larner, Waters couldn't hear what she said, and she was not allowed to speak to him. But the negotiator could see the tears streaking down her cheeks and the terror in her eyes as Larner preached at her and poked the shank in her face.

As the second hour of the hostage situation drew to an end, Larner gave Waters a piece of metal, which was seen as a positive gesture. Waters reported that Lisa Reynolds appeared to calm down after Larner asked Waters for aspirin because she had a headache. Larner gave her the aspirin and some toilet paper to wipe her face. But then he covered the door window with a sheet and the outside window with a blanket so no one could see into the cell. No further sounds came from that room.

Halfway into the third hour, the other prisoners in the cellblock began shouting, "The police swat team is here. They're comin' in ta get yah, Larner."

"Waters!" Larner shouted through the covered window. "I don't wanna talk to the police—just you. If you stay and they don't come in, I'll come outta my cell around noon."

Waters checked his watch. It was 11:30. He agreed to wait. At noon, Larner walked out of his cell and was immediately apprehended by two officers.

Shaking and naked from the waist down, Officer Reynolds was lying across Larner's bunk. She had been raped. Later she reported that Larner used the lead pipe to threaten her when he raped her.

Officer Reynolds was helped from the cell by the state police psychologist and a woman police sergeant. They took her to the prison infirmary where she received preliminary medical attention. Shortly after that, they took her to the local hospital. It was the last time she would be in Huron Valley Men's Prison. While at the hospital, Reynolds told the state police what happened to her during the four hours she was held hostage. It would be the first of many times she would be forced to go over every painful minute of that dreadful day.

II

I became more anxious each mile of the drive from Charlevoix to the prison, where I had to face the aftermath of the hostage taking. I wanted to help Lisa Reynolds, though I didn't know how, because nothing could ease the humiliation of being raped. And I wanted to hurt the prisoner, Paul Larner, and make him pay for the pain he caused. But selfishly I also wanted to turn the car around so that I would not have to face another investigation into a critical incident at the prison.

When I finally arrived at the prison, I had my secretary assemble the administrative staff in the conference room while I read the incident report. As I read the report, I was angered by the laxity I saw in the overall officer performance in Larner's cellblock, where the most dangerous and difficult prisoners were incarcerated. I had a lot of questions that needed to be answered before I could submit my report to central office. But the way things looked at that moment, it seemed to me the hostage/rape could have been prevented if the officers in the cellblock had done their jobs. All they had to do was follow the standard security measures outlined in the post orders. Those procedures appeared to have been ignored, and that oversight would forever plague the employees of Huron Valley Men's Prison.

I finished reading the report, made some notes, and went to the conference room to meet with the administrative staff gathered there. It was the beginning of what would become an intensive seven-month investigation.

As I placed the incident report on the conference room table, I looked at the exhausted group gathered and asked, "How did Larner get out of his cell?"

My question was met with silence, which added to the tension I had already perceived. Then Deputy Bentley cleared his throat and explained, "We think one of the prisoner porters disengaged the deadbolt at the bottom of his cell door. We have no idea how long it was in the open position, or whether officers making rounds missed it. Our guess is the porter slid it open, and then got Officer Reynolds over there by asking for supplies. But of course, he denies this."

"That only explains the deadbolt. What about the door lock? How was Larner able to unlock his cell door without officers knowing it?"

"He apparently tampered with the locking mechanism, using the pieces of metal he'd removed from the radiator in his cell. He worked at the lock until it no longer functioned."

"But that's exactly how he was able to get out of his cell the last time. How could it happen again?" My voice became louder with each word, and I no longer cared whether I showed my anger.

The normally vocal administrative staff sat silent, fidgeting and looking down at the table. They were willing to let Bentley do the talking. He looked at them and then back to me as he answered in a low voice, "Apparently, the officers failed to follow the post orders to shake down Larner's cell and check the door lock each time he was taken from the cell and during rounds."

I was appalled. "Their negligence allowed Larner to make weapons and breach security. What made staff feel this guy was no longer a threat? Or are they that lazy?"

Someone cleared his throat, but no one answered. I shook my head in frustration. I looked at each person and reminded them, "Lisa Reynolds will have to pay for this negligence for the rest of her life. It will be on my conscience for a long time, and it should be on yours. I hope you realize this session today is only the beginning of an investigation?"

All the employees nodded as I continued. "I expect everyone to cooperate and tell the truth—don't hide anything. Any mistakes that have been made will be corrected."

As the employees left the conference room, I thought about the barrage of questions from central office administrators and reporters that would follow. But mostly I thought about State Senator Jack Welborn. This whole nasty business was tailor-made to bolster his accusations that the Michigan Department of Corrections was out of control and needed new leadership. Of course, the department's unprecedented expansion in the past six years, which included an increase from thirteen to thirty-two prisons, might explain the difficulties. But I doubted the senator was interested in the obvious.

I had grown tired of the constant intrusions of the Senate Corrections Committee, the Legislative Ombudsman and the media. I was also frustrated by the lack of support from my supervisor. I felt that both Senator Welborn and my supervisor would look for a scapegoat to extricate themselves from any possible blame for the rape, the third in the past ten years in Michigan prisons. I also felt the scapegoat would be me, since the warden is ultimately responsible for both prisoner and staff behavior.

The conversation I had with Chet while driving from Charlevoix came back to me. He told me, "You know, you can get out of corrections any time you want. We have enough money for you to do something different. Why should we have to put up with this? You'll only end up taking the blame and beating yourself up because of it."

I wondered if Chet was right. Was it time to get out? I felt I was losing my objectivity, that I could no longer tell who were the good guys or if there were any.

In the last week of August, I received a notice from Senator

Welborn stating he was holding a public hearing at Huron Valley in September. I had the notice distributed and posted throughout the prison so that interested employees could attend. Though the senator was looking for people to blame, I sensed the hearing would only expose our pain and self-imposed guilt for public record.

III

September, 1990

Senator Jack Welborn, chairperson of the Michigan State Senate Corrections Committee, sat at the head of the table in the prison conference room. A microphone attached to a tape recorder was placed in front of him, and I sat to his right. He and his six person entourage had completed a tour of Huron Valley Men's Prison. Their focus was Unit One and the cell in which prisoner Larner had raped officer Lisa Reynolds just four months before. That rape was the reason for the public hearing about to take place, and was the first I had ever attended. I knew that it would also be the most difficult one that I would ever have to face.

As I watched employees drift in and fill the packed room, I thought about the previous day, when many of these same employees had come here to celebrate my forty-eighth birthday. The room was filled with laughter then; today it was filled with tension.

Six people had accompanied the Senator, but only one person from central office was present for the hearing, Deputy Director for Media and Legislative Liaison. My supervisor, Charlie Lathrop, was not present because he was on a stress leave of absence. I had filed a harassment complaint against him, and he was warned by the deputy director and director to back off. In response to that warning, my supervisor went on leave, and filed a grievance against the department for not allowing him to supervise as he saw fit.

While waiting for the hearing to begin, I thought about the events that led to my complaint against my supervisor. I had discussed my many concerns about Charlie with the deputy director almost a year before, but no action was taken and the harassment only increased.

223

It was the hostage/rape incident that forced me to file a formal complaint. When I reviewed my initial report about the incident with Charlie, he threatened, "You better make it a good one because it will be your only salvation." I knew from the way he said it that I was going to be the scapegoat, and decided I would have to do something to protect myself.

This statement, not overly intimidating on its own, was only one of numerous verbal and physical threats he made toward me and other wardens. What he asked us to do often violated polilcy; we would then be disciplined for either violating policy or disobeying orders. In one case, he interfered with an under cover investigation because he was angry at the warden for not informing him about it (at the request of the police who did not trust his discretion). His interference and the disciplinary action he took against the warden jeopardized staff and prisoner safety. On another occasion, a male warden was thrown against the wall during a wardens meeting because he asked Charlie to clarify a new policy, apparently embarassing him. I believe that my supervisor's irrational and often dangerous behavior resulted from his attempts to cover up his lack of intelligence and knowledge of corrections; he felt that his large physique alone would force his subordinates to submit to him. One state senator told me that many others had complained about Charlie, and some of them had even left their jobs because of him. It was the number and diversity of the complaints that was eventually my supervisor's downfall.

Before Lisa Reynold's rape, I had been subjected to daily interrogations about prisoner Larner's first hostage taking in January, from my supervisor and from Rob Stanger (staff representative from the Legislative Corrections Ombudsman Office). At that time, I was being threatened with disciplinary action because I had placed Larner on Top of Bed Restraints until a secure cell could be vacated for him. Stanger and my supervisor claimed I had violated policy because they didn't think that Larner's actions warranted such severe consequences. TOB status was usually reserved for self mutilators. I explained it was a two hour temporary measure to prevent a hostage taker from committing any other heinous act until an adequate cell could be found.

Neither was happy about the rest of my response. "Besides,

224

Warden Lowman has been allowed to waive the TOB policy for prisoners who trash their cells at I-Max. I can't imagine how that could be seen as more dangerous. I think, instead, it is a double standard which borders on being gender biased, favoring a male warden."

After that conversation, Warden Lowman was asked to head a committee rewriting the policy to accommodate his exception.

Now Stanger and my supervisor were questioning me about why Larner had been allowed to remain at Huron Valley Men's Prison rather than having been transferred after the first hostage situation. I explained, "First of all, he was transferred to Huron Valley from I-Max as a segregation prisoner who needed out-patient mental health treatment. Since we are the only institution at this time providing such treatment, and Larner assaulted staff, he can't be transferred without central office approval. That approval was asked for and denied to accommodate the state police investigation in the first hostage situation. In other words, I can't make that decision. It is up to my supervisor and the deputy director to authorize his move. And furthermore, no one seemed to care about how dangerous Larner was until he raped an officer. Remember, you two are the same ones who got on my case for placing him on TOB because I thought he posed a threat."

The department's investigative committee decided not to distribute any of our draft reports, but make available only the final comprehensive report with recommendations for needed changes. However, shortly after the first draft was reviewed, someone gave a copy to Senator Welborn. It happened at the same time my supervisor went on stress leave, and the committee felt that he'd leaked the report as retaliation. Perhaps the reason the Senator decided to have the public hearing was because the draft report was not damning enough.

The Senator brought the public hearing to order and spoke into the tape recorder. "This is Senator Jack Welborn at Huron Valley Men's Prison. I'm conducting a public hearing on the hostage situations here, especially the most recent, which ended in the rape of Officer Lisa Reynolds."

Since I had been interviewed in private before the Senator toured the institution, my main role in the hearing was to listen to employees, who had been notified of the hearing during role calls and by a posted memo. I was uneasy about what the employees would report and was prepared to be raked over the coals.

The employees presented a litany of complaints and concerns as I expected, but I was amazed to see that none of them placed blame on institutional employees or on me. Instead they faulted the legislature for not funding needed security equipment, and shouted their concerns and bitterness about having to work with extremely dangerous prisoners at Huron Valley Men's. The prison, they felt, was inappropriate for a mentally ill and segregated population, because the cells were not secure enough and the officers were not trained to deal with the mentally ill.

One nurse, however, addressed me specifically. "These prisoners are very assaultive and dangerous. They shouldn't be here, but you accept them anyway. You won't do anything when they hang their arms out the food slots and grab at us. We can't even get down the gallery. Something's got to be done."

Feeling powerless after the nurse's statement, I hid my shaking hands under the table and answered, "There is a procedure that should be followed when prisoners refuse to close their food slots. Also, we have to accept all prisoners transferred to us. They can only be sent back if our medical personnel decide they have not been diagnosed properly. However, I know many who remain are difficult."

When I finished my defensive statement, I waited for others to follow the nurse's lead, anticipating the worst. But the other employees who spoke praised the administration for sexual harassment education, employee training, and attempting to make the prison safer, even with the shortage of resources.

As the employees made their comments, I noticed the Senator kept looking at his watch. He finally announced, "I have to leave at four-thirty because I have another appointment." That gave the many employees only an hour more to explain their anger, fears, frustrations, and guilt.

I felt sure that the employees' surprisingly favorable testimony, and not an appointment, was the impetus behind the Senator's need to leave. He wasn't getting the negative information he had come for— proof that women should not manage men's prisons and that the department needed new leadership.

Just as Senator Welborn brought the hearing to an end, Officer Mewler walked into the conference room carrying a foot high stack of paper work. I chuckled to myself, thinking that if the Senator had not been in such a hurry, he could have had the information he wanted. Mewler, an ex-offender, had never been a friend to any supervisor at Huron Valley Men's. He was an endless complainer, and no doubt the stack of papers he held detailed the persecution he felt he'd suffered over the years. The Senator missed his chance that day. I was the last person to leave the conference room, and I was met by my secretary who asked, "How'd it go?"

"I almost want to quit this job so I can run for political office and fight people like Welborn. He doesn't want to get to the bottom of a problem; he just wants someone crucified so it looks like he's doing his job. I wonder if he really heard anyone today?"

At that moment, I realized I had already made my decision to leave corrections. I no longer felt I had the support of my superiors or that they had the support of the legislature. I envisioned most of my time in the future being spent defending myself against misleading, hurtful and demeaning accusations, rather than humanely managing a tough prison. Under those circumstances, I feared I would get to be paranoid rather than remain objective, and therefore be a less productive leader. I was tiring of battles and couldn't picture the next ten years under such stress.

In my office, I sat at my desk and reviewed the dynamics of the public hearing. I wondered if other wardens were as sensitive as I, or if I was being foolish. I thought over the testimony given at the hearing and Senator Welborn's reaction to it, which led me to believe his mind had been made up. He had found us guilty before the facts were presented. Guilty of what? That the sixth hostage situation at Huron Valley Men's Prison had not ended successfully and the other five had?

As I filled my attache case with that evening's reading, I recalled the testimony that distressed me the most. It reflected the guilt that employees felt at being helpless, and their feeling that if I had not been on a holiday, the victim would not have been raped. I had to fight off the conviction that I alone could have made a difference in the incident. But I still couldn't help asking if I had done all that I could have.

One of the male officers on duty in the unit at the time of the hostage taking cried, "I shoulda been quicker. If I was quicker, I coulda saved her. It shoulda never happened."

Another male officer pointed in my direction, saying, "When she was here the last time, Larner gave up. He didn't hurt nobody. I wish you'd been here in May. It woulda been different."

"But," a third officer interrupted, "we gotta remember that anyone of us could be the victim. Prisoners don't care if you're man or woman. We gotta do something to stop this, so no one else gets hurt."

Although debriefing was offered to all employees after the hostage/rape, I spoke in private with many of those who gave testimony and suggested continued counseling for several of them. Some followed this suggestion, and a few took stress leaves of absence. All came back to work, including the victim Lisa Reynolds. However, she went to another prison where she had no prisoner contact.

Could I have done more, and if so what? How could I have trained people to never let their guard down; that rules were made to keep them safe, not to harass them; that it really is okay to have a personal life and legitimate time away from the job? It was something I had to ask myself, because of employees' views about the impact my absence had on the outcome of the hostage taking. My absence was also an issue on which both Welborn's special investigator and Rob Stanger dwelled when questioning me and others. This didn't help to ease my guilt feelings.

I walked toward the door of my office shaking my head, thinking no other incident in my career had had such a negative and depressing influence on me. A rape touches every nerve in the bodies of those involved, and is the most savage and degrading form of assault. We all knew that any one of us, male or female, could have been the victim. Anyone of us could have been held in that cell for those four interminable hours by a prisoner armed with a homemade weapon. We were all afraid it would happen again.

A few days after the public hearing, several employees came to my office and reported that Welborn's special investigator had been pressuring them to meet with her off prison grounds. I encouraged them to meet with her and tell her the truth as they knew it. I feared she was looking for any damaging information that could be used against the institutional and central office administration, and knew if she looked hard and long enough, she would find someone like Officer Mewler to give her what she and the Senator wanted. I would have been a fool to think otherwise.

One warden told me that the investigator and the ombudsman were trying to get him to say that I had broken some policy by not being available on Memorial Day weekend. He told me, "They were relentless. Wanted me to testify that I always gave my whereabouts and phone number, even when I was on leave. I told them that it wasn't policy unless we were on call."

Neither Lisa Reynolds nor her husband appeared at the public hearing. If I had been the victim, I would not have attended either. But Reynolds' husband made an appointment to see me and came accompanied by his shift commander. Reynolds stared at me through red rimmed, narrowed eyes throughout the session. I began by asking how he and his wife were doing.

"There's little that can be done now. I guess...," Reynolds began, twisting his hands, "I guess I need to know why it all happened, and why you didn't give a shit? You're always on the side of prisoners. Look what it got yah."

We all sat in silence for a minute. I thought I would give him more time to continue getting whatever he had to off his chest, but he just stared at me.

"Well, Lieutenant Reynolds, I don't think I can give you any answer that'll make things better for you or your wife. But I suggest that you and your wife get counseling, separately as well as together. You each have needs right now that are independent of the other's. It may sound selfish to the other partner, but they must be addressed before you address your needs as a couple. I know you're both in a lot of pain as individuals and as partners..."

"You can cut the bullshit. We're in counseling together. Our therapist didn't recommend going it alone. Who do you think you are, some kind of expert in everything?"

"I'm not an expert, but I have done some counseling, and I certainly don't want to interfere with the therapy you're receiving. I just wanted to...."

"I'll take care of my marriage. You just get me outta this prison. Have me transferred some place else."

"I have already begun the request. It..."

"That's not what I heard," he interrupted. "I heard you won't do nothin'."

"I'm not sure where you heard that, but I'm only waiting for the deputy director and central office personnel to act on the move. Part of the problem is finding a vacancy. If you'd like, look at it as a purely selfish gesture on my part. You'll do me no good working in this institution except as a reminder. So for that reason alone, it's smart to have you transferred."

"If that's the case, I appreciate it."

"Lieutenant Reynolds, I sent a note to your wife. Do you know if she received it?"

"I got it, but won't let her have it. You can't say anything that'll help her, so I threw it out. I don't want her to have any contact with this place."

"That's a shame because she needs to know that we support her and want to help her recovery."

"Like I said, I'll see to the recovery for both of us. Thanks for your time. Let's get outta here." Reynolds stood up and motioned to the shift commander who shrugged his shoulders at me.

The shift commander returned a few minutes later to apologize. "I'm sorry for the way he treated you. It wasn't fair."

"What can possibly be fair in this situation. He needs to blame someone, and I'm as good a target as any." I thanked him for his support and he left. But I felt empty; I needed to help Lisa Reynolds, not just for her sake, but to make things better for myself.

I had only one more contact with Lieutenant Reynolds, just before I retired. He telephoned and asked if he could transfer back to Huron Valley Men's Prison. Neither I nor central office felt it was a good idea, and he did not return.

To my knowledge, no formal report was ever issued by Senator Welborn. But the report submitted to him by his special investigator appeared as part of the evidence in the law suit filed by Lieutenant and Lisa Reynolds. I didn't see the report until I was preparing for my deposition in that suit. I was not surprised by the misleading information it contained, but one statement really got my attention. "Due to this person's [department of corrections (DOC) official] perception of Miller's failure to adequately administer the facility, he recommended that DOC place her on administrative leave."

I thought, at first, that it was strange that the DOC official was not named in the report. But then I realized that the official was my supervisor; if he were named, the report would lack credibility because his alleged recommendation to put me on administrative leave was made two days after the deputy director and director told him to stop threatening me.

Although charges were filed against several employees of Huron Valley Men's Prison as a result of the department's investigation, none was brought against me, and none was upheld through Civil Service proceedings. Central office administrators were attempting to appease and defuse Senator Welborn's investigation by finding prison personnel to blame for the rape of a rookie officer. In that process they went after Deputy Bentley as the acting warden and person in control during the rape. And they went after the primary prison negotiator who had successfully negotiated all but that one hostage situation. I never understood what made them think any negotiator could perform miracles.

As I had predicted, there was not enough evidence to support anything except the fact that these employees had used their best judgement and acted within the scope of policy as they knew it. None, even the worst employee, would have wished such an assault on a colleague.

Within a year of the public hearing, a new governor was elected, the corrections commission was dismantled, and the director retired under pressure. The corrections commission had acted as a buffer between the governor and the director, thus reducing political influences. The new governor appointed Senator Welborn to head the corrections transition team, which included two of the men who had accompanied Welborn at the public hearing. They hired the new director for the corrections department.

The new departmental reorganization plan that had taken two years to develop, using input from corrections employees at every level and from all over the state, was replaced with one developed by the new

231

director. His replacement plan abolished many positions, the majority of those affecting minorities and women, under the guise of being fiscally responsible. But the two white males from the transition team were brought into the Department of Corrections in unclassified positions, replacing two people whose positions had been abolished.

The reorganization was the subject of legislative and civil service hearings. It was investigated by the Department of Civil Rights which ultimately ruled in favor of those who filed the complaint. Although compensated, they were not returned to their positions, and the two new positions remained.

I was notified on Valentine's Day, 1992, that the Reynolds' law suit against the department and me had been dismissed. Though the involved employees were vindicated on paper, they had suffered a great deal from the unrelenting accusations and disciplinary charges. The hostage negotiator suffered from depression; the central office administrators never let up on the harassment of Deputy Bentley, forcing him into retirement; and I left corrections a year sooner than planned. To this day, I am tormented by my decision to leave when I hear about the struggles still facing the women and minorities who remain. I have said many times that I admire their strength, but I do not envy them.

IV

Five mornings a week, my Golden Retrievers and I walk six miles around the lake nestled in the rolling hills of the rural county where I live. It is the perfect way to awaken my brain and escape from the nightmares that still push their way into my sleep. In one, I open the front door to my home, and am met by a faceless human figure who shoots me. In another, I am walking and grabbed from behind by an unknown person carrying a knife. Neither nightmare goes beyond these points because I awaken in a sweat, whimpering.

One morning, a month after I retired from corrections, I took my usual six mile walk in the rare February sunshine. The silence of this serene winter morning was interrupted only by the comforting sounds of snow crunching under my feet, songs of the hardy winter birds, and the occasional bark of a dog.

I was tired from lack of sleep and had slowed my pace, but picked it up when I heard a slow moving vehicle approaching from behind me. Images from my nightmares flashed into my mind. My heart started to race and I thought, not here, not in the country.

A black Ford pick-up truck moved into my peripheral vision and I could see two white males sitting in the cab. I watched the truck approach from the corner of my eye, thinking—please don't let this be what I have been fearing, an old enemy hunting me down to kill me. Please don't let this happen. Not when I am just starting to feel free.

When the truck got alongside me, the driver, a young man in his twenties dressed in work clothes, rolled down the window and leaned toward me. "Pardon me, ma'am, have you seen two cows? They're black and white and got out of our field. We're on the farm over the hill."

I wanted to laugh out loud with relief, but knew the two men wouldn't understand. Instead I answered, "No. I'm sorry, I haven't. But I know your farm. If I see them, I'll come tell you."

It is a four hour drive to Charlevoix from my home. When I was a warden, I looked forward to this drive, knowing my destination brought me peace, removing me from the intrusion of the office telephone. Now I find the drive tedious, and it often serves to remind me of the prison. Official state signs dot the freeway along the route, warning: "PRISON AREA, DO NOT PICK UP HITCHHIKERS."

I agonized for a year over the guilt I felt about leaving corrections. I was bothered by my lack of self-worth, once I had lost my title, income, power and authority. I floundered through that year feeling I had deserted both the women's movement and my personal fight against gender bias.

I finally found peace when I admitted that I had loved my work in corrections, but didn't like the changes I was forced to make by others who had little concern for the human element, whether prisoner or employee. I learned that I could lead battles for human rights more successfully from outside a department that chose not to listen to women. I learned I could be more successful fighting gender bias when I didn't have to fear retaliation from supervisors and legislators.

I also admitted that I needed a break from the oppressive world of the incarcerated. I especially needed a break from the kinds of prisoners who could never change and would forever remain in the growing mound of human waste. Those prisoners had become blurred, unidentifiable faces behind scratched, narrow windows framed in a metal door. I realized that I could not rescue every one; that I must choose my battles with care and stick to them, so as not to burn out again. And most importantly, I learned not to feel guilty about people I didn't have the energy to help.

I have to be counted among the lucky women because I have had a husband who understood my need to be independent and to succeed in a challenging career. Chet offered the support, patience and sense of humor a prison warden's mate needs. If it weren't for these, I'm sure I would never have been as successful a warden or as confident a woman as I am.

Chet endured in silence the many times our sleep was interrupted by calls from the prison, and neither of us could go back to sleep. And on those occasions when I had to make unexpected trips to the prison because of some crisis, he would get out of bed, clean the snow off my car in winter, and prepare something for me to eat while I got dressed. He would wait up on evenings when a crisis kept me at the prison late, greeting me with dinner and a non-critical ear as I carried on about the incident. He helped me work through my self doubts when officers were hurt, prisoners committed suicide, my boss harassed me, Officer Reynolds was raped, employees and prisoners submitted unending grievances, and when I was not welcome as the warden at Huron Valley Men's Prison. He never once made me feel unworthy. And when I considered leaving corrections, he said, "Do whatever will make you happy."

V

Today, when I become most unhappy about negative personal and work relationships between men and women, I remind myself of my retirement party. There were songs sung by the Pointless Sisters, of course, but others who spoke and roasted me that night were men, and some of them cried. I realized that evening that there was hope for narrowing the gender gap. Those men and I had used our differences to complement each other, and had developed a formidable working team of women and men.

Perhaps the most surprising comments that evening came from several wives of the men I had supervised. "We just want you to know that we are probably more unhappy about you leaving than our husbands. They have never been as happy at a job or enjoyed working long hours before now. Because of you, they always felt they belonged and were a part of a team."

One of my favorite moments during my retirement party was when Director Brown finished his flattering remarks by asking everyone to join him in honoring me with a twenty-one oink salute. The entire room of people oinked twenty-one times.

I told a story on myself that evening that describes the open and comfortable relationship I had with most of the employees, including the men I supervised. Detective Sergeant Norman, who attended the retirement party, was the state police prison liaison. One day, months earlier, he had invited me to observe a demonstration of the drug dogs' and their trainers' abilities. He had scheduled two dogs to sniff for drugs in employee and visitor lockers located in the prison lobby.

Several prison employees and I gathered in the lobby to watch. Our attention peaked when one dog stopped at an employee locker and began scratching wildly at it.

"He's got a hit!" Sergeant Norman pointed to the German Shepherd who was pacing and whining in front of the locker. "Can you get the employee up here so we can open the locker?"

I looked on the locker roster and found the employee's name. I told the desk officer to have Ms. Dyer, a teacher and union president, report to the lobby.

Ms. Dyer arrived and I explained the situation. She smiled, nodded at me, and opened the locker while everyone stood around in silence.

Sergeant Norman closed in on the locker to watch. "The dogs will be rewarded today."

"Indeed they will," I said.

The locker door was flung open and the German Shepherd

pounced on a plastic bag on the lowest shelf. "Stand back," Sergeant Norman ordered Ms. Dyer, and he grabbed the bag.

I couldn't contain myself any longer and began to laugh. Sergeant Norman's face turned red as he produced his evidence, a large bag of dog biscuits. He turned to me, eyes narrowing, but with a slight smile on his face. "You knew. You knew all along it was only dog biscuits."

Ms. Dyer was the trainer for the prison's dog handling program. Everyone laughed, and Sergeant Norman gave each of the dogs a biscuit.

A couple of weeks later, Sergeant Norman returned to the prison with new dogs and trainers. He asked me to meet them in the lobby for introductions. After they completed their search, Sergeant Norman, the trainers and dogs came to my office to report their findings. "We didn't find anything, but would like you to see our new dogs in action. They're the best we've had."

The dogs began sniffing around my office, starting at the shelves near the conference room door and working along the wall to my credenza. Suddenly they stopped and scratched at the sliding door that hid my telephone directories. They scratched and whined at the door while the trainers and Norman stared at me.

"Go ahead and open it. I have nothing to hide," I said to them, hoping I had dog biscuits stored there.

Norman opened the sliding door and pulled out a pound of marijuana. My heart was in my throat. I thought that Rick Mayer had finally got me—had set me up. I felt nauseous and scared.

But my thoughts were interrupted by Sergeant Norman's laughter. "Paybacks are hell."

Then several employees came into my office laughing. I discovered the marijuana had been hidden in the credenza by employees while I was in the lobby meeting the dogs and trainers.

"You SOB, Sergeant. This isn't over yet." And we all laughed.

I miss those moments.

Today, I look forward to yet another adventure, being a grandmother for the first time. Perhaps if I'm lucky, people will say to me, "Funny, you don't look like a grandmother."

You have scolded some,
You have given advice.
To some you only gave
The time of day.
We all know that
You, above all, have earned
Your pay.
We will miss you and
Think of you often,
So to you we all raise
Our glasses to drink.
After all, you were the
Warden who wore pink.

Captain Dalton, January 4, 1992
Warden Tekla Miller's Retirement Party

When Tekla Dennison Miller received her degree in elementary education from Cazenovia Women's College in New York and UCLA, she never dreamed she would end up as a prison warden in Michigan. However, Ms. Miller's experiences teaching children in South Central Los Angeles after the Watts riots, and working for the U.S. Special Services in Germany training "mentally challenged" soldiers helped to prepare her for corrections. After receiving a Master's degree from Oakland University in Michigan, Ms. Miller worked as a probation officer and a halfway house agent in Detroit.

She was the first female probation officer in Oakland County, and among the first women in the country to manage male felons on her caseload. Ms. Miller then served as the Supervisor at the first Prison Camp for women in Michigan, and was a leader in fighting for job and program equality for women employees and prisoners.

After four years as warden at Huron Valley Women's Prison, initially Michigan's only prison for women, Ms. Miller was appointed warden of both Huron Valley Women's and Huron Valley Men's Prisons. The men's prison was the only maximum security facility in Michigan to house self-mutilators and the mentally ill segregated population. Ms. Miller was the first warden in Michigan to undertake the responsibility of simultaneously managing two maximum security prisons.

After twenty years in Michigan corrections, Ms. Miller retired, and now lives in Colorado with her husband. She continues to be a community activist, feminist, writer and speaker. She is active in several social justice organizations and enjoys every minute of being a Harley-riding grandmother.

ORDER FORM

Please send

_____ copies of **The Warden Wore Pink** @$11.95   — — — — —

Shipping: $2.50 first book, .50 ea. add. bk.   — — — — —

Sales tax, Maine residents only, .72   — — — — —

TOTAL   ————

Send check or money order to

Biddle Publishing Company
PO Box 1305 #103   207-833-5016
Brunswick, Maine 04011

Name_____

Address_____

_____

Visit Biddle Publishing Co. on the World Wide Web
http:\\www.maineguide.com\biddle